May Need Renovation

For Mary O'Mahony

MERCIER PRESS
Douglas Village, Cork

Trade enquiries to CMD Distribution
55A Spruce Avenue, Stillorgan
Industrial Park, Blackrock County
Dublin

© Pamela Rowan, 2007

ISBN: 978 1 85635 541 4

10 9 8 7 6 5 4 3 2 1

A CIP record for this title is available
from the British Library

≋arts
council
≋chomhairle
ealaíon

Mercier Press receives financial
assistance from the Arts Council/
An Chomhairle Ealaíon

Typeset by Dominic Carroll,
Co. Cork

Printed by J.H. Haynes & Co,
Sparkford

May Need Renovation

Pamela Rowan

MERCIER PRESS

WHAT YOU NEED TO READ

CHAPTER ONE

Crumple a Jaguar

*E*nding up on the front page of the *Star* in black French underwear and four-inch Prada heels was never Sullivan's plan. I mean, ending up there in nothing but the black underwear and the four-inch heels.

Not that Sullivan ever has a plan. I'm her shovel friend, so I can tell you that for sure. Shovel friend? The one you could ring at midnight to say 'I have a body that needs burying' and they'd be around in ten minutes, no questions asked, carrying a shovel. Since we were both eight years of age, Sullivan Spencer has needed that shovel. The girl has a capacity for disaster that amounts to a brand like Nike. She just does it. My job is to undo it or explain it or get her the hell away from it, depending on the nature of the most recent cock-up.

This particular cock-up started at get-out-of-jail time, Friday evening. The two of us were standing at the pond in the middle of the bank's grounds. Pleasant spring evening. Sullivan was telling me something amusing about Hugo, our esteemed mutual boss, whose car was parked in front of us. Telling it to

5

me as if he was *just* her boss. I may be her shovel friend, but she still hadn't come right out with it and told me she was having an affair with him. Hugo is big and bullet-headed and a part time rugby referee. He also drives a cream Jaguar the size of a hearse. The sort of Jag you expect will be occupied by a celeb. I don't know how he stands the looks of disappointment that must cross people's faces when they draw level and find he isn't one. If I was him, I'd get blacked-out windows and let the onlookers live in hope.

So there's me, standing there listening. And there's Sullivan, towering over me, talking. Story of our lives. Well, not true, exactly. When we were in school together, she didn't tower over me. She just loomed, until the year she was allowed to wear high heels. From that point on, we're talking tower. But then, when you're 5' 3" like me, pretty much everybody towers over you.

Sullivan's telling me about the hot-stone treatment she had the previous weekend in some country mansion where they throw freshly harvested herbs in your bath and throw edible flowers at you for breakfast. The stones were *so* good for relieving her stress, she tells me.

What stress? I think. Why is it always the gorgeous women every man falls over, the ones who get into the inner circle in Reynards without an argument, the ones who pick up Miu Miu bags in a sale for €30, who believe they live lives of torch-hot tension? It's like they're Red Cross workers in the middle of a battlefield, picking up random limbs and exhaustedly trying to stitch them onto the poor hoors who originally owned them.

'There's Bryan,' I say, as his bull-bar fronted SUV comes horsing over the speed bump at the security kiosk like the Stena ferry hitting rough seas.

Sullivan turns, sees him and bends down to retrieve her bags, which is why she misses the first collision.

As I'm doing a 'Hi, Bryan' wave, the SUV accelerates. Now the SUV does not have open road in front of it. It has a bloody big cream-coloured Jaguar in front of it. So it connects with the arse of the Jag at maybe fifty miles an hour. The SUV kind of half climbs up on the back of the Jag (up on the crumpled back of the Jag, I should say) and then, because Bryan jams it in reverse, falls back down, bouncing on its oversized wheels. He reverses nearly as far as the courtesy kiosk, the engine doing that high scream of protest cars do when you drive them fast in reverse, and then he clunks a gear change and comes at the Jag again.

By now, I'm pretty clear, this is not an accident. It's like the trend on radio news bulletins when two cars make bits of each other outside Mullingar, and the announcer says 'Three people died in the incident.' *Incident*? This repeated assault on the Jag is the first crash I've seen that amounts to an incident, rather than an accident. An undiplomatic incident.

Bryan comes at the Jag the second time around with such speed, he overrides its handbrake and lurches it straight into the lamp post in front of it, which snaps its bumper in two. I'm standing there thinking this wouldn't happen to any modern car, because none of them *have* bumpers; it could only happen to a vintage car. Sullivan's screaming and crying and waving one of her many handbags at Bryan, and people are pouring out of all the doors of every section of the bank.

On his third run, the Jag gets a seriously accordion look to it, and the next thing I realise Hugo is standing beside me, pointing his phone at Bryan's car and taking pictures. This is surprising and impressive, since Hugo is the kind of age where guys don't do their own e-mails but get their personal assistant to send them instead. Him being able to take pictures on his phone is like finding your father making smoothies on the sly: admirable but surprising.

Bryan promptly stops the SUV, leaps out of it, grabs Sullivan one-handed, snatches the phone out of Hugo's grasp with the other hand and is back in the car before any of us can react. The SUV is out the gate maybe thirty seconds in advance of the squad car nosing in at the other entrance.

The two guards are female, which causes Hugo problems. Hugo thinks women are for only one thing. It's odds on which happens first, the sexual harassment case against him or his retirement. He even put his hand up *my* skirt once, in the lift. He had to sort of reach down and then up to do it.

I was really proud of my response. I pushed the emergency button so the thing stopped between floors.

'I take it this means you support my promotion?' I asked him, knowing that he hadn't up to then. He withdrew his hand, I pushed the button to free the lift and I got promoted three weeks later.

This Friday afternoon, though, he was so distracted by Bryan's departure, he hardly registered the gender of the two navy-uniformed guards. Hugo would probably call them *ban ghardaí*. Banners. The two banners walked around the Jag with interest written all over them. One of them flipped a notebook and asked who the owner was. Hugo advanced, for some reason pulling me along with him. Feck.

'I won't be making any complaint,' he told the garda.

'You're shitting me?' she responded.

Hugo's mouth went all pursy. He'd get up on a cracked plate, but he doesn't like women to get drunk or swear. Pre-war, he is. As in First World.

'This is an internal matter,' he said quietly.

When Hugo says things quietly in the bank, shivers run down spines, questions stop being asked and things get done.

'How d'you mean, an internal matter?' bellowed the banner.

Hugo winced and gave me a nudge.

'The thing is,' I said, getting close to the garda and talking hoarsely, like I had laryngitis, so I could whisper and not be overheard by all the wankers from Corporate Services and Pensions crowding around. 'The thing is, one of Hugo's friends is going through a bit of a problem in his private life at the moment, you know how it is?'

It was stretching it a bit to describe Bryan as Hugo's friend, since the only point of contact they had was Sullivan, a bridge over very troubled waters, a stepping stone between two banks. (Bryan works for the opposition, down in the Financial Services Centre.) The two gardaí looked at me as if I needed medication.

'He just lost it, the friend. He just needed some way to – to–'

Suddenly, Sullivan's hot stones popped into my mind.

'To relieve all the stress that had built up in him,' I said triumphantly. 'So he really was – was –,' The two gardaí looked at each other expressionlessly as I ran out of steam. 'Venting,' I said, reviving a bit.

'The point is,' Hugo started up again, this time in take-no-shit, take-charge mode, 'I would not dream of taking action against Bryan. Once he calms down, nobody will see quicker than he will that –'

The garda who hadn't yet spoken cut across him.

'Your personal intentions are irrelevant,' she told him. 'This is disturbance of the peace, dangerous driving, destruction of property and quite possibly a number of other things, too.'

'Wasting police time,' suggested the first one.

'I'll have your name and address,' the second one said.

She took him firmly by the elbow and steered him into the lobby.

'Move along there,' the other garda told the bank gawkers, of whom there seemed to be an endless supply, as later workers arrived to survey the wreckage and get told the exciting details by the ones who'd been around when it happened. They all made ineffectual shuffling movements to placate her while not actually shifting position much at all.

She then started to interrogate me. Who was the driver of the car that had totalled Hugo's? I told her. His address? I ground to a halt, debating which I was most scared to piss off, this garda or Bryan. Bryan, I thought, having seen him do his Survive My SUV act.

'Well?' the garda asked, pencil poised. (My father always maintains the guards use pencils so they can rub out anything they decide would be better replaced by a lie, if and when someone bribes them. My father has a jaundiced view of the world. Everybody's out to get him. Especially people from Clare, God alone knows why, and cops.)

'How would I know Bryan's address?'

Now, *there's* an answer that shows you what a rotten liar I am. I could have wriggled out from under with one word: Dunno. But I *do* know his address, so I couldn't lie. God help any kid that ever asks me if Santa really exists. I'll traumatise the toddler for life with my ungovernable truth.

'His address, please.'

No question mark, you will notice. This was a statement: you're going to give me his address. So you are. Which, of course, is the wrong way to play me. When you're not two hands higher than a duck, you've a lot of experience being bossed around by anybody who *is* hands higher than a duck. By the time you're hitting thirty, you have a Rambo response to even a hint of boss-tactics.

'I don't know I'm at liberty to share that with you.'

I know, I know. Not just a vomitous truth-teller, but pompous with it. I began to check her belt for handcuffs, certain she was going to arrest me for obstructing the cause of justice, but then the other one came back and told her she'd got it from Hugo. Not that she called him Hugo. She called him 'that baldy bastard'.

'You're not allowed to call him that,' I said, trying to add to the distraction.

'Yeah, I am,' she said comfortably.

'You're not, actually,' the first one said before moving on from disturbance of the peace to abduction.

'You can't call it that,' I said, beginning to sound like a CD with a scrape on it. 'He just grabbed her and put her in the car with him. That's not abduction. She's his girlfriend, for God's sake.'

'Did she indicate she wanted to travel with him?'

'She was expecting to travel with him. He collects her every evening.'

The two of them turned and looked at the newly crumpled Jag.

'Normally, he does it a bit more quietly,' I admitted.

11

I swear to God, I saw 'Duh' forming on the first one's mouth.

'Bryan's an old pet, really,' I added, desperate to wind this up.

'Is Ms Sullivan safe with him?'

'No, Sullivan is her first name. She's Miss Spencer.'

'What kind of a name is that?'

'Sullivan's parents believed you should give kids names they had to live up to because they were unusual. Her brother is named Rupert.'

'And they're from where?'

'Leitrim.'

The two of them considered the problems of growing up in a place like Leitrim with a name like Rupert Spencer. I didn't point out that a) Rupert was out of Leitrim when he was four, and b) his name is the least of his problems.

'I thought she was baldy's girlfriend?'

I made vague noises about us working for Hugo.

'But why would her boyfriend attack the other guy's car?'

'I told you he's under a bit of pressure at the moment.'

The leader of the two looked at me with such slaty coldness, I could feel my cheeks getting chapped.

'So he responds to stress by destroying someone else's treasured possession, drags his girlfriend into his car, and you're telling us she's safe with him?'

Sullivan, I thought, where are you when I need you? In this kind of situation, Sullivan would introduce some total irrelevancy without knowing it was one, and in the confusion I'd escape.

'Of *course* she's safe with him,' I said, trying for a casual laugh and producing something that wasn't either casual or a laugh.

'By the time they get home, she'll have him in stitches.'

The two of them looked at each other and at me as if maybe the person they should be arresting was this looper in front of them, never mind the SUV driver or the bald one.

'Well, maybe not in stitches,' I backtracked. 'But oh, you know, a meal calms everything down.'

For the first time, they looked as if I'd said something half-way intelligent. Which, as it turned out, was not the case.

CHAPTER TWO

Deep-fry a Phone

*T*he minute she got into the car, she told me later, Bryan started swearing at Sullivan to put her effing seatbelt on, did she want him arrested? To which the answer, if she'd had her wits about her, was a resounding 'Yes.' But she didn't have her wits about her – assuming she ever does, which I don't – and so she just buckled up.

Not that her buckling up shut him up. The bull bar on the front of the SUV had got bent in its repeated assault on Hugo's Jaguar and every time the vehicle turned right, it scraped the tyre on the driver's side. Helpful pedestrians pointed this out to him at traffic lights, not knowing how lucky they were he didn't get out and smack them. Sullivan smiled and twinkled her fingers at them to indicate her appreciation of their wonderfulness – until he caught her at it. His look withered her hand down into her lap and the smile off her face.

'If you just went straight or turned left you'd be all right,' she told him after a few minutes' silence.

Bryan closed his eyes and breathed deeply.

'You'd need to watch the road,' she suggested and he told her to shut the hell up. Or worse. By the time she was telling me about this, she couldn't quite remember. It had silenced her, though. She did remember that. Well, she would, it happens so rarely.

When they got to the apartment, for some reason he dragged her up three flights of stairs rather than take the lift. They live in one of those high-tech apartment blocks where owners get an electronic door opener. Bryan pointed Hugo's phone at the lock and pressed send repeatedly before he realised it wasn't the right gadget. In spite of her terror, Sullivan would have laughed except she was so breathless from the three flights of stairs.

The minute they got inside, he started yelling and she started cooking. Now, Sullivan does not cook. She occasionally nukes, and even then fails to poke holes in the ready-mades before she nukes them, so they either blow up or come out of the micro-wave so swollen with heat and steam, they have to be left for five minutes to calm down. But somewhere at the back of what we'll laughingly call her brain is the memory of her mother putting on the kettle for tea to prevent shock and baking cakes to cope with bereavement, so she turned on everything and started taking things out of the freezer. The only things Bryan and Sullivan have in the fridge are low fat milk and ground coffee. The coffee is in there because otherwise she can't find it first thing in the morning. She wakes in stages. Walking around she can do quickly. Thinking takes longer. Memory takes twenty-five minutes and even then is patchy. She some-times calls me Rupert, if she gets to the office without enough caffeine in her.

On the Night of the Crushed Jaguar, once she had everything

powered up, she left frozen food on the surface and stripped, knowing that sexy French underwear and high heels is a killer combination for Bryan. It might have worked, too, if she had remembered to fill the kettle before she fed it power. As it was, Bryan got distracted from any possibility of underwear-related lust by the rusty growl it gives when it's empty and filled it so full even Sullivan could see it was going to overflow when it boiled, but was too afraid of him to do anything about it.

Instead, she stood dithering in her undies, holding a packet of frozen baguettes in one hand and a brick-hard Lean Cuisine lasagne in the other, confused by the number of cooking possibilities outlined on the lasagne packet and bothered that they didn't include deep-fat frying. Neither of them had ever used the deep-fat fryer, but, having turned it on, she felt it would be hurt if she turned it off again, unused. Sullivan worries a lot about inanimate objects. When she bumps into furniture in the early mornings, she apologises to it. When she tries on shoes before realising that her credit-card status is Red Alert, she pats them when she takes them off, for fear they'd lose self-esteem.

Bryan's loss of self-esteem wasn't going to be solved by a pat, she could see that. He got launched on the sequence justifying his Jag-crushing by telling her he had been in a pub at lunchtime and heard her name mentioned and someone else asking who she was. The answer had come back immediately: she was 'the girl who's fucking Hugo the Boss' and the person who so described her then got launched on a description of the kind of sex they probably shared. Hugo was the kind of bossy bastard, this informant opined, that probably got his rocks off by being whipped or tied up.

Another voice (Bryan was scrunched down, staring at a

drink-stained cardboard coaster which reminded him to drive safely, so he couldn't tell which girl owned any of the voices) said you never get bondage in marriage, which gave rise to general discussion about why married couples don't handcuff each other to the sleigh bed that much. The consensus was they didn't have time, once they had kids, and also no sensible married woman would trust a guy because men lose things so you couldn't be sure he wouldn't mislay the handcuff key.

Bryan sat there, a mouthful of unchewed sandwich gluing his jaws together, and played back in his head everything Sullivan had ever said to him about Hugo. Or rather, everything she'd ever said that he could remember. Bryan never paid that much attention to what Sullivan says because there's so much of it. He just did pick-and-mix when she'd grind to a halt and feed her a few of the words he remembered so she'd get going again. Like my nephew, who says he can't study unless he has heavy metal on in the background. Sullivan was sort of Bryan's heavy metal, allowing him to think while she talked.

All he could remember was her describing Hugo's wife as 'very Four Seasons' which hadn't meant anything at the time and meant even less now he was faced with the probability of Sullivan having an affair.

In their galley kitchen, that Friday night, he asked her how did she think it made him feel, to hear a total stranger describe her as fucking Hugo the Boss? Sullivan, already confused by the lasagne, tackled the question from the wrong end.

'It sounds like millions of times and it was only twice,' she said reasonably, and he went completely ape-shit, snatching the frozen packages out of her hands so suddenly she was sure chunks of her skin went with them.

At this point, his mobile phone went off, and he grabbed what he thought was it off the surface, discovering when he pressed the right button that he had picked up the wrong (as in Hugo's) phone and casting it from him with such force that it hit the surface, bounced once and went straight into the deep-fat fryer.

'Ah, now,' Sullivan said, in that mild way she has with people who have done something unreasonable. Bryan yelled a greeting into his own phone and was starting to tell the caller he'd ring them back when Hugo's phone blew up in the deep-fat fryer. An arc of boiling fat sprayed up, catching fire on one of the bright red circles of the lit-up hob so that the whole kitchen was suddenly alight.

'Call the fire brigade,' Bryan yelled at his phone caller, as he dragged Sullivan out of the kitchen.

'Why don't *you* call them?' she asked.

I figure the caller was asking the same question. I mean, he (or she) had rung Bryan, taken ages to get a response, been yelled at, heard a bomb go off, been told to call the fire brigade and then got cut off. The caller probably didn't even know Bryan's address.

Bryan then dialled 999 and bellowed the address at whoever answered. It was as if his volume control had got stuck on High. Sullivan ran through the smoke to their bedroom to retrieve her dress and Bryan followed her and then they couldn't get back out because the big open-plan area was black with smoke. Bryan slammed the bedroom door closed with the two of them inside and watched the black smoke curling up like an Irish dancer's ringlets from the bottom of the door. He ran to the floor-to-ceiling window letting out onto the tiny balcony and tried to open it.

'Where's the effing key?'

'Second drawer on the left beside the hob,' Sullivan told him.

When it comes to knowing where things are, she has an idiot-savant genius. In the office, if she misfiles something (which she does 80 per cent of the time) she can tell you precisely where it is without thinking. Which doesn't make her misfiling any easier to bear, but at least speeds up the confusion.

'I'll get it,' she added obligingly, and opened the bedroom door.

The handle burned her hand, the door blew in and knocked her down, and Bryan started to bellow like his earlier offerings had been just a trial run.

He dragged her by the hair across to the window, smashed it with his shoe, and pushed her out onto the balcony where, she told me afterwards, the nice thing was she could hear the fire brigade on its way.

The bedroom was now a mass of roaring flame.

'It's good that it's raining,' Sullivan said to Bryan, who was shouting at the fire brigade and waving his arms, like they might miss the floor where the flames were coming from. A ladder banged against the balcony, and one of the lads was up it in a flash. Bryan lifted her up and before she could protest that she could get onto the ladder by herself, the fireman took her on his shoulder like a pashmina and started down. This – we were soon to know – was the moment the *Star's* photographer captured.

Bryan stood, steaming, for a minute watching her descent. He was steaming literally, because the heat from behind him was vapourising the rain that was lashing down his back. He kicked off the other shoe, climbed onto the ladder and went down it as if it was something he did every day.

At the bottom, Sullivan hugged him, which caused the tin-foil blanket they'd wrapped around her to fall off. This gave rise to a round of applause from bystanders and Bryan would have gone over and thumped every one of them if his mobile phone hadn't gone off. Again.

'Thank you,' he roared. 'They're here.'

'Who's here?' I asked, because it was me ringing, looking for Sullivan.

'The fire brigade,' he told me, as if it was obvious.

'Oh, Jesus, Bryan, what did you do to Sullivan?'

'I saved her fucking life, Patricia, if you must know.'

'Oh, and got the fire brigade as witnesses?'

'Listen, the cops are here, too.'

'I don't give a shit if the Archbishop of Dublin and the seven dwarves are there, Bryan, you put Sullivan on to me this minute.'

'It's all right,' Sullivan's shaky voice told me. 'I'm just a bit scorched down the back.'

'What?'

'Bryan had clothes on, so he's not so bad.'

'*What*?'

'They're taking me – where did you say?'

A calm male voice came on the phone.

'We're taking her to the Mater A&E, but they probably won't keep her. You a friend of hers?'

'Yes.'

'You might bring her some clothes.'

At that point, the phone went dead. I got jeans, a jumper, shoes and a coat and jumped into my car. We'll gloss over how long it took me to park at the Mater and get past their patient-protection systems. I was still standing, clutching the clothes, when Bryan came out through the double doors, followed by a group of gardaí. He hugged me and began to cry, which of course convinced me that Sullivan was dead or in a vegetative state, not that the latter would make much difference to her IQ. Dropping shoes and jumpers, I shook him off my shoulder and demanded promises that she was OK. He snuffled and nodded.

'Jesus, you again,' a female voice said.

Standing right behind Bryan was the garda I'd encountered earlier in the bank's grounds. Bryan went back to crying on my shoulder, which was a serious pain, because he's one heavy dude. The garda picked up the shoes and scrunched up her eyes at me and Bryan.

Then she did a pointed finger at him and raised her eyebrows: *This* the guy who totalled the Jag? I ran out of discretion at that point and just nodded. She stood and did a 'whooo' of quiet admiration: this guy has an exciting life. She prodded him gently.

'We need to get some information, Sir.'

Bryan wiped his face on my shoulder (thanks, friend) and straightened up. The garda handed me the shoes and when Bryan saw them he burst into tears all over again. She rolled her eyes at me and began pulling him by the arm.

'Can you get me in there?' I asked her and she opened the doors without losing her grip on Bryan's arm and nodded me in.

Sullivan was sitting up on a chair the way Christine Keeler, that famous call girl in the spy scandal used to sit, facing backward with a leg hanging either side. A doctor was laying strips of something white over what looked like Vaseline on her very red back. She wasn't paying any attention to him, because directly in front of her, a team of medics were bellowing in a helpful sort of way at a beautiful girl with cornrow hair. They seemed to be trying to wake her up and I could have told them, just by looking at her, that they hadn't a prayer. Every time they got her upright, her head would fall heavily to one side.

I came around Sullivan and she hugged me, spreading whatever ointment was on her all over me. The doctor tut-tutted at me as if it was my fault. I was laying out the clothes when the double doors banged open and a man briefly appeared, bellowing something. Two or three porters followed him and dragged him back out.

The medics dealing with the black girl gave up on trying to wake her up and rigged up an IV. The doctor working on Sullivan went over to check it. Just as he came back, the two gardaí reappeared. One of them got totally distracted by seeing me in A&E. I figured the other one hadn't got around to telling her I was there. The other one, meanwhile, was all business, demanding from the doctor who was wallpapering Sullivan that he admit the spouse of the black girl. He carefully and silently laid the last strip on Sullivan before standing up and turning around.

'Suit you better to arrest that bastard,' he told the two gardaí crisply. 'No bloody way is he getting in here. Why? Because a) we have no evidence that he *is* her spouse or partner, b) we have no idea why a seventeen-year-old would voluntarily ingest a litre of pure whiskey or if she did it voluntarily, c) she carries considerable evidence of recent injury, not self-inflicted and d) that bastard has already assaulted two of my staff and I have a duty of care to patients and staff alike. Any further questions?'

Sullivan clapped her hands to applaud this speech.

'Need to talk to the two of your staff who claim they were assaulted,' one of the gardaí said briskly.

'No, they don't *claim* they were assaulted. I *state* they were assaulted, and everybody in this room will support me.'

'That's true,' Sullivan said. 'Although I didn't see that much because I was facing the other way.'

'Shut up, sweetheart,' I said helpfully, and the doctor nodded as if I should go to the top of the class.

He pointed silently at a pair within the team working on the comatose teenager and one of the two cops went over to them and started making notes. The other muttered that the doctor could be pretty sure yer man would not bother them again tonight. Yer man clearly being the putative spouse/partner/poisoner/batterer of the unconscious cornrow girl. It wasn't clear what she planned to do to the guy, but the doctor seemed mollified by the general intent.

'You're done,' he told Sullivan, who immediately came away from the back of the chair she was straddling and demonstrated that the black French bra had been taken off earlier to facilitate the medical wallpapering of her back. I shoved the jumper at her and she began to put it on without hurry. Privacy and modesty are not concepts of which Sullivan has much of a grasp.

'I'd love your job,' she announced to the cop, who – oddly – looked at the doctor for an explanation. She probably figured he'd injected Sullivan full of hallucinogenic painkillers. He shrugged and started to write notes.

'Do you *have* a job?' the cop asked.

'Wrong question,' I told her. 'Right question: Do you *still* have a job?'

It was the doctor's turn to look confused. As in: why would a beautiful if brainless girl lose her job because her apartment goes on fire?

'course I have a job,' Sullivan said, as insulted as Sullivan ever gets by the suggestion that she might not have one.

'Remind me,' the doctor said. 'It was a chip pan set your kitchen on fire?'

'Well, it was the mobile phone, really,' Sullivan said. 'Bryan threw it into the chip pan. Not his own. Hugo's.'

'Hugo's chip pan?' the doctor asked.

I shook my head. I might not know much, but I knew that if Hugo had a chip pan, it had no role in a fire at Bryan's apartment.

'Why'd he throw your boss's phone into a chip pan?' the cop asked.

'Well, he didn't mean to, it just bounced.'

'What did?'

'The phone.'

'Whose phone?'

'Hugo's. I told you.'

'Hugo's the big baldy oul fella with the accordion Jag,' the cop told the A&E medic, who started to write it down before he caught himself.

'He's only in his fifties,' Sullivan said, defensively.

'What did Hugo's phone bounce off?' I wanted to know.

'Bryan threw it in the kitchen because it wasn't his when it rang.'

We all three considered this.

'Of course, it wasn't it that rang,' Sullivan said, with an air of clearing everything up.

'What did you give her?' the cop asked the doctor.

'I can't tell you because of patient confidentiality,' he responded. 'But believe it or not, nothing, yet.'

'This isn't a new symptom of shock,' I said. 'Sullivan is always like this. I think she means Bryan mistook Hugo's phone for his own and threw it away when he realised.'

'And it bounced into the deep-fat fryer,' Sullivan finished. 'It blew up the whole thing. Hugo's going to be furious about his SIM card. I mean, the Jag is bad enough, but without his SIM card, he'll be helpless.'

'Who's Hugo?' the doctor asked, trying not to get sucked into this but failing.

'I told you,' the cop said severely. 'Big baldy oul fella. Had a real nice Jaguar until *her* very best friend assaulted it this afternoon.'

'Why did you assault a Jaguar?' the doctor asked me.

'It was Bryan,' Sullivan said. 'Not her.'

'The guy who throws phones?'

'Exactly.'

'What did he assault it with?'

'His own car. SUV.'

The doctor considered this and decided he was never going to understand any of it. He handed me a couple of prescriptions and announced he was going to give Sullivan an antibiotic shot. Did she have a penicillin allergy?

'No,' she told him. 'But I used to have a very bad egg allergy when I was a child. My tongue used to burn in a peppery way whenever I ate an egg. Even if I didn't know I was eating an egg. In sponge cake, even.'

He silently injected her and taped Elastoplast over the site. I held out the jeans to her and she put her hand on my shoulder to get her legs into them. She didn't seem to notice the mucky damp on that shoulder, earlier donated by Bryan. I put the shoes where she could step into them. The jeans were six inches too short, but other than that, she looked fine. Feck it, let's be honest. Even with jeans that were way too short, she looked breathtaking. Put the same jeans on me, they'll fit me perfectly and you won't notice me.

'Where is the phone-thrower now?' the cop asked as her colleague rejoined her.

'He'll be back at the apartment,' Sullivan told her.

'What – revisiting the scene of the crime?'

Sullivan looked totally confused.

'Not his own apartment. Bryan will have gone to stay with his brother,' I said.

'Is this Rupert the Bear?'

'No, that's *my* brother,' Sullivan said. 'I can't even ring him,' she added to the doctor. 'Because my mobile phone got left behind in the fire.'

'I hope it's insured.'

'Oh, it is, and I know exactly where the form is.'

'In the apartment?'

'Yes, it's – '

The realisation that everything in the apartment was history struck Sullivan all of a sudden and she began to cry. I put the coat around her and pointed her at the door. Otherwise, she'd have given them a full inventory of every framed photograph of herself and Bryan in every exotic holiday resort they were unlikely to revisit in the foreseeable future.

I glanced back before the doors closed and sure enough, the doctor was looking after Sullivan with an air of wistful longing. Some other time, fella, I thought. Right now, her romantic life is as overpopulated as Bangladesh.

CHAPTER THREE

Water Damage

S he slept the way you'd expect someone to sleep after the day she'd had. She didn't really lie on the bed, just fell across it and got in my way while I pulled the jeans and shoes off her. When I turned out the light, I could hear her saying 'Night, night' like a four-year-old and five minutes later she was snoring like a sixty-year-old. She snored even in her teens. I remember having a nightmare, the year we were in the Gaeltacht, that she'd get us expelled for not snoring in Irish.

I went out at about ten on Saturday to get papers and coffee. The papers mentioned a fire in an apartment block which had caused the evacuation of all residents, but it didn't name the perpetrators. Or speculate about the cause.

My phone never stopped ringing and doing the squawk that says it's receiving e-mails and texts. All of them wanting the inside dope on the dope inside my house. I sent a standard text to everybody saying nobody had been badly hurt, which I imagine annoyed the hell out of them, because even though each of them started by asking about Sullivan's state of health, that wasn't what they were after. Knowing the Dublin rumour machine, the word on the street by that stage probably included her and Hugo having sex on a trampoline four times a night.

She was wandering around when I got back. I put the papers down and pointed to the stories.

'Why would they put all those people out of their homes?' she wanted to know.

'It was quite a fire,' I said mildly. 'There'd have been water damage. Smoke damage. The electrical system is probably buggered. Maybe structural damage.'

'Well, at least it showed the fire brigade are good.'

She said it like she was a spy shopper who had found nothing but positive things in her experimental conflagration. She drank her own coffee and then drank mine as well without noticing. Good, I thought. At least she's not going to keel over from dehydration. I fed her antibiotics and asked if she needed painkillers. She shook her head.

'I didn't get burned, just a bit hot. I have to have a shower.'

'You can't have a shower. The doctor said that stuff has to stay on you.'

'Have you got a raincoat?'

'Sorry?'

'I could wear it in the shower.'

'Sullivan, do you know anybody these days who has a raincoat?'

'My mother has a raincoat.'

'Your mother lives in Leitrim.'

'My hair is filthy.'

'That's true. We could wash it in the sink.'

'And then I could have a bath.'

'As long as you just sat in it.'

'As opposed to what?'

'Lying down in it, for Chrissakes.'

When we were ready to do the hair-washing, she baulked at my shampoo.

'I can't believe you use something so harsh.'

'D'you want your hair washed or not?'

She put her head in the sink with a big sigh and I scrubbed the smoke and smuts out of her long, expensively highlighted locks.

'D'you know the worst bit?'

'Of what?' I asked, rinsing thoroughly and waiting for her to whinge about me not having conditioner.

'Nobody's ringing me.'

I towel-dried her hair and handed her the dryer.

'You don't have a diffuser?'

'What's a diffuser?'

Another sigh. It was like she had been dumped in the middle of some developing country where the water gave you parasites the size of sheep.

'Everybody's ringing you, probably,' I said, ignoring the diffuser issue. 'They just don't know your phone fell victim to the fire.'

She nodded, pleased with this. I could see her rehearsing it to say to other people: *my phone fell victim to the fire.*

'Should we ring Bryan's brother?'

'No, we shouldn't.'

I was expecting an argument, but she headed for the bathroom and started to run a bath.

'Promise me you won't lie down in it?'

'Promise.'

'And that you won't lock the door?'

Stupid instruction. She never does. What am I talking about? She never locks the door of the loo. You can be halfway into the room before you realise you have company and have to back out, apologising like hell for what is not your fault.

This time, she didn't even close the bathroom door. Conversation was easier with it open.

'Do you think this is the end for me and Bryan?'

'The fire or the Jag or discovering you've been at it with Hugo?'

'You *know*.'

'Probably.'

'Really?'

'Well, he didn't really take the news lying down, did he?'

'But that just shows he cares.'

Out of the mouths of blondes, I thought.

'Well, doesn't it?'

'A Jaguar and a luxury apartment both written off in one day would certainly indicate a move away from neutrality,' I agreed. 'Does that mean he'll come around here with a bouquet of red roses and an engagement ring? Not sure. Ask you a question?'

'Sure.'

'What possessed you to go to bed with Hugo?'

'Well, why do *you* go to bed with men?'

That question was so porcupine-shaped, I didn't know where to start. Plus, if you must know, I was kind of flattered by the present tense and the plural. I haven't quite got to the stage of celibacy-surrender and a cat, but I'm close. We may be the same age, but Sullivan is twenty-eight going on eighteen. I'm twenty-eight going on forty.

'I was sorry for him, in a way, because his wife is such a bitch.'

As described by the unfaithful swain, the wife is always a bitch, I thought but didn't say. The other thing I didn't do was repeat the remark about Hugo's wife being very Four Seasons, mainly because it didn't sound such a bad thing to be. Who'd want to be very Jury's Inn?

'Plus, she's so *old*,' Sullivan said, at the end of a stream of stuff about the wife.

'Same age as Hugo, surely?'

'Oh, no, she's a lot older. Two, three years at least. And anyway, it's different for men.'

Put it on a t-shirt, honey. One of life's great truths. One of ageing's inescapabilities. Age is different for men.

'You screwed him because you were sorry for him?'

'You don't have to talk like that.'

I do, I thought. Because if I said 'you made love to Hugo' I might get good and queasy.

'He's very masterful.'

'Dogmatic bossy bully, you mean.'

'Whatever.'

'Is he good in bed?'

'He's the same as he is out of bed.'

No offence to Hugo, but I'd have thought that was a pretty potent *anti*-aphrodisiac, if there's such a thing.

'Sullivan, tell me something. Has Hugo ever bought you anything?'

'A gift, you mean?'

What the hell else, I thought.

'He's taken me to dinner twice.'

'What's he actually bought you, though?'

'Nothing.'

'What does that tell you?'

All that emanated from the bathroom for the next few minutes was splashes. I could almost hear Sullivan thinking. Hugo spends money on old cars. Other than that, his reach-for-the-wallet reflex is so poorly developed that some of the guys in the office maintain he'll never retire because he couldn't bear having to stump up for his own newspaper in the morning. They think he simply couldn't manage without his bank-donated free copy of *The Irish Times* each morning.

Bottom line about Hugo is he has beer tastes on champagne money. I was once on a flight to Milan with him and not only did he take the little metallic envelope of Hellman's light mayonnaise off his tray, he took mine off *my* tray, too. And then slowed up a line of passengers as we exited the plane, picking up sections of the *Financial Times* left behind by others.

'Sullivan?'

'Hmmm?'

'You don't love Hugo?'

'No!'

She laughed, as if I'd suggested she might be in love with Pope Benedict.

'Why do you scr – why do you go to bed with guys you don't love?'

'What's love got to do with it?'

'Most of us don't go to bed with total strangers.'

'Everybody does at the weekend. Well, maybe not people like you.'

'Sullivan?'

'Yeah?'

'Do you realise it's a scientific fact that if I went in there and grabbed you under your knees, I could have you underwater and drowned within two minutes and nothing you could do would save you?'

'How do you know?'

'There was a famous murder case where they did it to a policewoman in a bath in the middle of the court and she went unconscious immediately. Even though it was only a demonstration and she was expecting it.'

'Did she have her uniform on?'

'Why does that matter, for Chrissake?'

'Why did you tell me in the first place?'

'I've forgotten.'

I could hear her getting out of the bath and hovered nearby in case she got weak. After a minute, she padded out, barefoot, looking better in my towelling robe than I ever looked.

'You go to bed with people because you like them, because you're sorry for them, because you're feeling horny. It doesn't have to mean anything,' she explained.

'Oh, and you'd have been thrilled if someone told you me and Bryan were hard at it behind your back?'

'Nobody would tell me that.'

'Why not?'

'Because you'd never have sex with Bryan.'

'What's wrong with him?'

(Other than attacking Jags and apartments, I mean.)

'Nothing. He's a bit fast, though.'

I *so* didn't want to go there. The orgasmic speed of other people's near-boyfriends is not something I care to think about a lot.

'But you wouldn't anyway, you're not the type.'

'I thought you said everybody did?'

'Yes, but not under-sexed people.'

'Sullivan?'

'Mmm?'

'You are so lucky I am your best friend, you know that? Because anybody else would have killed you long ago, you're such an insulting bimbo.'

'But you know I don't mean it,' she said comfortably, and gave me a hug. 'Like, I wasn't suggesting you weren't attractive enough to get a man, it's just your pheromones are low.'

That's it, then. Wonder if you can get a pheromone supplement on the VHI?

'I'll have to see Bryan anyway over the insurance.'

'That'll be good. Continue the relationship over the claim forms.'

'He dragged me by the hair, you know.'

I waited for some atavistic cave-girl viewpoint. Some masochistic he-beats-me-he-loves-me comment.

'Yes,' Sullivan said, looking, dreamily, into her own dramatic recent memories. 'I was thinking it's lucky I got rid of the extensions.'

You have to admit she has a point. You don't want your extensions to fail just when your life depends on them.

CHAPTER FOUR

Monday is the Root of all Evil

Sullivan was still asleep when I left for work on Monday. I left the car keys for her, together with a note to remind her how to use a manual gear change. On Baggot Street, I went into the shop to get a coffee, working out in my head how to allocate some of the work she'd normally do, when I suddenly found myself looking at Sullivan in her underwear, in full colour, on the front page of one of the tabloids. Some earlier customer had left the newspaper behind them.

It winded me, it was so unexpected. I mean, Sullivan is always in trouble of some kind, but it doesn't usually reach the tabloids. The sight of it made me ask for a third shot of espresso. The story was continued on an inside page and mentioned an earlier but obscurely related confrontation on the same day involving two cars, illustrated with several shots of Hugo's Jag, from every possible angle.

Not good, I thought. The number plate had not been destroyed by Bryan's vigorous assault. It was readable. Anybody who knew Hugo would know the car. Plus there was a smaller shot showing the exterior of the bank with the sign identifying it. The designer who had come up with the new brand (5 million euro's worth) would be delighted. The board of the bank would not.

I passed that same sign a couple of minutes later, swiped myself in to the building and got into the lift with an improbably handsome strange man who raised his matching beaker of coffee to me in mute salute: we band of brothers, we band of Vente brothers. I got off at the third floor. He was obviously going on to the fourth, where the movers and shakers live. He had a cashmere coat.

At my desk, I folded the *Star* over and shoved it into a drawer, took a deep breath and logged on to my computer. The inbox in my e-mail started to behave like Niagara Falls. Not just the usual messages offering me bigger penises, cheaper flights and instant loans. This particular morning, as one message after another fell into place, it was obvious from the subject lines that 90 per cent of them wanted the dirt on Sullivan. Half of them called me Patsy. I hate Patsy. Trish I can live with, but Patsy is my aunt's name and I don't want to share anything with her. Not a country, a century or even an oxygen supply.

I wrote a preachy little paragraph to the effect that the bank's rules on use of the Internet precluded me from answering questions about non-bank issues. And then deliberately sent it to a list of people so they could all see they were one of a squirming bunch of maggots living on an open wound. I really enjoy reverse networking. How To Lose Friends and Piss Off People.

One of the messages gave me pause. It was from our Head

of HR, asking me to make sure Sullivan dropped into the HR Department as soon as possible. I rang the house but got no answer. After four rings, I cut off – no point in dragging her out of sleep, I thought.

Wrong again. She wasn't asleep. She was on her way into work, stopping off at the Mater to get the wallpaper stripped off her back. Which was why everybody else had arrived when she pitched up at my desk with my car keys. They all watched her like she was Paris Hilton. Or worse.

'They've take away Hugo's Jag,' she whispered. 'Every bit of it.'

'I know.'

'The lamp post is at a bit of an angle, though,' she murmured in a satisfied way, like a tourist who visits the site of the Battle of Waterloo and finds a rusted bayonet, thereby linking themselves to a significant historic event.

'Lego Littleton was looking for you,' I told her.

'Why'd she ask you?'

'She may have started with your boss, but I'm not sure he's on the premises. Or it could be as simple as her being aware that you and I are friends. Who cares? She's probably heard about the fire and wants to give you access to some special emergency fund.'

'No,' Sullivan said. 'Whatever she wants, it isn't that.'

My phone rang. I looked at the screen.

'That's her now.'

Sullivan did a 'you talk to her, I'm not here' mime. I picked up the phone. Our head of Human Resources, Lucy Littleton, is known as Lego Littleton because she looks like one of those little figures kids put in the houses they build with plastic bricks. Hard. Roundy. And with a plastic helmet of hair that wouldn't move even in a hurricane. She's Lego Littleton except when she's Lethal Littleton. Which is most of the time.

I picked up the handset and greeted her neutrally. She came on like a battalion. Had I seen the *Star*? I had.

(I groped in the drawer and pulled it out to show Sullivan. She spent rather too much time drinking coffee and examining the front page picture, I thought, when she could more profitably have been considering the corporate and career implications of the inside story.)

Lego Littleton cut to the chase, as she always does. Not much for small talk, our Head of Human Resources. She wanted to see Sullivan in her office right now.

'I presume you've telephoned her extension?' I asked, brightly unhelpful.

'I know she's with you and not at her desk.'

'The secret cameras are working, then?'

'Patricia. Put her on to me.'

'A "please" would be good.'

'Please put her on to me.'

'Here's a compromise. Why don't I bring Sullivan to your office in about ten minutes?'

'Sullivan knows where my office is.'

'True. Very true. But you will appreciate that a girl who's suffered such a trauma might benefit from the presence of a close friend during any meeting with the Head of Human Resources.'

Sullivan looked startled. I put a finger across my mouth: say nothing.

'What am I to take from that?' Lego Littleton asked.

'Oh, I think someone of your intelligence and education would apprehend the full meaning of what I've said.'

'Get her up here.'

'Please?'

She cut me off.

'Why does that bitch want to see me?' Sullivan asked.

That she called the Lego Lady a bitch said a lot about our Head of Human Resources, because Sullivan gives everybody the benefit of the doubt. In Hugo's case, rather too much benefit of not a lot of doubt, but who am I, pheromone-deficient as I am, to judge?

'I suspect she wants to terminate you with extreme prejudice.'

Sullivan goggled at me.

'Fire you.'

'Why would she want to fire me?'

I took the *Star* from her and opened it to the page celebrating Bryan's Jag-destruction. She winced at the sight of it.

'But what's that to do with her?'

'Picture? Of bank? With sign?'

'So?'

'Sullivan. This is *so* not good PR for the brand.'

She understood that, all right.

'But it wasn't my doing.'

'No, but she can't fire Bryan.'

'He doesn't work here.'

'True. And Hugo's just a bit too senior for her to do anything to him. Although, between you, me and the burned-out walls of your apartment, if Lego Littleton had her way, I suspect she'd have Hugo out the door along with you.'

'I'm not going.'

'You're bloody right you're not going. That's why I'm attending this meeting.'

'You're my guardian angel.'

At this, my PA, who up to now had been drinking her coffee and pretending to see no Sullivan, hear no Sullivan and speak no Sullivan, did a reverse snort that put cappuccino all over everything. I left her to mop herself up and marched out into the corridor, followed by Sullivan.

'When we go in there, I want you to do one thing for me.'

'OK.'

'Just ask questions.'

'What questions?'

'Any questions. Ask. Don't answer. Don't answer anything. Not anything. You clear?'

'I can ask questions but not answer them.'

'Anything else, I'll take care of.'

The two of us headed off. When the doors parted on the fourth floor, the handsome guy who'd saluted me with the coffee was outside, waiting for the lift.

'We can't keep meeting like this,' he told me.

'Why not?' I asked. 'It's been good so far.'

He laughed and got into the lift as I told the receptionist we were expected by the Head of HR. The receptionist fought down her self-evident urge to say 'I know, and I know why, too,' and just ushered us in.

Lucy Littleton got up and came around her big desk to greet us, gesturing us to sit at the little oval coffee table in the corner. Sullivan looked flattered. It wouldn't occur to her that the little oval coffee table is for softening up edible humans the way a boa constrictor softens its lunch before ingesting it.

'So how *are* you?' Lucy asked, sitting down on one of the soft chairs. I'm always surprised that she can. She's made up like a snowman of three circles, and I worry that the middle circle will be scrunched or burst when she sits down, but it never does. Pity.

'How are *you*?' Sullivan asked in return, taking my instructions literally. Good.

'Oh, I'm fine,' Lucy said, laughing lightly. Like a tin can rolling down a metal staircase. 'But then, I didn't have the kind of tough weekend you did.'

'Did you have a good weekend?' Sullivan asked politely and the smile froze on Littleton's face while she tried to figure out if Sullivan was being a smartarse.

'I had a fine weekend,' she said in the tone of voice you'd use to announce an outbreak of bubonic plague in the canteen. 'Maybe you'd like to fill me in on *your* weekend, though.'

'Why?' Sullivan asked.

Lucy the Lego Lady fixed me with a look of pure hatred. I examined my French manicure. Needed renovation. In common with almost everything else in my life.

'Sullivan, you will appreciate that what has happened has wider implications.'

'Wider than what?'

'Oh, come *on*.'

Sullivan looked at me with an expression of pure terror, and I realised she had run out of questions.

'Perhaps I could help, here,' I said softly. 'Maybe we could first establish the objective of this meeting.'

Sullivan nodded happily. Sounded good to her.

'The objective of this meeting is to find out what precisely led to two major incidents which have had and are likely to continue to have considerable negative implications for the bank,' Lucy told me.

'Where would you like to start?' Sullivan asked.

You brainless blonde bint, I thought. I wanted you to ask questions, but I didn't mean you to ask that kind of open question.

'At the beginning,' Lucy said, as if Sullivan was four and a half.

'Well, on Friday evening, we were outside waiting for my boyfriend Bryan to pick me up and – '

'I'm not clear why Sullivan is being asked about an incident that didn't involve her,' I intervened. 'We both saw Mr Eglinton's car being destroyed and very regrettable it was, too, but neither of us was involved. I'm sure you have access to lots of other witnesses who can recount exactly what happened.'

'But maybe you want to know about the fire?' Sullivan prompted and at that stage I gave serious consideration to choking her. Particularly when Lucy nodded agreeably with a 'now we're sucking diesel' expression on her hard doll face.

'A statement has already been given to the Garda Síochána on that,' I said.

'But maybe they wouldn't give it to HR,' Sullivan told me. I gave her a look that promised broken teeth. Hers, not mine.

The three of us sat in silence. Lucy pushed her fringe up off her forehead, with surprising results. She had one of those rigid black bobs with a fringe that came to within millimeters of her black eyebrows. It never moved. When she pushed it back, I could see why she might choose such a godawful haircut. Her hairline came halfway down her forehead. Or, if you looked at it another way, she had only half a forehead. Her entire fore-head was maybe an inch from hairline to eyebrows.

'You might usefully reflect on this,' she said eventually.

'How do you mean?' Sullivan asked, happy to be back in questioning mode. She looked across at me for approval.

'Just,' Lucy said firmly. 'The bank is happy to provide you with leave which would not be drawn from your annual allot-ment to facilitate this.'

'Gardening leave,' I said.

Lucy shrugged.

'I don't have a garden, any more,' Sullivan said, suddenly teary-eyed at the loss of waves of romantic bluebells in springtime.

'You never *had* a garden,' I snapped.

'But I don't garden is the point.'

'You don't understand gardening leave. It's just a phrase. You don't have to mulch. The bank really sends you home to exam-ine your conscience. That way you don't pollute any of the rest of the staff and they don't look like they're approving of you prancing around on balconies in your thong.'

'It wasn't a thong. I don't like thongs. I don't think women do, really. It's men who are turned on by them, isn't it?'

Why she directed this to Lucy Littleton I couldn't imag-ine. The Lego Lady's image, inside the bank, had never been tainted by association with any member of the opposite sex and the size of her ass would have swallowed up even an oversized thong, no bother.

I stood up and Sullivan stood up with me.

'Tell me, off the record, Lucy,' I said, 'what do you figure is going to happen as a result of all this?'

She smoothed the fringe back into place over her forehead deficit and looked at me with calm contempt.

'Off the record,' she retorted in a kind of spit. Meaning: forget it.

'All right,' I told Sullivan, heading for the door. 'Let's go reflect.'

CHAPTER FIVE

Lawyering Up

*A*s we approached the lift, the handsome guy was approaching it from the other side. The two of us began to laugh. Sullivan smiled to indicate she wanted to join in but didn't know the punchline of the joke. The guy pressed the lift button, then held out his hand.

'Mike Kearns,' he told me.

'Patricia Gogarty,' I responded. 'And this is Sullivan Spencer.'

'The girl who wears the coolest underwear in the hottest situations.'

Sullivan glowed. She looked like she was getting ready to make an Oscar speech when the lift doors opened and disgorged three oversized members of top management, Hugo in the middle. I looked to see if he was attached to either of the other two by handcuffs, but no. He looked into the middle distance and strode purposefully away. We three got into the lift.

'He might at least have asked how you were feeling,' Mike Kearns said to Sullivan.

'He's probably under a lot of pressure,' Sullivan told him.

'Pressure is no excuse for abandoning good manners. Quote from my mother, repeated down the years at appropriate intervals.'

The lift doors opened at our floor and he followed us out.

'You don't belong here,' Sullivan told him.

'How d'you know?'

'Just,' she said. Picked that one up from Lucy the Lego Lady, I thought.

Mike Kearns was fumbling in his jacket pocket. He produced a business card and handed one to each of us.

'You're a lawyer,' Sullivan said, impressed.

'An employment lawyer,' I said slowly reading from the card. 'No doubt you have been called in to advise Them Up There on how to get rid of Sullivan without a fight?'

He leaned against the wall and laughed out loud.

'What's so effing funny?'

'You,' he said, looking down at me. 'Squaring up to hit a man a foot taller and forty pounds heavier than you are.'

'And it all pure muscle,' Sullivan said admiringly.

That made him laugh even more. I gave Sullivan the 'run along' look and after a minute's argument-by-facial-expression, she ran along. Probably because she knew everybody in her office would be only dying to get the full story. She should tell them nothing, I thought, but it was too late to do anything about it at that stage.

'I was dealing with corporate banking, up there,' Mike Kearns said, getting serious. 'Nobody as much as mentioned the girl with the legs up to her armpits and the Prada shoes. Reason I give you my card is I suspect you may need me. Or she may.'

47

'You're good, are you?'

'You know that old Saatchi ad that goes "d'you want me working for your opposition?" I'm that good.'

'But if you work for Sullivan, they'll hate you, upstairs. You'll never get another case out of them.'

'When you're as good as I am, they expect you to work for whoever books you first. They wouldn't hold it against me. They couldn't afford to hold it against me. Think cutting off nose to spite face.'

'Should I be giving you a euro or something to retain you?'

'I'll just consider myself retained. What's your relationship with Gorgeous?'

'The foil. The straight man. The plain-looking best friend. The shovel friend.'

He obviously wasn't familiar with that term, so I explained it.

'You don't have a card?'

I found one that I'd written a shopping list on. He read the shopping list.

'Black olive pâté?'

'It was in a recipe I was going to make. Never got around to it.'

Sullivan appeared beside him, glowing.

'TV3 have invited me to go on their breakfast programme tomorrow morning.'

'No,' Mike Kearns and I said, together. 'No, no, no.'

Sullivan looked so crestfallen, I rushed to explain.

'Honey, you have a load of legal and insurance problems to sort out before you can go public on this. There'll be other opportunities later, trust me. It would just be so dangerous for you to go on telly right now.'

She stood, her lower lip beginning to jut in the general direction of defiance.

'Presumably all your very best clothes were destroyed in the fire?' Mike Kearns said.

This made much more sense to Sullivan.

'I'll wait until I get new things,' she nodded and disappeared.

'You're very clever,' I said to Kearns.

'Empathy up the kazoo,' he said briskly. 'We'll talk. And in the meantime, keep her from talking.'

This was a difficult mission. Since our schooldays, Sullivan has believed in the talk cure for everything. If she punctured the tyre on your bike, she was convinced that telling you the story of the drawing pin she'd run over would make you feel better about walking the two miles home from school. If your boyfriend fell for her – and they always did – she would tell you who his uncle in Castlebar was. Like you cared. It had taken me years to understand that talking, for Sullivan, equated to living. As long as words were coming out of her, she could not die. Whenever she was scared of anything, she talked as if any three-second pause would cause her to disassemble. Which was why all of her friends made sure, when they went on skiing trips with her, that they sat at the other end of the plane. Total strangers got the full blast of Sullivan's output and seemed to quite enjoy it. I suppose if it was the first time you'd experienced a stream of unrelated anecdote infused with goodwill and delivered by a stunning blonde, you wouldn't mind too much.

The rest of that day was filled with phone calls from media people to Sullivan, to the PR Division in the bank, to other workers in the bank. One of the guys who reached me was a radio producer whose sister I knew.

'Not telling you anything,' I said when I picked up the phone to him.

'Knew you wouldn't, but keep talking to me anyway.'

'Why?'

'Have to convince my presenter that I'm busting my ass and yours to persuade you to give up the First Secret of Sullivan. He's watching me even as we speak.'

'How long will this last?'

'God alone knows. Slow news day today. If something major breaks tomorrow, it could fade.'

'Ever hear of Michael Kearns?'

'Oh, yeah. Oh, really, yeah. Way to go, legally. The guy's shit hot. Gay as Christmas, but not even the old fart judges seem to hold it against him.'

I sat there, thinking about this. It felt oddly freeing, to know the handsome guy was gay. Me and the radio producer bantered a bit before I put the phone down. It immediately rang again.

'Mike Kearns.'

'I've just been checking you out with a radio producer.'

Hell, I thought. Why did I say that?

'What did you get told?'

'That you're shit hot and gay as Christmas.'

He roared laughing – a great rollicking unguarded laugh that made me laugh too.

'That radio producer has a future. Listen, a thought struck me. Where's Sullivan Spencer living, these days?'

'In my house. Redbrick. Ranelagh.'

'Good purchase. Worth millions already.'

'Should be, the mortgage I'm carrying.'

'The thing is, this country has suddenly developed papparaziitis. Wouldn't surprise me at all if the two of you encountered a phalanx of snappers when you go back home this evening.'

'So you want me to get Sullivan to refresh her make-up before she leaves the office?'

'Be no harm. Don't want a shot of her captioned "a drawn-faced Spencer takes refuge in the home of a female friend".'

'Be a lot better than a shot of her beaming and waving like she's just won the lottery.'

'You're absolutely right. Tell her to keep a serious face on her and look fixedly at something about six feet away at her own eye-level and not get distracted no matter who calls out to her. You, likewise. Or the two of you can talk to each other as you walk.'

'No, that wouldn't work.'

'You'd make each other laugh?'

'No, Sullivan would fall over something if she wasn't looking ahead. Can I ask you something?'

'Sure.'

'Why d'you care?'

'She actually seems a nice kid.'

'She is. But the world is full of nice kids.'

'Not wearing chic underwear, Prada heels and back lit by a bonfire.'

CHAPTER SIX

Look this Way

*T*he way I explained it to Sullivan, she was giving a performance.

'You know when you see photographs of Paris Hilton, she's never smiling and waving or making faces? That's because she knows the cameras are going to be there and she has to control what they deliver to the publications, because that's how she makes her living.'

'She doesn't have to make a living. She's an heiress. That's what her perfume is called.'

'Heiress?'

'Yes. I have some of it.'

'But she wants to be a singer or something?'

'I think she's given up on that,' Sullivan said, as seriously as if she was talking about the war in Iraq.

'The point is, she controls the pictures they take.'

'Nicole did the same when she got busted.'

'Nicole who?'

'Richie. She was busted for DUI on Oxycodone.'

Sullivan got launched on Nicole Richie's anorexia, drug history and the pharmaceutical properties of Oxywhateveritwas. This was how she got through exams, I realised. She retained everything like a blocked-up sink.

'The thing is,' I said urgently, as we entered Ranelagh, 'the pictures have to show you looking tranquil and beautiful and uninvolved, OK?'

'What about you?'

'What *about* me?'

'You'll be in the pictures, too.'

For a mad minute, I surveyed myself to see if the suit I had on would stand up to camera scrutiny.

'They'll probably crop you out, but,' Sullivan said, with blunt accuracy if not good syntax. I even got cropped out of a photograph in our secondary school yearbook, the final year. You could see my arm, linked into Sullivan's, but the rest of me had been amputated.

'I'll look into the middle distance, too,' I said. 'There they are.'

She drew in her breath like she'd been told Santa was halfway down her chimney.

Half thrilled. Half scared.

'Stop looking at them. Start searching for something in your handbag.'

That was a good idea. Sullivan has one of those handbags that cost half the industrial wage and could hold a Great Dane. It has gold rings and pleats and pockets front and back. She started to search in it. I drove carefully through the photographers and parked in what used to be the garden of my little house, before I had it bricked over. The two of us got out into a storm of instructions. Yells of her name. Calls to turn this way or that way. She walked to the front door as if she'd been recently anaesthetised, which was some achievement, because they were literally in her face. I got the door open and pushed her through it, resisting the temptation to turn around and give them the finger.

'Stand there,' I told her and went into the front room to pull down the blind.

'I felt it was rude not to say "excuse me",' she said, still standing inside the front door. 'But I knew you wouldn't want me to.'

'You can come into the kitchen,' I said, realising too late that one of them was in the back garden. I pulled the tie-backs off the curtains of the kitchen window and the light fabric fell across the glass, cutting out his view of us. First time I had ever released those curtains and it showed how much they had faded.

'You have a lot of post,' Sullivan said, handing it to me.

I rummaged in the freezer and found something to nuke for the two of us.

'Most of it's shite,' she added, segregating the direct post from the real stuff and handing me the latter.

'Make us a cup of tea, would you?' I asked her, sitting down to open the post.

The landline started shrilling. She reached for the receiver, then shrank away from it. I lifted it.

'Well, I hope you're happy,' a female voice shrieked.

It's a funny thing. Whenever someone says they *hope* you're happy, it always means they actually hope you're in misery-meltdown.

'Who is this?' I asked neutrally.

'You know bloody well who it is,' the voice yelled, and I

did. My cousin Goretti. Named after an early Christian martyr. Born with the sense of entitlement and injury implicit in borrowed martyr status.

'I hope you never have a moment's happiness in it,' she went on. 'You sucked up to that old fool deliberately. Think I didn't notice?'

'Goretti, what are we talking about?'

'Oh, yeah, play the innocent.'

Sullivan took the Lean Cuisine out of the microwave and divided it into two bowls. I gestured to her to take the three tea bags out of the mug she was making for me. The tea was already the colour of Ribena. She fecked them into the sink. Goretti was in full spate. I held the phone out so that Sullivan could hear it. Her eyes widened in appreciation. I put the receiver to my ear.

'Goretti, I'm going to put the pho – '

'You cut me off and I'll come right around there,' she bellowed.

Sullivan shook her head violently. Neither of us might know what was eating Goretti, but it wouldn't help the situation if she allowed it to eat her in front of all the photographers in the front garden.

'I could challenge this, you know. I could. I've taken legal advice,' Goretti went on.

'That makes two of us,' I told her. 'My lawyer is shit hot.' And gay as Christmas, I didn't add.

'Oh, and you were letting on not to know anything about it,' she hissed.

No, Goretti, I genuinely don't know anything about it, I thought, but by coincidence, I have a lawyer who'll fight your lawyer. If and when. My lawyer is probably bigger than your lawyer, too.

'I wouldn't demean myself,' she said, in a self-reverential way.

'Good,' I said. 'Anything else you want to get off your chest before I let you go?'

Now that, you should know, was a really low blow. Goretti and I are the same age. Three weeks separate us.

We went to the same school, and it drove her nuts that I always did better in exams than she did. But what really galled her ass was that I got boobs in the adolescent lottery and she didn't. It's not that she's flat-chested. She does have something, up top. She has two flattened blobs like someone stuck bits of chewing gum on her front when they'd finished chewing it.

I, on the other hand, have great boobs. Not much to look at otherwise, but the boobs are good. Which drove Goretti around the twist, although my mother always called her Harpic, in reference to some loo cleaner that claimed to 'clean around the bend' so maybe the comparative boob deficit just confirmed her problems. I had always known, though, that any reference to chests would set her off. When I was a decent convent school girl, I used to do it by accident, the way you tell a bald guy that you're going to get out of his hair or can he tell you something off the top of his head. But by the time we'd done our Leaving Cert, I was doing it deliberately. As was the case at that moment. She banged down the phone on me.

'They're still out there,' Sullivan said, coming back into the kitchen from the front room.

'They're going to get a picture of you, you know, peeping around the curtains.'

'D'you think they'll stay all night?'

'Perfectly honest with you, I don't give a shit.'

'But nobody should have to tolerate this.'

'You are right, Sullivan. But you did make yourself more interesting than the average bank clerk in the last few days.'

I tasted the tea. It was so strong, it tasted like an iron supplement. Sullivan was ploughing through a novel called *Something Primavera*. I began opening and sorting the post. My Aer Lingus frequent flyer miles entitled me to a free drink. As long as I kept the coupon, flew within the next week and didn't share it with anyone else. I glanced up. Sullivan had finished and was looking lost.

'What d'you think of frequent-flyer programmes?' I asked.

Anything to get her going. Off she went like a good 'un. She was even able to tell me that some politician said they should be banned because air travel was contributing so much to global warming. I went on opening envelopes while she discussed the benefits to Dublin night life of global warming: outdoor cafés, evenings fit for spaghetti-strap dresses right up to October.

The third envelope was from a solicitor's office and for one horrible minute, I thought it might be about Sullivan's problems. Then I saw it had a line about the estate of George V. Minton. George V. was my grandfather, an irascible old fart cordially loathed by everybody who knew him, with the exception of his wife (my beloved Nan) and me.

I've no idea why my Nan tolerated him. I enjoyed him because he was ready to fight with someone every minute of the day. When you're placid by nature, as I am, it's very exciting to hang around fighters.

'D'you remember my granddad?' I asked Sullivan.

One of the good things about her flow of talk is that she never minds if you cut her off. I suppose she knows from experience how easy it will be to get started again.

'No, but I've heard of him,' she said solemnly.

'Heard what?'

'My father thought he was awful.'

'Why?'

'He said he'd argue over two flies walking up a wall. Never even bothered to learn the names of his own children.'

That was true. He'd never called me by my name, either. 'You' was his all-purpose form of direct address, and 'that halfwit' his preferred term of third-party reference. You knew where you were with him. Nowhere.

'He's dead a long time?'

I pondered the question she clearly intended. Got it, I thought. Sullivan deals with today, with living people, preferably cool living people, ideally rich living people and if the wind is in the right direction and the force is with her, rich, cool, *famous*, living people. There's no room on her agenda for the dead, except maybe as Any Other Business.

'Six or seven years. I don't know why they're writing to me about his estate.'

The preamble to the letter made that formally clear, once I concentrated on it. My grandfather's will had been written before the car crash that killed my mother and her two brothers but after something else and –

'Maybe he's left you money.'

– this had caused delays and –

'Oh, get to the bloody effing point, would you?' I asked page three of the letter.

– it was only now I could be informed that George V. Minton had bequeathed The Tower, Sloe Head, County Dublin to me, this being a Martello tower on three-quarters of an acre.

'Where's Sloe Head?' I asked Sullivan.

'It's that pokey little place near Baldoyle.'

'My grandfather's left me a Martello tower there.'

'Oh.'

'You're thrilled for me. I can tell. No, no, don't fight your enthusiasm.'

'What would you want it for?'

'Same thing whoever built it wanted it for.'

'The early Christians?'

'What?'

'They used to put those things up so when the Normans came on those boats looking for stuff they could climb up ladders and pull the ladders after them and survive.'

'Remind me again, did you do history in the Leaving Cert?'

'No. I hated Miss Brady.'

Sullivan would have hated Miss Brady because Miss Brady always painted two Toblerone peaks on the skin below her nose to extend the illusion that she had an upper lip. Bad make-up, to Sullivan, is a crime against nature.

'That may explain why you don't know the difference between a round tower and a Martello tower. The ones the early Christians hid in were Round Towers. And it wasn't the Normans they were hiding from – they were Catholics, too. It was the Vikings. Martello towers were much later.'

She pulled her laptop out of the powder-blue satchel and opened it up.

'Where'd you say it was again?'

I told her and she Googled it.

'Oh, it's that funny flat tower like the Joyce museum,' she said, turning the screen around so I could see it.

'Is that a picture of the Sloe Head one or just a general one?'

'It's one in England. Hey, listen to this. "Martello towers were built throughout Britain, Ireland and Canada to protect against coastal invasion by Napoleon. They were named after a tower on Cape Martella in Italy."'

'*Canada*? Why the frig would Napoleon want to invade Canada?'

'Why would anybody want to invade Canada?'

There was no answer to that, although I was a bit offended on Canada's behalf. I think of myself as a human version of Canada. Competent. Discreet. Easily overlooked.

I reread the letter. Having never owned anything unencumbered in my whole life – I even owe €5,000 on my car, and the bloody thing is five years old – I couldn't believe that my grandfather had snuck me this bequest. The letter didn't indicate that he'd been rich, just that he'd owned this tower since 1937. Never told any of us. Held it quietly until he could use it to give the finger to anyone in the family who had hopes he'd leave them anything in his will and surprise the hell out of the one person he knew *wouldn't* have hopes. It wasn't that he was doing me a good turn. He was using me to do everybody else a bad turn. As in life, so in death.

'It says here that the Sloe Head Tower is in poor repair and hasn't been inhabited ever.'

'Ever?'

'No. These yokes were built, it says, at the beginning of the nineteenth century – 1807 and around that time. Along the coast where one could light a fire and be seen by the next one so they'd all know if Napoleon's ships arrived. Hey, this is *cool*. They all had a ring of iron on the roof with a big canon on it, so two of them could co-operate and get a ship in crossfire.'

'How many ships did they sink?'

'Hang on. None. This site says they never fired a gun in anger. Any of them.'

I rooted in a few drawers looking for a map. There it was, sitting on the poking-out bit of a tiny promontory. It even said, in tiny print, 'Martello tower'. I jammed the map in front of Sullivan and hugged her.

'Jaysus, Sullier, I own a little beach. I *own* it.'

She hugged me back.

'Mightn't be a beach. Might be just rocks. You wouldn't want to get your hopes up too high.'

'But I actually *own* this old tower, this thing that soldiers lived in, on the coast. It must have a fabulous view.'

'You'll have to light a candle for your Grandad.'

This caused me some confusion. Sullivan's grasp of religion failed somewhere around her confirmation. Now, you might think it sweet that she still remembers rituals like lighting candles for people, but I know better. Sullivan may not have been responsible for the apartment fire, but she's an arsonist from way back. One day when we were doing our first or second confession and had to hang around while the rest of the class did theirs, she noticed that there were half-burned candles on the silver foil under the metal grid that supports all the little white candles in the back of the church. She rescued them and started lighting one from another. She didn't notice she'd dropped one and that it had stayed lit, until all the wax spills of weeks went up like napalm. The school gave serious consideration to not allowing her to do her first holy communion as a result.

'If I lit a candle for my grandfather, he'd haunt me,' I told her. 'He was an atheist before atheism was cool.'

'Why don't we go and look at your tower, since we have the time?'

'Because those wankers are still outside and we don't want them taking pictures or following us. It'll keep. Nobody's going to run away with a tower overnight. Jaysus, no wonder Goretti's pissed off at me.'

'Why would she want it?'

The bluntness of the question took me by surprise. Wouldn't everybody want to own an historic tower?

'She could live in it.'

'Why would she want to? Would you look.'

She turned the computer around again. This time, the photograph was of a Martello in Sutton, sitting on a rocky base near a cliff, self-contained and threatening.

'They must have had windows.'

'Maybe on the other side,' she agreed.

The two of us looked at this stump of a building, and Sullivan turned to me to see how I was taking it. I suddenly stopped being Canada. I squealed, threw up my arms and ran around the kitchen.

'I own an effing bit of history,' I yelled. 'I'll find out all about it. I'll become the greatest living expert on Martello towers. I'll do it up. I'll live in it. It'll be fantastic.'

'God, it's not like you to get so enthusiastic –'

'And he was so bloody right not to leave it to Goretti…'

'– in fact, it's not like you to get so enthusiastic about anything.'

I sat down again and tried to control the excitement burbling inside me. Sullivan looked at me very seriously.

'You'd need to be realistic,' she said solemnly.

At that, I just lost it. The idea of Sullivan telling anybody to be realistic. She had the good grace to laugh, too.

'No, but seriously. It probably doesn't have a damp course.'

'What the frig is a damp course and why should I care?'

'You don't want mildew everywhere. I can't remember what a damp course is, but my dad will tell you.'

Sullivan's father is a builder. Not a household-name builder, the kind you'd meet in the Fianna Fáil tent at the Galway races or see as a brand name outside a site where fifty apartments are replacing what used to be a neat little local pub. He has always described himself as building small projects that don't fall over.

'Ring him,' I said. 'Ring him and ask him. Right now. Please.'

She stood up, took down the wallphone and dialled.

'Dad? Hi. Listen, I wanted to ask you about Martello towers. What? Oh, listen, don't mind that, it's not important. No, I wasn't burned. No, don't put Ma on, please don't put Ma on. Da? I –'

Sullivan rolled her eyes to heaven and put the phone on speaker. I could hear her mother's footsteps rushing to the phone and then a die-away voice.

'I can't believe you would take this long to telephone when you must have known how anxious your father would be.'

'Ma, Da doesn't do anxious.'

'Oh, and your mother is of no account?'

'Ma, I've been kind of busy.'

'That's obvious.'

'I knew you wouldn't read a rag like the *Star*,' Sullivan said, winking at me, 'So I didn't think you'd hear about it.'

Even for you, Sullivan, I thought, that's dumb. Your parents live in a rural town in Leitrim and you didn't think every neighbour within a radius of a hundred miles wasn't going to arrive, hot foot, with the news of your performance damn-near naked on the front page of a newspaper?

Oddly, her mother didn't even seem flattered by Sullivan saying she knew Mrs Spencer wouldn't read the *Star*. Mrs Spencer gave her to understand that Ger Colleran, the editor of the paper, came from the same town in Mayo as she did and was an admirable human being who was just serving his time. I wracked my brains to try to remember why Ger Colleran would be in jail and then realised she meant the *Star* was just a stepping stone on the way to him editing *The Irish Times* or maybe *The Guardian*.

'Mrs Spencer, this is Patricia,' I said. 'Your daughter is in great nick and the real reason she didn't get to ring you sooner was that I've just got great news.'

She made noises of civil tolerance towards me and without quite asking me to cough up the news, indicated that a good productive cough would be timely. I told her about the Martello.

'On how many acres?' was her question.

Never mind the building, suss out the land.

'Half an acre. Three quarters.'

'Tsk tsk.'

I could feel myself getting red in the face and Sullivan made 'calm down' gestures at me.

'Ma, why's that bad?'

'Well, she won't be able to do anything with the building and there won't be space to build anything else on it. I'll put your father on.'

'Mr Spencer, why would I not be able to do anything with the building?'

'An Taisce,' he said. 'And the Planning Board. Something as old as a Martello, they wouldn't let you fart in.'

We could hear Mrs Spencer making disapproving noises. Presumably she didn't know about farting or if she did, didn't want it talked about.

'I could live in it, though?'

There was a long silence.

'It might be a bit short on mod cons.'

'Mod cons?'

'Modern conveniences. Like inside sanitation.'

'A toilet, you mean?'

'A toilet, a shower, a bath, a sink. Hot and cold running water. Electricity.'

'An Taisce wouldn't stop me putting in electricity, would they?'

'Probably not, but putting in *anything* into a Martello wouldn't be easy.'

'Why?'

Mr Spencer let a long patient sigh out of him.

'The entry is eight feet above the ground, if I remember rightly, and the walls are eight feet thick.'

'Oh.'

I was beginning to think maybe Goretti wasn't that unlucky after all.

'The State should really buy all those yokes back from their private owners and make them into museums,' Mr Spencer said. 'For ordinary people like you, owning a Martello is like owning a boat. It's just something to pour money into in an unbroken stream.'

'Thanks a bunch.'

'Well, you did ask me.'

'I did. Thank you. You're wonderful.'

I hung up the phone and tipped our dishes into the dishwasher. Sullivan was yawning and logging off. It was half eight.

'I have to stay here all day tomorrow because of this gardening leave, right?'

'We can decide that in the morning.'

'But aren't *you* going to work?'

'Listen, I'm a rich Martello-tower owner. I might have to inspect my new property, and let the bank muddle along without me for one day. I could bundle up a duvet and carry it as if it was heavy and put it in the boot before driving off, and the photographers might think I'd done you in.'

'Do you know, Nicole Richie's dad says he knows when to put on the coffee when she's due to visit him because there'll always be a helicopter directly overhead?'

I stopped and considered this. I'd a vague memory that this Nicole's father was the singer Lionel Richie, but what that had to do with helicopters or with Sullivan's gardening leave, I couldn't imagine. Undeterred by my blank face, Sullivan went right on.

'He says that they just follow his daughter everywhere. To take pictures of her. Especially since she got the anorexia.'

I didn't buy that 'getting' anorexia, like it was an ambient virus, but I said nothing.

'They're running our lives, the paparrazzi,' Sullivan said, her eyes full of tears.

I swear, I didn't know whether to laugh or cry. Laugh at the idea that Sullivan Spencer, having once appeared in a local tabloid, was up there alongside Nicole Richie having her life impinged upon by relentless stalking photographers, or cry at Sullivan being upset by the commitment of photographers whose output went into precisely the magazines she couldn't live without. I turned my mobile phone on and about eighty text messages fell into place. I scrolled and erased. Second last was from my pet radio producer.

Long sht, I know, but wd Sulliv like 2 be I/Vd tom about Mrs Baldie's barrage?

For just a moment, I considered asking Sullivan what she thought it meant. For another moment, I considered texting back or going on the web to find out who Mrs Baldie was. Then sense took over.

'You know what?' I asked. 'I'm going to bed. I'm shagged.'

'I'll not be long after you,' Sullivan said. 'I'll print out some of this Martello stuff for you before I head off.'

CHAPTER SEVEN

Warning Shots

I swear to God, it was like a mini-Starbucks outside the following morning first thing.

Some of the snappers arrived on motorbikes (which they
parked inside my front wall, presumably on the basis that we
were now friends) some of them in taxis and a few of them
walking. The walking ones seemed to have been told to pick up
coffee and they were holding out those papier-mâché trays and
indicating which was which to their colleagues. I was tempted
to lean out and ask for one, but my phone distracted me.

'Mike Kearns.'

'The very man,' I said.

'I get told that all the time,' he said comfortably. 'What
embarrassing problem would you wish me to solve for you
today?'

'Two. No. Three.'

'Well, who'd have thought?'

'First of all, I now own a Martello tower.'

'That's a *problem*?'

'Well, everybody else seems to think it is. It's never been inhabited and it doesn't have a damp course and the walls are eight feet thick.'

'On the sea side. They're only six feet thick on the land side.'

'How the hell do you know?'

'There was one around the corner from where I grew up. I used to break into it all the time. Me and my friend Ray. Rusty iron hoops coming out of the walls and ferns growing on the inside because it was so damp. When they were built, they had to have thicker walls on the sea side to withstand cannon fire. I dunno if it's true, but someone told me that when spice ships came into Dublin Bay, they'd light signal fires on the roof of one and then the next one would light a fire and the next and an hour later, Donegal would know cinnamon and cumin were on the way.'

'Wonderful. So the roof is probably all burned, too?'

I could hear him laughing and shouting goodbye to someone.

'Can I come and see your Martello?'

'Gave up breaking into them, did you? Yes, of course. Today?'

'I'll look at the diary and come back to you. What were the other two problems?'

I outlined for him Lethal Littleton's attitude to Sullivan's media exposure.

'Complicated, of course, by last night's outing.'

'Which?'

'Your friend's lover's wife. Was apparently listening to one of those late-night phone-in programmes and someone came on and said that the guy on the balcony with your friend had already that day destroyed another guy's car and the presenter got worried about libel and switched lines and the other guy's wife got on and said it was true and she'd turfed him out and he was a shit from way back.'

This left me speechless. The wives of high-ranking bank officials don't usually spill all to radio programmes. But then, I suppose, not many wives of high-ranking bank officials have to put up with what Hugo would have put his wife through, down all the days.

'She said bonking made him believe he wasn't bald as an egg.'

'Well, it would, I suppose.'

'Briefly, dear. Briefly. A transient illusion, I would have thought. It does rather complicate your friend's position, however. Would you like me to have an exploratory word with Lethal?'

'Do you know her?'

'Oh, yes.'

'Go for it. Remember, though, Sullivan is but a lowly e4. She probably couldn't afford to pay for thirty seconds of your time.'

'She has rich friends, though. One of them owns a Martello.'

'Which, I'm reliably informed, is going to put me in the poorhouse. Anyway, the most immediate problem is that my front garden is filled with photographers and their motorbikes.'

'Harleys, no doubt. Media people can be relied on unfailingly to choose the obvious.'

He said he'd get to sorting my media inundation after he'd

dealt with the other problems and would get back to me. Sullivan appeared on the landing and came halfway down the stairs, wearing my chenille dressing gown. When I wear that thing, it makes me look like an unmade bed. She looked like she was posing for an ad.

I told her about Hugo's wife and the invitation to answer her back on radio. She shook her head. Thanks be to Jaysus, I thought, she's got that message.

'She used to be a model,' Sullivan said. 'This is her chance to relaunch her career. Modelling for older women is a growth area. Demographics.'

I could tell that this was something someone else had said to her and that if I asked her to tell me what she meant by demographics, we'd run aground very fast.

'I wouldn't have thought saying your husband's bonking made him believe he wasn't bald was going to get her much business.'

'It's already got her attention.'

'True.'

'And Hugo's never rung me.'

I selected Expression A: head to one side, puzzled sympathetic face. As in: how upset are you by this?

'OK with you if I use the shower?' she asked.

Not that upset, then. I nodded and started to bustle around the kitchen. The temptation to pull open the curtains was enormous. It was like what happens when there's an ESB blackout. You know you can't use the cooker, so you think 'I'll boil a kettle for coffee' and then you realise the kettle won't work either, and you're halfway across the kitchen to the microwave before the penny drops about how useless it's going to be.

The guys knocked on the door a couple of times and one of them started to shout through the letter box just as Sullivan came down the stairs, wearing a pair of my jeans and a t-shirt. She stood on the stairs for a minute.

'C'mon Sullivan, I can see you, be a star and just give us three seconds,' one of the guys called through the letter box.

I had to give him brownie points for effort. The letter box in the doors in these houses is about two feet off the ground, so he must have had to twist himself like an acrobat to see through it.

'Hang on a minute,' she called, and ran back up the stairs.

A second later, she was back, clutching her yesterday's blouse. She ran down the stairs and knelt by the letter box. Asked the guy's name. He gave it, nearly choking with the excitement of having netted her.

'I don't want the others to know, and it may be no use, but I've been writing down my thoughts about the last few days,' she told the inch-deep slice of him we could both see. 'Would you like to see them?'

Would he what?

'Slide your hand in.'

The slice of face disappeared and a big brown hairy hand slid in, palm upright. Like a shot, she wound the blouse around the wrist several times and knotted the sleeves at the top. This made his hand so bulky, he couldn't withdraw it. We could hear him bellowing in the garden. I walked across the tiny hall and shook hands with her.

'Nicole Richie needs you,' I told her. 'She *so* needs you.'

'I didn't tell him any lies, though,' she stressed in a worried way. 'I *have* been writing down my reactions. I didn't actually promise him that's what he'd get, if he put his hand in.'

While we had breakfast, we left the kitchen door open so we could see what happened the hand. Your man clearly organised some of the others in the garden to help him. At one stage a much smaller, female hand slid in and tried to free the bigger hand, but failed. We could hear the big hand owner yelling that his circulation was stopped. Sullivan went out to the hall to check.

'No, you're grand, actually,' she called. 'Lovely and warm, it is.'

She patted his palm in a comforting kind of way and he called her an awful name.

'Take that back,' she told the hand.

Most of its fingers curled up, so that only the middle one was left pointing upwards.

'Take it back and say you're sorry, or I'll do awful things to your hand.'

The finger jabbed in the air even more vigorously: up yours on steroids.

Sullivan stood up and went into the kitchen. She searched the food presses until she found strawberry jam, took the pot together with a spoon, went back out to the hall, forced open the three fingers that were closed, ladled three spoonfuls of the jam into the palm of his hand and stepped back. I shoved a paper napkin underneath the now bright red hand, decorated with lumpy strawberries. I didn't want the doormat mucked up.

'Now, you can just guess what I've put in your hand,' Sullivan called out to him. 'Just as well you can't see it or smell it.'

Some of the other guys laughed and we could hear him swearing at them. My phone rang. Mike Kearns.

'OK, I've talked to Lethal, and she's agreed to meet you tomorrow in some pub of your choice for an off-the-record chat. I can be at your house in about ten minutes. When I get rid of the photographers, you'll give me a cup of coffee and then we'll head off to look at your Martello. How does that sound?'

'D'you not have to be in court, convicting someone?'

'Not today. See you soon.'

I clicked off the phone.

'You didn't tell him about our friend in the letter box,' Sullivan pointed out.

'No, I thought it would be interesting to see how he handled it when he arrived, not knowing. See how he copes with the unexpected.' (Because, I thought but didn't say, if he tries to save your ass, he's going to have to deal with the unexpected on an hourly basis.)

Mike Kearns drove up a few minutes later in a Lexus that managed to be the size of the Isle of Man but subtle with it. I was peeping from the front bedroom.

He got out of it very slowly. Slowly enough for his height to become gradually impressive to the guys milling around. Slowly enough to convey his astonishment at the condition of my front garden, awash as it was in photographers, motorbikes, newspapers (each having brought their own) tossed coffee beakers and papier-mâché trays. Slowly enough for those in the know to tell the others who he was. Slowly enough for the ones clustered around the trapped guy to abandon him and step away from the front door, leaving him like a beached whale, facing the wrong way and flailing with fury.

By now, I was standing just inside the front door, straddling the blouse-wearing hand, one eye glued to the security peep-hole.

The lawyer closed the door of his car quietly and didn't lock it. He walked slowly into my front garden, ignoring the questions coming from the hacks who had pulled themselves together and remembered that asking questions was their job. He stopped. The questions didn't. He looked, steel-eyed, from one to another until they all wavered away into silence.

I realised something was happening between my ankles and looked down to see Sullivan with a warm face-cloth, cleaning the jam off the invading hand and towelling it dry. When she was finished, she kissed the palm gently, undid the knotted sleeves and unwound the blouse. The hand made tentative movements, as if it couldn't believe its luck, and then withdrew.

'What are you doing here?' the lawyer asked, so quietly, I could hardly hear him from the inside of the front door.

'Our job,' a voice responded. This got a murmur of approval from the others.

'Trespassing is your job? Littering private property is your job? Stalking an individual at their home is your job?'

I could hear a few murmured smartarse comments, but they didn't amount to much. With silky courtesy, the lawyer assured them that, as representatives of responsible media outlets, he had no doubt they would all, inside five minutes, be outside the front gate of this premises, taking all of their property with them. He also had no doubt that they would speak to their editors or producers and check with them about how far away from a private house they should be and how that would conflict with the rights of pedestrians on a public thoroughfare.

Some of them were up for giving him an argument, but, when they noticed that the others were quietly picking up coffee containers and moving motorbikes, they got resentful at being abandoned to fight the good fight on behalf of the fourth estate all on their own, and decided to surrender.

I could see them, one by one, sliding outside. I could also see one of them getting into an abortive argument with a garda who had appeared without warning and who did the unmistakable gesture that says 'Not here, not now'. In no time at all, my little front garden had nothing in it but my car and the lawyer who advanced towards the door and raised his hand to knock.

I opened it so his upraised fist got left in mid-gesture, and Sullivan pulled him in and hugged him. I shoved them to one side so I could get the door closed and then hugged him, too.

'The Law Library was never like this,' he observed. 'Now, I'd give those lads ten minutes or so to disperse and then we can head off to the Martello. My car or yours?'

'Oh, yours,' Sullivan said decisively.

'He was asking me,' I pointed out.

'You'd prefer a Lexus too,' she assured me.

When we belted across the garden to the car, it was all choreographed in advance, just in case any photographers were still lurking in the vicinity. He and I shielded Sullivan, who got into the back and flung herself along the seat, head down, as if she did this gig regularly.

'She has a future,' he murmured. 'Knows all the moves of the furtive famous.'

'I'm getting her a job advising Nicole Richie.'

'Who's she?'

Sullivan, straightening up in the back seat, looked so stricken I thought she was going to ask if she could be dropped off near the LUAS, rather than share a car with someone so out of touch with the influential cultural figures of our time.

'She's an *icon*,' she told him, disapprovingly.

'So's every nonentity, these days.'

Sullivan went silent, crushed.

'They sent keys, this morning,' I told him, showing him the oversized set. 'The girl from An Post had quite a time getting them through our letter box.'

'Your letter box must be exhausted,' he said. 'What gave you the idea of imprisoning that guy's hand?'

'I used to do political canvassing at home,' Sullivan said.

Kearns glanced at me with slightly narrowed eyes: this make sense to you?

'Well, it was my boyfriend at the time, really. He was Fianna Fáil.'

'And you were?'

'Oh, politics,' Sullivan said dismissively.

'Not New Age enough for you,' he said sympathetically. 'I understand completely.'

'He had this system where if he knocked at a door and there was no answer, he'd knock again and if the third time nothing happened, he'd take out this signed card from the candidate, saying, "I'm really sorry to have missed you when I dropped by, but I'd be delighted to talk to you about blah blah, signed Joe."'

'Joe was your boyfriend?'

'Of the time?'

Sullivan rolled her eyes. The two in the front of the Lexus were clearly too stupid to live.

'Eugene was my boyfriend.'

'Of the time.'

'Joe was the candidate. He was a Minister too.'

'So your boyfriend,' Mike said amusedly, 'was setting out to mislead the voters by convincing them the candidate had been on their doorstep, when the candidate hadn't been anywhere near their doorstep.'

'Well, I don't *care*,' Sullivan said. 'He was only my boyfriend until I went to university.'

'Time-limited ethics,' he murmured, giving the car a little acceleration, now he was on the straight road north by the sea. Sullivan clearly didn't know what he was on about and disregarded the comment.

'It made voters feel much better to know that a Minister had been there than that Eugene had. I mean, Eugene wasn't anybody. They felt really bad at missing the Minister.'

'I thought you said they felt better?'

'But bad too and that makes people vote. Except this one night was very wet and one house had a low letter box like and a brambly kind of a tree near the doorway and when he bent down to put the note through the letter box, his umbrella got tangled in the tree and his hand got caught in the letter box and he got into a complete panic because he thought "they're going to come home, the people who live here, and what are they going to find?"'

'Your brief boyfriend impersonating someone more important than himself,' Kearns suggested.

'Absolutely.'

Sullivan lost interest in the story and began rooting in the powder-blue handbag, from the innards of which her phone was giving the squawk that said it had either a text message or an e-mail for her.

'Wait a second,' I said. 'What happened Eugene?'

'I went off him,' Sullivan said, which I had already figured out, but which still left the poor hoor spancelled at some voter's front door.

'I suspect,' Kearns said casually, 'that he remembered he could let go the handle of the umbrella.'

'Right!' Sullivan said, suddenly poking him in the back with approval.

I told him about the intruding hand in my own letter box and how Sullivan had trapped it and smeared jam on it.

'Peanut butter with nuts in it would have been a better texture,' she murmured, attending to her messages. 'But the soft strawberries must have felt awful when he didn't know what they were.'

I explained that she had thoroughly mopped all the jam off the guy's hand before releasing it.

'How kind,' Kearns said, sardonically.

'No, it was really nasty,' Sullivan said happily. 'He'll never be sure what he had in his hand while he was stuck there.'

'And because journalists have filthy minds, he'll imagine the worst,' I said.

'Forever and ever,' Sullivan confirmed.

'Amen,' said the lawyer.

CHAPTER EIGHT

A Rocky Proposition

*T*he Lexus was now heading around a rough rocky area on Sloe Head. The road was somewhere between poor and dire. He drove more slowly and we breasted a hill and there it was. Squat. Dark. Round. Bleak. My Martello.

'D'you see that sticky-out bit?'

He gestured and I realised for the first time he was wearing pale leather gloves. I dragged my gaze off the gloves and saw the bit towards the top of the tower being indicated.

'That was where they boiled water or pitch to pour down on any invaders brave enough to scale the walls,' he said.

'How could anybody scale those walls?' Sullivan wanted to know.

'Nobody ever did,' he said, releasing the car so it moved softly forward. 'Never in military history has so much money been spent on such an elaborate method of defence without it ever being put to use.'

'What about nuclear power stations?' Sullivan wanted to know. 'I mean, shelters. Nuclear power shelters. Shelters for nuclear war. Shelters to go into if there was going to be a nuclear war. Bomb shelters for nuclears. Or maybe atoms. Fallout. Half-life. Plutonium. You know yourself. Hiroshima and stuff.'

Kearns pulled the car up beside the Martello and turned off the engine.

'A fallout shelter is a hole in the ground with stud walls hammered up. It costs virtually nothing. A Martello tower was one of the most costly structures ever built. It cost, for its time, roughly what a Trident missile would cost in today's money.'

Sullivan got out, belting her trenchcoat about her and turning up the back of its collar. When that girl is dying, she'll give of her last ounce of strength to arrange the pillows in the most fetching way possible. I could see her view of the tower had improved. It might still look like an upturned cast-iron stew pot, but it was an *expensive* cast-iron stew pot. Possibly even a *designer* cast-iron stew pot.

A metal fire-escape-type stairs had been thrown up against the wall under the raised entrance. Mike Kearns tested it and climbed to the entrance. Sullivan went around the front to look at the sea.

I tossed the keys up to Kearns and he caught them in that leisurely way sportsmen and athletes catch thrown objects. Sullivan came back around from the sea side of the tower, shivering.

'There's something like a big garage door on that side,' she announced, before taking the metal steps three at a time. I thought the whole fire escape was going to come away from the wall, it rocked so much. Kearns had the door unlocked and Sullivan was about to plunge past him when he gently but firmly restrained her.

81

'You must ask the owner's permission,' he told her.

I came up the stairs behind them and cursed myself for not having a torch. The three of us moved inside the door. Into a kind of tunnel of rough-hewn stones.

'This is how thick the walls are,' I said, stretching my arms from the outside and not able to reach the inside.

Mike Kearns removed his gloves and put them in one pocket of his elegant overcoat. From the other pocket he took a small torch and turned it on. It was amazingly powerful, and – combined with the light coming from the door and from a slit window on the other side, showed the circular shape of the interior of the tower. The floor was littered with rocks. He turned the torch overhead to show an arched roof, made of the same stones as the walls.

We stood, hushed by the sense of the tower's quiet strength, by the solid certainty of it. I could imagine the first people inside it using candles or maybe torches of brushwood.

The moving torch revealed a broken, blackened space in the wall across from where we stood. Fireplace, I realised.

'It's been used,' I said. 'Someone *did* live here.'

'Soldiers may have been billeted here briefly. It could take twenty five of them. But the fire might just have been used by the guys who built it.'

'Wonder if it's still functional?'

'Can't see why it wouldn't be,' Mike said. 'The rest of the structure seems completely intact. Except – '

The light from his torch played on a wooden structure.

'That's the kind of garage door thing I told you about,' Sullivan said.

It didn't look as if it had ever been opened.

'Now that's probably the best thing you could imagine,' Mike observed. 'At some point in the distant past, but probably in the twentieth century, someone broke out the wall over there. That break is probably – what? Ten feet across and twelve high. The planning authorities wouldn't let you do it now, but because it's already done, therein lie your possibilities of an extension. A way to get more light into this place. More natural light.'

Sullivan got very excited.

'There's plenty of flat space directly outside that door,' she told me. 'You could build anything you wanted.'

'D'you know what I think?' I asked.

The two of them looked at me. I tilted Mike's torch down towards the ground again.

'I think those rocks are actually the lumps of the wall they broke out.'

'Very bad workmanship,' Sullivan said unexpectedly. 'My father would never tolerate that. He always says you have to clean as you go, if only for health and safety reasons.'

'I think you're right,' Mike said to me. 'You can see some of the masonry stuck to the bigger blocks.'

'Which means we could do a fantastically authentic job by reusing those stones on whatever we do outside.'

'Take you a long, long time to get them all out,' he warned. 'I suspect they're six or seven feet deep all the way across the width of the tower. Lot of rocks. Lot of big rocks.'

I stood, flummoxed by the scale of what I was looking at. He tactfully shifted the light off the mountain of rubble on the floor of the tower and picked out a stone staircase moving up the wall from the platform we were standing on. The staircase was spiral, disappearing into the wall. Sullivan was halfway up it before I had even considered an ascent. She disappeared around the corner.

'Wait, for God's sake,' Mike said.

'There's no light here,' Sullivan's voice announced, slightly muffled.

'Gimme a second,' he said and handed the torch to me before shrugging out of his coat. He turned it inside out, exposing its silk lining, folded it neatly and put it on the side of the platform.

'Your suit's going to be equally destroyed,' I said.

'Not worried about my coat being destroyed,' he said, looking slightly wounded. 'I just don't think I'll fit up that spiral staircase with the coat on. Those soldiers were a lot smaller than we are.'

He then took off his jacket and folded it the same way.

'They couldn't be smaller than me,' I said.

'Maybe not, but they weren't much bigger.'

'Soldiers?'

'Soldiers are always picked from the poorest elements of any society. The undernourished. But anyway, *everybody* two hundred years ago was smaller than we are today.'

He took the torch from me and led the way up the spiral staircase.

'What a view,' he said lightly, playing the light on Sullivan's ass.

'I was actually thinking of getting push-up jeans,' she told him seriously.

'Not yet,' he responded. 'May come a time, but not the smallest sign of cheek-prolapse at this point.'

'There's a banister,' she called down to me. 'On the right.'

Sure enough, a metal bar ran along the wall. Iron. Pocked and puckered with rust, so that bits of it flaked away when I put my hand to it. But I needed to use it, no matter how dirty it made my mitts. The spiral stairs were deep and narrow.

The three of us proceeded until Sullivan encountered a wooden door with heavy old fashioned bolts. She tried them but couldn't shift them, then slid sideways to let Mike Kearns have a go. He struggled for some time.

'Gimme a shoe,' he told her.

She pulled off one of her shoes and he beat the bolts vigorously with the heel of the runner.

'Thanks for that,' I muttered, trying to shake rust flakes out of my hair.

He put down the shoe and embarked on another epic struggle with the bolts. This time they shifted. It required more shoework and Sullivan kicking the door with her other foot – the one that still had a shoe on it – helped, too. He handed the shoe back to her.

'Never saw that kind of sole before.'

'Oh, Masai Barefoot Technology,' she told him. 'Just walking in them for twenty minutes tightens your buttocks.'

'I *have* to have a pair,' he murmured and pulled the door open, flooding the circular staircase with daylight. The three of us climbed up the remaining, non-spiral steps, which were three times as deep, emerging onto the roof of the tower.

'Omigod,' Sullivan said, forgetting about the Masai. 'Omigod. I mean, *OMIGOD*!'

The roof of the tower, completely and perfectly circular, was ringed at chest level with a protective wall inside which ran a step at about two feet higher than the rest of what you could

call the floor of the roof. Sullivan ran across the slightly conical space – in the middle was some kind of iron machine like a
rusty pompom on a hat – and hopped up onto the step.

'Jesus, I can see Wales,' she announced.

'Who would want to?' asked Mike, *sotto voce*, turning off his
torch and setting it neatly down on the nearest ledge.

The three of us stood on the raised platform and, eyes water-
ing from the wind, scanned the incredible view. It seemed to
extend as far as Carlingford to the north, included islands,
one of which had its own Martello tower on the side facing
us, and moved on to the Bull Island and right across to the
Wicklow hills. It was breathtaking. I could be sure of that. It
had taken Sullivan's breath and speech away. It has to be some
view before that happens. I was with her when she first saw the
Bay of Naples and it didn't happen there. I can still remember
the details of the saga she was telling me about how the dry-
cleaners destroyed her one and only Escada dress and tried to
compensate her as if the garment had been bought in Dunnes
Stores.

'There's animals on that island,' she eventually said.

'Wallabies,' Mike Kearns responded.

'*Wannabies?*'

'No, real ones. Marsupials. Like kangaroos only smaller.
Wallabies. Lambay Island has had them for years. Thirty years
back, Dublin Zoo got crowded, so they landed them out there
and they went feral.'

'Oh, look,' Sullivan said, losing interest in marsupials and
stepping off the ledge onto the roof itself. 'See the iron?'

She was pointing to a big ring of rusted iron running around
the conical roof.

'That's what allowed the cannon to pivot and point at anything on any side.'

'What would you do with this?' Mike Kearns asked, his snowy shirt billowing like a sail in the high wind.

'Haven't a clue.'

'You could put a jacuzzi up here,' Sullivan said.

'You could,' Mike nodded. 'It's on the flight path to Dublin airport. I'm sure passengers would pay extra just to catch a glimpse of you in it.'

'Well, it would be Patricia, not me.'

'Nobody's going to pay to see me from overhead in a Jacuzzi,' I said. 'And anyway, there ain't gonna be no Jacuzzi up here. I will have you note,' I told her severely, 'that I *do* have a beach.'

'It's not a private one, though,' she said, pointing to a man and his dog traversing the sand. When they reached the other side, the man stood patiently while the dog peed on a post sticking up from the rocks.

'All that has to change,' Mike laughed. 'The Lady of the Tower is going to institute new rules.'

'Rasputin, isn't that who she'll be?'

Mike closed one eye and concentrated on Sullivan.

'Rasputin?'

'Don't tell me you've never heard of Rasputin,' Sullivan ordered him. 'What kind of a childhood did you have?'

'I have to admit, Rasputin didn't play much of a part in our bedtime stories at home. It was only when I got to my teens I fully appreciated him. What a guy. They poisoned him, shot him, tied him up, dumped him in the river to drown and it took the cold to kill him.'

'Smelly, though,' I offered.

'Was he? Didn't stop the Tzarina climbing aboard, did it?'

'Oh, that's a filthy slur. She didn't fancy him, she just relied on him to cure that thing her son had.'

'Homophobia,' Sullivan said helpfully.

Mike Kearns leaned against the wall of the roof and shook his head wonderingly.

'I never fully appreciated how completely a conversation can lose its way until I met you two,' he said. 'It's like the time my GPS was first installed, and it didn't know it was in Dublin. It took me all the way through London. Even got me to cross the Thames at one point without the benefit of a bridge.'

'Haemophilia,' I said.

'I didn't mean Rasputin the man,' Sullivan said. 'I meant Rasputin the girl with the long hair people could climb up.'

'Rapunzel,' Mike Kearns told her, before disappearing into a darkened alcove on one side of the roof. A mesh metal curtain hung in front of it. I pulled it slightly to one side and shone the torch in on him, crouched as he was, looking around.

'I think this is where they stored the cannonballs,' he said. 'Don't know why there's a divider wall though.'

He put his head around a hole in the wall.

'Howya, lads,' he said and I could hear a bustling ruffled noise like someone falling out of bed wrapped in a duvet.

'Rapunzel owns a pigeon loft,' he told me, climbing back up out of the deep recess. 'And they're not used to visitors.'

'Rasputin, to you.'

'I'm beginning to have a lot in common with the mad monk,' Kearns said. 'I'll probably die of cold if I stay here any longer.'

Sullivan had already got bored with the Omigod view and disappeared down the spiral staircase. I followed her and Mike beat the bolts back into position.

'It's not actually cold, inside,' Sullivan observed.

'Fair bit of insulation in eight foot thick walls,' I said.

'Can you imagine how cosy you could make it if you lit that fire and fed it all day long?'

The two of us watched Sullivan, who was stroking the stones nearest her as if they were tame cats.

'Imagine,' she whispered. 'Soldiers two hundred years ago touched these same stones.'

'If they were billeted here,' Mike said, with a rigorous concern for accuracy.

'Well, *somebody* two hundred years ago touched these same stones,' I said. 'Because otherwise the bloody things wouldn't have been built into a tower.'

'They're local stones, too,' Mike said, trying to dust rust marks off his shirt and failing. 'You'll nearly always find a quarry somewhere close to a Martello. A disused quarry. Each Martello's unique, just follow the same basic principles: circular, on the coast, massive, in line of sight with two others.'

'There wouldn't be a quarry out on Lambay,' Sullivan suggested.

'Not only was there a quarry on the island,' Mike told her, 'But it was in use in Neolithic times.'

'How the hell do you know that?'

'Client work, a few years back.'

I found myself doing the same thing that Sullivan was doing. Touching the stones as if they connected me with people long dead. People as small as me. People who had built a structure that stood, undamaged, undiminished by storm and seaspray over two centuries, and who were remembered not even with a plaque. Hewers of wood and drawers of water, they were, press-ganged into service in a wider cause. The cause of an empire threatened by another empire, neither of which connected in any real way with the anonymous labourers whose leathery hands had carried and hammered and cemented these stones into place.

I hated to go, but had no reason to stay. If you're thinking of buying or renovating an old house, you'd usually have heat and light and an auctioneer blithering on about the great possibilities of the place. Here, there wasn't a place to sit down, other than freezing your ass off, as Sullivan was now doing, by planting it on the broad end of the triangle that was one of the steps of the spiral staircase. There wasn't even a path through the rubble on the floor. I would probably, I realised, have to clear all that rubble out before I even got a surveyor to come and look at the structure.

'Is there anything underneath a Martello?' I asked nobody in particular.

'The pictures on the web showed a cistern – reservoir? Big amount of water, anyway, stored in the cellars, except there wasn't cellars, there was just this huge space and the water came down in a lead pipe from the roof, rainwater, you know? But I don't know if that cistern was in all of them.'

'Big cistern, if so,' Mike Kearns said. 'Because it would have been built in the expectation of having to withstand a siege. Now, if the force in the tower was twenty five strong and a siege lasted even a month, that's an enormous water requirement.'

'And no flush toilets,' Sullivan said, shuddering fastidiously. 'How could they manage?'

'Go outside,' I said.

'In a *siege*?'

'Oh, I don't know. Pee over the edge of the roof?'

'Too small, they were, for that, dear. Unless they stood on a platform and set themselves up as targets. I'm going with chamber pots.'

Now it was my turn to shudder. Twenty-five guys living in one big stone room and doing the needful in chamber pots made me feel suddenly warm and cuddly about the twenty-first century.

'Don't knock the chamber pot,' Mike said. 'Great development in civilised living and proud position in the history of warfare, personal and national. Long before we had nuclear warheads, we knew how to repel boarders with the well-aimed contents of a chamber pot.'

He stood courteously back to let the two of us out past him and quickly slipped into his jacket and overcoat before tackling the closing of a creaking door that was being asked to do more exercise in one day than it had done in years.

We retreated to the car and stood looking at the stolid vastness of the tower.

'Isn't it lucky Napoleon didn't arrive?' Sullivan said.

'Why? You prefer speaking English to French?'

'No, he might have knocked down Patricia's tower.'

I noticed that the tower had developed a capital T, the way Sullivan talked about it. Right and effing proper, I thought.

'Not a chance,' Mike said, handing her into the back seat of the car and coming around to open the door on my side.

'He had cannons.'

'True. But these yokes were well built.'

'Still, cannons.'

'Not that accurate.'

He slowly turned the Lexus in a three-pointer to head back to the motorway.

'Just as well we have An Taisce to protect ours,' Sullivan said.

'Ours?' he queried, looking quizzically at her in the rear-view mirror.

'Patricia's,' she corrected, self-consciously.

Isn't it funny, I thought. I prefer 'ours'. This tower is too big and important to be owned just by me.

CHAPTER NINE

Getting Roots done in Newtownmountkennedy

*M*eeting Lethal Littleton off site presented all sorts of problems. We couldn't meet in any of the pubs I frequented. We couldn't meet in any of the pubs *she* frequented. We couldn't meet in pubs favoured by management of the bank. We couldn't meet in pubs favoured by minions from the bank. We had to pick one that didn't involve the M50 or making a southsider (her) cross the Liffey.

I'd never heard of the pub that eventually got picked. It was named after some Dublin footballer. Which meant I had great difficulty remembering it, because what I know about sport of any kind would fit on the head of a pin with loads of room to spare.

By this point, Sullivan was getting cabin fever from being stuck in my house, because she was convinced that even if Mike Kearns had intimidated the snappers into retreating a bit, they were probably nested in a tree somewhere along Ranelagh Road, waiting for her to put her head out. And it was her head that was bothering her most. Roots.

'Roots are fashionable, these days,' I told her.

That was a mistake. It got her launched on the Comparative Study of Emerging Roots. Black at the root of blonde hair is OK up to a point, but that point is measured in millimetres, and one millimetre beyond right positions you as Slapper. This from a girl who'd been pictured nearly naked in a tabloid?

'There's supposed to be a brilliant new colourist in Newtownmountkennedy,' she said at the end of the thesis.

'That's halfway to Wexford.'

'Is it?'

Thank God, I thought, my car has GPS.

'He used to work in Bloomingdales,' she added.

'That's a decider,' I agreed, knowing irony goes over her head in a soundless whiff.

Then it struck me. Newtownmountkennedy mightn't be halfway to Wexford, but it was a long way away from a) the bank, and b) the media.

'Tell you what,' I said. 'You drive me to this pub and then go on to Mr Bloomie and get gorgeous.'

'But how will you get home, afterwards?'

'I'll make her give me a lift.'

I had no intention of even trying, but I knew this would impress Sullivan. It did. She made an appointment and off we set.

'What do you want me to achieve?' I said.

'Recalculating,' a disembodied voice said, and Sullivan started as if she'd been stung.

'It's the route finder,' I said. 'You didn't go the way it likes.'

'I'm sorry,' she told it. It told her to drive three hundred metres and turn right. I leaned across and turned off the sound. Sullivan wouldn't know three hundred metres from three hundred gerbils.

'What do I want you to achieve? I don't know. You know stuff like that.'

'Sullivan, this is your career.'

Laughter offstage. Sullivan was never going to have a career. She would have *jobs*, but none of them would ever add up to a career. Not in banking, anyway. Head of corporate banking in twenty years? Right. And if my aunt had a willie, she'd be my uncle.

'I don't want to be fired,' she said, decisively.

'They'd have difficulty firing you.'

'Well, then.'

'Sullivan. In three years' time, what do you want to be?'

I could almost hear her brain announce 'Recalculating'.

'Well, I'd – I don't know, I suppose, really. I've never… Do you know what you want to be in three years' time?'

'Alive would be good.'

'But apart from that?'

'I don't know.'

'Well, why are you asking me?'

'Because this wagon I'm meeting on your behalf has considerable power over your immediate future.'

'Well, I don't want to be fired, is all.'

I looked at her sideways. Sullivan is breathtakingly beautiful, even with roots. Stop-you-in-your-tracks beautiful. Solid gold goodnatured. Generous as hell. A memory like a computer – everything gets saved but someone else has to make sense of the data. And, on the cusp of thirty, all she wanted was not to be fired.

'If you could wave a magic wand, what would you want out of life?'

'I'd like to be happy,' she said, as if this would solve all my problems. 'I mean, I *am* happy, really, not at the moment, like, because it's awful my mother having to deal with nosy neighbours talking about my underwear and stuff and I wouldn't say my Da is that pleased, but guys'd be too afraid of him to say it really. But generally I'm happy. I'd like to be happy.'

'With Bryan or with Hugo?'

'Oh, neither, really. They don't make me happy. I never realised that before, but if Bryan never comes back it would be the best thing for me and for him. Bryan was always worried about something to do with work and what people thought and he was always telling me to go and change into something less revealing if there was going to be people from his office around even though he thought my boobs were the best thing about me except for my legs but even then, he didn't like me wearing shoes when his boss might be present that'd have toe-cleavage. He said it was overtly sexualised.'

The notion of toe-cleavage as a come-on had never struck me before. Now and again, I think Sullivan and I live on different planets. Mine is duller but safer.

'Hugo will just plain hate me by now. Do you know they're selling t-shirts with that comment his wife made about him bonking to make himself forget about being bald? I read it on the web. I've just destroyed him and that's so bad.'

She was crying like the rain and I told her to pull in to the side of the road. She put her head down on the steering wheel and broke her heart sobbing, although I couldn't see why t-shirt sales justified emotional meltdown.

'She'll get everything she wants in money terms and that's dreadful for poor Hugo, but his reputation matters to him more than anything and now he's just a laughing stock and it's not Bryan's fault, I shouldn't have caused it I can *so* understand why he hates me.'

'Hate to say it, but it does take two to tango.'

'Tango?'

Sullivan can't dance.

'Have sex. Hugo was never really behind the door in his sexuality, long before you arrived with your toe-cleavage. He was a hand-up-your-skirt merchant from way back.'

'Most of them are, but it doesn't mean he should be humiliated for it. He was just doing what comes naturally to him.'

'And you weren't?'

'Well, he really enjoys it.'

She began mopping herself down and I produced a packet of tissues, noticing too late that each had a sad smiley face on it with one tear and the caption *Sniff!* Sullivan blew her nose like a ten-year-old with a cold and didn't notice the caption.

'Sullier?'

A strangled sound somewhere between a snort and a sob came out of her. I took it as permission.

'Do I get the sense that you may not have actually – how can I put this? You may not actually have enjoyed sex with Hugo that much?'

'It was only twice, I told you.'

'What's frequency got to do with it?'

She balled up the tissue and tucked it into her bag. Typical Sullivan: don't leave your germs in someone else's vehicle. Then she examined herself in the mirror of the sun visor. Also typical Sullivan.

'You're going to think I'm very stupid.'

'So what's new?' I asked and was immediately sorry. So hard to take anything back once it's said.

'What's an orgasm?'

I scrabbled in my own bag for chewing gum and offered her a piece.

'Sullivan, you know what an orgasm is.'

'It's the thing you get with sex.'

'Right.'

'But what *is* it, exactly?' she turned big bloodshot but still beautiful eyes on me. 'Maybe you don't know, either.'

That riled me, with its suggestion that I haven't been made love to by hordes of handsome orgasm-deliverers. It riled me mainly because it was true.

'I don't really know what's supposed to happen. They never show it in films. All they ever show is stars –'

'I know, I know,' I said. 'It's like. Like. Well, it's like you're trying to get a car up a hill and you take a load of runs at it and you're getting edgier and edgier and then suddenly you're over the top and flying like a character in a cartoon just in mid-air, you know?'

This, I could tell, was not working. I always loop back to car references. Comes of growing up with a bunch of brothers. You either learn cars or sport or both. I learned cars. Sullivan looked at me bleakly.

'Whenever I have sex it's like when my mother used to make us chew everything forty times. I'd start out liking the food, but I'd be dying to swallow it and by the time I was let, the flavour was all gone out of it and I didn't care.'

'Orgasm is like swallowing the best food in the world several times.'

'Oh.'

'Sullivan?'

'Mmm?'

'You telling me sex for you is like chewing and never swallowing?'

'Always.'

'*Always?* In that case you haven't had orgasms.'

'I thought there must be something wrong with me. I even made myself think about my favourite shoes, but nothing happened. It gets really tedious. I know you're not supposed to want guys to – to – finish fast, but it's less boring, especially because you don't have to keep making noises to make them think they're doing a great job, because it's not their fault and it might make them impotent if you let out that – '

'You're thinking of shoes in order to get through this god-awful experience.'

'Well, it's not godawful completely,' she said in a fair-minded way, getting the car moving again. Traffic parted like the Red Sea to let her out. It always does. 'It's always exciting at the beginning and afterwards falling asleep in a hug is nice. It's just it kind of goes nowhere, you know?'

Now, as I told you, I have spent most of my life rescuing Sullivan, but a solution to her orgasm-deficit didn't immediately strike me.

'I'm going to have to think about this,' I told her, and then lost whatever restraint I had on the subject. 'Why the hell,' I blurted, 'do you keep fucking so many men if you get nothing out of it?'

She didn't even get offended by the implication that her lovers numbered thousands.

'It's part of the deal,' she said. 'Here we are.'

'Sullivan, it's not part of the deal.'

'How would you know? You're not in a deal.'

'Sullivan, have I ever given you bad advice?'

She considered this very serious, despite the line of traffic drawn up behind my car.

'No, I don't think so.'

'Well, trust me on this. Sex is not a boring duty like washing dishes that you have to do as part of a relationship. And if you've been having washing-dishes sex, it's not your fault.'

'Maybe I should stop for a while.'

'Sex?'

'Yes. That English actor Stephen thingie did and it didn't seem to do him any harm. And you don't, either.'

'Not right now. I haven't taken a vow of celibacy, I just don't know anybody fanciable. The point is that – yes – me and Stephen Fry have managed to survive bits of our lives without sex. Nobody ever died from a shortage of sex.'

This seemed to surprise her.

'Nobody,' I confirmed.

Cars were beginning to beep behind us.

'Never mind Stephen Fry,' I said in a moment of inspiration. 'Think Marilyn Monroe. Sexiest star who ever lived, right?'

'Oh, yes.'

'Never had an orgasm in her life. Did sex the way you do sex: gave it away like a present. Well, fuck that, Sullivan.'

I was halfway out of the car and she was shaking her head the way you do when you want to get rid of a wasp: totally confused.

'We'll sort that later. I have to go in here and make sure you don't get fired.'

'That's right. But I don't want to keep that oul job, either,' she said as my door closed and the car left me standing outside the pub thinking that with the mandate I now had, the best thing to do would be to hail a taxi and go home.

Except that I knew I couldn't.

Lethal Littleton
in a Sports Pub

*E*ven with the brief sojourn on the side of the road for
Sullivan to cry, I was still way too early for my appointment with Lethal the Lego Lady. No way was I going to arrive
in, breathless and flustered. I selected my position, laid out my
stuff, ordered a soda water with a twist of lime, and waited, trying to establish priorities for the meeting and totally distracted
by thoughts of the tower.

She arrived on the button of the appointed time, saw me
immediately and looked pissed off that I was there before her.
She blended in with the surroundings, which were brownish.
I would believe Littleton went to one of those Colour Me
Beautiful people and got told she was an Autumn, except I
know bloody well she wouldn't waste her time and money on
anything to do with her appearance. Littleton's appearance has
'take me or leave me, preferably the latter' written all over its
dun brown totality.

She stopped at the bar and ordered coffee before coming
over and sitting not directly opposite me (HR professionals

know that this would be confrontational and not likely to lead to a win/win negotiation) or beside me (HR professionals know that this would lead to unrealisable expectations of God knows what) but at a slight angle to me.

'Well?' she demanded.

Suddenly I turned into all my brothers.

'Well fucking what?' I demanded.

The barman thought this was a great way for two women to start having drinks together. He was so chuffed, he asked me if I'd like a cup to have some of Lethal's coffee out of the big pot she'd asked for.

'Why not?' I asked rhetorically.

She waited until he was out of earshot before speaking.

'What are we here for?' she asked, wearily.

'You know bloody well what we're here for. We're here because you agreed to have an off-site conversation with someone who wants to save Sullivan's arse from the mangle you want to put it through.'

'Why would I want to put anybody's arse through a mangle?'

The barman reappeared at this point with the second cup and it was all he could do not to sit down and join our conversation, he thought it was so cool. Lethal fixed him with a look that microwaved his entrails and he retreated.

'Because, shorn of all the shit, you work for the bosses. Hugo's a boss. Get rid of Sullivan, embarrassment around Hugo ceases. QED.'

She surprised me by pouring coffee for me, having first questioned me with a look: Hot milk in first? I took it and drank.

'Hugo's not a boss.'

'Oh, puhlease, can we not play semantics, here?'

'Hugo's resigned. Retired. Gone.'

'When?'

'Yesterday.'

'Gone?'

'Gone.'

'Well, of course, that makes it worse for Sullivan.'

'Why?'

'All the guys upstairs will blame her for bringing a good man down, blah, blah.'

'Not really.'

It wasn't the next offering in an argument. It was a tombstone marking the death of an argument.

'The guys upstairs would, however, have an ongoing concern about Ms Spencer.'

'D'you talk like that at home?'

'I live alone.'

She looked at me from under her Lego helmet of hair in a completely neutral way.

'I shouldn't have said that.'

'No, you shouldn't.'

'I'm sorry.'

'Your apology is accepted.'

Oh, Jesus, I thought, I don't believe I heard that. I looked up at her and she looked at me without expression.

'You were saying they've other problems with Sullivan?'

'We're not having this conversation, right?'

'Well, Jaysus, we could be wearing wires all over the two of us for all either of us has said that couldn't be broadcast.'

'So far.'

'Oh, make my day. Say something indiscreet.'

'Unless Sullivan enters a convent, she's going to be a continuing challenge to the brand.'

'If she joined a convent, she'd be the *ultimate* challenge to the brand. My God, can't you see the story?'

'True.'

'So get rid of her. Get rid of any association between her and the bank. So that any time someone from media rings the PR people, they can shrug and say "nuthin' to do with us, she's history".'

'Precisely.'

'And that doesn't bother you at all?'

'Why should it?'

'Ending someone's career because of an accident?'

'I'm not ending anybody's career. It wasn't an accident, either, it was the culmination of a series of behaviours.'

'You know something, you spend too much time reading HR regulations.'

'You know something? You may be right.'

That was so unexpected, I laughed out loud. Surprised the knickers off me that she did, too. It encouraged the barman to make another foray. More coffee and hot milk? Sure.

'Patricia, let's be honest with each other,' Littleton said, leaning forward a bit. 'Sullivan *has* no career in the bank.'

'She's very bright and has a good degree.'

'I haven't seen much evidence of brightness, but let's concede the degree. Let's concede, also, that she's attractive, likeable and hard-working. So are babies, but you don't give them senior positions as bankers.'

'Babies don't work. They just eat and crap.'

You can see I yearn for motherhood.

'Babies work every minute of the day and night. They learn more in their first year of life than in any subsequent year.'

'If you're so keen on babies, why don't you work with them?'

'Do you know the salary levels of childminders?'

The barman arrived with more coffee and this time I did the pouring, surprising myself by my own civility and by the fact that I was quite enjoying this meeting, in spite of the fact that two different TVs were giving out commentaries on two different matches.

'Sullivan Spencer can spend the rest of her life in the bank, for all I care, but she'll drive herself bats and everybody around her ditto. I would have thought that this situation might predispose her towards the consideration of alternative career options and it might just be possible that the bank would be in a position to assist her positioning in relation to those options.'

'Meaning?'

'In confidence?'

'Look, can we lay it down in stone? I'm not here. You're not here. If I could hear you over all this sports crap, I wouldn't remember what you'd said. If you'd said anything, which you can't do because you're not here. Let's just talk honestly, and forget all the meaningless HR shite, OK?'

'Just to clarify. What's "all the meaningless HR shite"?'

'350-degree feedback and half-yearly reviews and career plans and mission statements and values and compacts of performance and grids for the evaluation of suitability for promotion and bonuses and blah and bloody blah when we know people in the bank and really everywhere get promoted by licking up to the right people and not complaining and being lucky enough to be in the right place at the right time with the right face and the right address.'

She looked both amused and flummoxed.

'Because, if you want to know what I think – '

'Don't sugar-coat it, you're playing a blinder so far.'

'I think if every HR department in this country burned to the ground it would save everybody a lot of time and hassle by removing pointless bureaucracy and effing systems and rules and regulations that get in the way of impulse, creativity and everything decent in ordinary human beings and waste so much fucking time. I'd rather be dead than have your job.'

She absorbed this so calmly, I felt guilty again.

'Not that my own job is any great shakes. Which is probably why the idea of Sullivan fecking off out of the department doesn't appeal to me, because at least she brings a bit of light into what would otherwise be so screamfest boring, I'd slit my wrists.'

'Did you always feel like that?'

'Listen, this is not about me.'

'But did you?'

'No, I didn't. When I got the personal wealth management job, I was banging off the walls with delight. Dealing with real people with real problems with real money and I was going to come up with great ideas for them and make them richer and happier and more secure. Took me a year to cop on that my real job was just selling them pensions and that if I tried to get them a loan or anything like that, all this personal relationship stuff I'd been trained to do didn't matter a shite, all that mattered was that a computer programme would rate them as a good risk or a bad risk based totally on numbers.'

'What else would you rate a risk on?'

'Talent. Personality. Drive. What their parents were like. Those are the things that let you work out whether someone's a goer and a doer or just filled with theory.'

'And are you a goer and a doer?'

'You bet your ass I am.'

'Well, why are you still in the bank, then?'

There was no answer to that other than hitting her, and believe me, I gave consideration to a smack upside the nut-brown helmet of hair. Like a smack upside my own head came a flash from the past: the day I got the job in the bank and my mother brought me around to my grandparents' house for congratulations. My grandmother enfolded me in talcumy hugs and told me I was a great girl altogether with a great future and sure she wasn't a bit surprised because I'd always been a great little worker, she'd always said that, even back when I was in primary school, so she had.

My grandfather looked at me over the top of his newspaper and said nothing. Until my grandmother nagged him to join her congratulations and he said flatly that nobody with gumption should ever work for the civil service or the bank and he thought I had a bit of gumption, but it just proved you could be wrong. It was perfectly clear he didn't think he was wrong. It was just that I had misled him as to my gumption level.

'There's nothing wrong with the bank,' I said to Lucy, weakly.

'But there's nothing right in the bank for you. Or Sullivan Spencer.'

'Oh, so you're going to purge the whole lot of us?'

For the first time, she looked both impatient and furious.

'Don't flatter yourself, Patricia,' she said, rising to her feet. 'I wouldn't devote the intellectual energy to – as you put it – "purging" either of you.'

She lifted her handbag and departed. I thought she was marching out of the whole meeting, but then realised she was headed for the loo. The barman came back and started clearing some of the detritus of the coffee so far.

'Ooops,' he said cheerily as the coffee pot slid on his tray and poured a neat stream of cold coffee on to the seat Lethal Littleton had just got up from. I grabbed her scarf and got it out of the way just in time. He scrubbed at the spill with paper towels, which is always a mistake because they shed all over the place.

When she came back, I explained what had happened and pointed her to the chair directly opposite me. By this time, of course, the coffee had caught up with me, too, so I had to pay a visit to the Ladies. When I came back, the barman had removed the paper shreds and filled the table with fresh cups and a big pot of coffee and milk. When I sat down, she fixed me with a look to die from.

'Is this your idea?'

Her gesture seemed to incorporate the new set-up.

'No, the barman spilled –'

'I mean *that*.'

I craned around to see what she was pointing at. Big framed photograph behind me of some football match.

'That?'

'Yes, that.'

'I'm sorry, I've lost you.'

'You know who that is.'

I got up and looked at the photograph. In the foreground was a guy with a rake of curly hair, legs like Schwarzenegger and a turn of speed that seemed to have been miraculously captured by the photographer. I leaned closer to read the caption.

Padhraic Stapleton kicks the 1971 decider.

I sat down again.

'I didn't know the picture was there. I don't know who Padhraic Stapleton is. I know nothing about sport.'

'You didn't pick this place deliberately?'

'This pub or this chair? Lucy, I don't know how we've got to where we are, but I didn't plan any of it.'

She looked at the photograph.

'Is he dead? Was he a relative of yours? I'm really sorry. You're obviously upset.'

She wiped her face with her hand and said it was all right, forget it, let's move on. I don't know what possessed me, but I baulked.

'No, I won't move on. Tell me. Tell me why that photograph gets to you so much.'

Nothing. Not a word. The two TV commentaries continued.

'I won't tell anyone if it's a secret. What am I talking about? I won't tell anyone, period.'

She looked at me with a weird kind of a smile even though her eyes were filled with tears.

'I've never told anybody else, so if I *ever* hear *anything* back, it has to have been you who spread it.'

'So send me a horse's head,' I said. 'Set Hugo's wife on me. Get me tarred and feathered.'

'He was the best footballer his county ever produced and he was my boyfriend.'

I worked hard to imagine this and it must have been obvious, because she sighed.

'I know you won't believe this, but in my teens, I was a tennis player.'

'A good one?'

'The best Ireland ever produced.'

'No messing?'

'By the time I was sixteen, I was competing internationally and American universities were negotiating with my parents about academic scholarships. I'm five-foot two.'

'Smaller than me by an inch.'

'I was seven and a half stone.'

No safe response to that.

'Our family were all into every kind of sport, and my brother played with Padhraic Stapleton, so I got to know him. At seventeen, I fell in love with him. Which didn't go down well with either set of parents, because he was only eighteen and we both had great sporting careers ahead of us. They used to liken me to a legend of tennis named Maureen Connolly.'

I shook my head, a bit shamefaced. Never heard of her.

'She was known as "Little Mo". They used to call me "Little Lucy Littleton".'

'That must have been a pain in the arse.'

'No, it was a pain in the arse later, but at the time it was magic. I made people in Ireland interested in tennis who'd never given it a thought. The way Ken Doherty made people interested in snooker. Half the time, I was out of the country competing, and when I was home I was studying twice as hard, because my parents were very strong in the belief that qualifications make you employable, whereas sporting success is a) transient, and b) can be cut short at any moment by injury, leaving you as "that girl who used to play – what's her name again?" In Ireland at the time, professional sport was just beginning to be understood, and the idea of making a fortune from tennis was unheard of. Particularly for a woman, but also for a GAA player. So he was studying, too, he was doing engineering.'

'So ye didn't see that much of each other, you and him?'

'No – and a lot of the time we spent together was in public. We were at big dinners and receptions and awards ceremonies. We were the golden couple. Literally. I'm naturally blonde and so was he, and him being so tall and me so short, it made for great pictures.'

'Did ye fight much?'

'Never. Every now and then, I'd get ratty about something, but he'd just laugh me back into good humour. The only confrontations he ever had were on the pitch, and even then he was a strong rather than a dirty player. Plus, I never had any reason to fight with him. He was a one-woman man. And I was that woman. If he wasn't with me, he was out playing football, or in the pub with the lads, or studying or helping his da on their farm. Or writing to me. He wrote me great letters. Great letters.'

'You still have them?'

She shook her head. The helmet moved, but only slightly. I tried to understand why someone with naturally blonde hair, if they were going to go brunette, would dye their hair the colour of a peat briquette.

'Go on.'

'My parents loved him. His parents loved me. Coming up to my nineteenth birthday, my Mum and Dad sat me down and said that they couldn't fault me on the way I'd stuck by their rules but that now I had another choice. I could go to university in Ireland or in the States. If I was going to the States, they didn't think I should get engaged, because…'

Her voice trailed off and I nodded. Too much separation would have either led to the breakup of the relationship or to her coming home when she missed him too much, abandoning the scholarship and maybe having to pay back some of the considerable sums of money involved.

'I said I'd tell them after the party. But I knew the answer. I was going to stay in Ireland, and study in Ireland, because our engagement was going to be announced at my birthday party.'

'I thought you said both sets of parents –'

'Oh, sorry, they'd said it was up to us once I reached nineteen.'

'So you were planning a great birthday party?'

'It was on a Sunday, and he had a match. Not an All-Ireland or anything, but he was going to play the match and then the whole team were going to clean up and arrive at the party. They were going to be a bit late, but.'

'Even more dramatic, to announce the engagement?'

'Right.'

'Had you picked the ring?'

She nodded and didn't describe it. Thanks be to Jaysus, I thought. There's only one thing more boring than girls – even fairly ancient girls – describing their engagement rings, and that's girls describing their dreams.

'The party was in a local hotel, which in itself was unusual, that time. Twenty-firsts, maybe, but ordinary birthday parties happened at home.'

Glancing up, I met the eye of the barman, who looked a

query: need anything over there? I shook my head fast but in a contained way so he'd get the message and she wouldn't notice.

'It was perfect. Everything was perfect. Music. Food. Friends who gelled from both sides.'

'And?'

'And he never turned up.'

'Was there an accident?'

'No. Some of the team turned up in the bus, because I think they didn't know what to do and didn't want me to feel that they were responsible in some way for what he was doing. He wasn't with them. Eventually, one of them said he'd got off the bus somewhere in the midlands.'

'Why?'

'Because there was a pub there.'

'There's pubs everywhere if he wanted a courage drink.'

'He didn't want a courage drink. He didn't want one drink. He wanted to be where he couldn't be reached, couldn't be dragged or drag himself to the party, where he could just blank out everything with drink and that's what he did.'

'He didn't telephone?'

'No.'

'What did you do?'

'I danced. I laughed. I made sure everyone had a great time. Because it was only me who knew about the engagement. Or so I thought until I was kissing his mother goodbye and she broke down and cried and said she was so, so sorry. "You're well out of it, honey," she told me. "Well out of it. That ring would have been an anchor dragging you down with him. God works in mysterious ways." So I knew his parents had known about the engagement plans. Which made it better, in a way.

Because otherwise I'd have thought he was just pretending all the time, playing me along, deliberately setting out to make a complete fool of me. The fact was, he had been so thrilled about the engagement, he had told them and sworn them to secrecy. Nobody else was to know.'

I put my two hands in between the coffee cups and pots and jugs and took hold of hers and she let me.

'And when I was going home with Mam and Dad, I told them I was going to America. My father'd had a fair few drinks that night and Mam was driving and I kept thinking we were going to be killed, because she was crying the whole way home. My father was just ready to go and find him and kill him and it was making him twice as mad that he didn't know where Padhraic was.'

She straightened up slightly and I let go of her hands, in the process tipping over the milk jug. The two of us began to laugh at the way we were wrecking this pub neither of us had ever been in before, and both of us stone-cold sober.

'I went to America and six weeks later had a fall so bad it shattered my left leg in three places.'

'End of scholarship?'

'Oh, no. This university believed you can encourage athleticism by giving scholarships, but you never forget you're an academic institution. So as long as I maintained my grades, I was fine. Which I did.'

'I wouldn't doubt you.'

'I came home after five years with a Masters and nobody would have recognised me. I was fifty pounds heavier and my hair was completely different. The Lego Lady.'

I think the blush started on me around my waistband and

surged north, gaining heat all the way. By the time it reached my forehead, I had no choice but to mop my sweaty brow. She watched this process with knowing interest.

'You thought I didn't know everybody calls me that? When they're not calling me Lethal Littleton? Patricia, every Christmas party since I became Head of Human Resources, someone has got pissed and made it his or her business to tell me the truth about how I am perceived.'

'It must bother you dreadfully.'

'Not as much as you'd imagine. Nobody who calls me Lego Littleton is ever going to remember I was once a little blonde dynamo on a tennis court and if they don't remember that, they don't remember anything else about that time. With every generation, every seven years, it gets further and further away. So it begins to feel like a story I was told, not that I lived through.'

'Let's have a drink,' I said.

'I don't,' she said.

'Neither do I,' I said. 'I meant anything other than coffee.'

I signalled the barman and it was only when he was halfway across that I realised it wasn't the same barman. It was like that scene in *The Devil Wears Prada* where Anne Hathaway is filmed in New York on the street and every time a taxi gets between her and the camera, when the footage of her resumes, she's in a different new chic outfit. Not that the replacement barman was any more chic than the first one. He had that sort of red hair you don't want to call carroty because everybody else does, but it's like nothing only a carrot.

'Soup,' he said.

That surprised me. It was kind of a statement: You two have been here for a long time, soup is the next step.

'Mulligatawny or carrot and coriander.'

We both opted for carrot and coriander. They're like Siamese twins, carrot and coriander. It's difficult to get a carrot that hasn't gone to bed with coriander.

'When did Padhraic Stapleton get in touch with you and what did he say?'

'Never.'

'But you lived in the same town?'

'I've never seen him in all the years since a week before my nineteenth birthday. I went to the states as soon as I could, and he never contacted me. The odd thing was, I expected I was always going to have to deal with newspaper stories about him, because he was such a star player with such a future. But his form fell off, and then he got into trouble for not turning up for matches and in no time, he was being written off before they started. So there was very little in the papers. Except, now and then, a story with a picture like that –' a nod towards the photograph behind my back '– in it. So it was a clean break. I knew he moved to Manchester and worked for a building firm there – he never finished his engineering degree – and he seemed to do all right. Got married. About eighteen months ago, one of his brothers e-mailed me to say that Padhraic's wife had died of kidney disease and he gave me his address.'

'Did they have children?'

She shook her head.

'I thought about it and decided not to write to him. But then, about six weeks later, I remembered something a priest in our church had said from the altar years before. He said everybody's great at doing the sympathy bit when someone is newly dead, but the suffering of the bereaved only kicks in after a few weeks, only *really* kicks in after a few weeks and at that time they're left all alone because they're no longer a couple and it's socially awkward and people just want them to get the hell over it. So I wrote to him then. A very short letter sympathising and wishing him well. I got a letter back a few days later saying that mine had been exceptionally generous and that he hoped we might some day run into each other. End of story.'

Of course, I was now sitting there, trying to look enthusiastic about bloody carrot and coriander soup (why doesn't anybody ever put the coriander first?) and wishing I was dead because of all the shit and derision I'd poured on HR and on the bank, when obviously both had given her a career and a place to belong.

She had her head down and I suddenly realised teardrops were falling in her soup. I handed another of those *Sniff!* tissues across the table to her.

'Don't pollute your soup with tears.'

She looked at the darker spots on the soup and then stirred them in and started to eat it.

'That's kind of cannibalism,' I said. 'You were a lot more than bloody generous. By Jesus, if it was me, I wouldn't even have sent a mass card.'

'We're always sure of what we'd do when it isn't us,' she said quietly. 'We're always sure what we won't tolerate until we're called on to tolerate it.'

'Have you been happy in the bank?'

She considered this for quite a long time.

'I haven't been *un*happy in the bank. It's been financially rewarding, it's given me the opportunity to travel and put me in a position of seniority and influence. For a half-life, it's been good.'

I think that was the moment I realised I had to get out of the bank. Not because I didn't have a good job. But because I could not continue to work inside the bank with her after she'd told me all this.

'Half-life?'

'Like a very good painkiller. Takes away the acute agony but leaves you at one remove from reality.'

'That must be helpful, given some of the things you have to do,' I said, more tartly than I intended.

'Very much so.'

She finished the soup-and-tears cocktail and sat back. Bundly little Lego Lady in her fifties. I glanced sideways and upwards at the picture. He must be in his late fifties, too. In Manchester.

'Be clear,' she said, reaching for some of the bossy certainty she had abandoned along with the tears. 'I've had the best of both worlds. I've had more of a life than many people dream of. Success, bit of fame, trophies, popularity in my teens. A lovely boyfriend who could dance as well as he played football. And success of a kind since then.'

'Of a kind.'

'He sucked the colour out of my life on that birthday,' she said. 'It's been black and white ever since.'

CHAPTER ELEVEN

Back on the Front Pages

*O*ne dropped mobile phone. That was all it took to put Sullivan back into the tabloids.

She'd found the Newtownmountkennedy salon. Bonded with Bloomie's hair stylist. Bonded because he immediately recognised her, hugged himself and then hugged her, and told her about American celebs he'd worked on who'd had similar problems/advantages. Once he'd established her as belonging up there with Jen, Angie and Drew, it was obvious that root-treatment was only the beginning of what her fame required. So, by the time she left, she had a new, slightly shorter, more sophisticated near-bob with straight tendrils falling seductively around her face, and just a touch of ashy lowlights. All of which took four hours and more money than she was ever going to admit to.

When she got out of the car in front of my house, her mobile slipped out of her hand, bounced on her boot, and disappeared underneath the vehicle. (You'd think she'd have worked on how to prevent phone-bounce after the fire, but no.)

So, as any normal human would do, she dropped to her

hunkers and went groping. Never noticing the single snapper who leaned over my tiny front garden wall to take a fast picture. Which appeared in the *Irish Mirror* the following morning, mainly because at the time of the photograph, she'd been wearing designer hipster jeans and a crop top, it being summer, and bending over made the top ride up and the jeans ride down, revealing Sullivan's infinite capacity for cleavage.

The story talked about her new hairdo, the cover pointing readers inside to page five for a shot of her glancing back through the tendrils, the number of my house *so* visible behind her: come stalk me, guys. It speculated that she was so depressed about being suspended by the bank (it was believed) that she needed to buck herself up with a new coif. I was quite surprised not to see Mr Bloomie in there, hugging himself and uttering psychobabble about her state of mind before, during and after the ashy lowlights.

A friend rang her at dawn to tell her about it. That's one of the things I noticed back in school about Sullivan. Maybe it's true of all spectacularly beautiful women. All other women want to be the one to bring them bad news.

'Paula was so good to let me know,' Sullivan said, making instant coffee because neither of us had remembered to get ground.

'Hmmm.'

'No, she really was. She said it was awful that when all I'd been doing was getting my hair done, that this should happen.'

Red lights. Sirens.

'Sullivan, what did you tell Paula?'

'Nothing. There was nothing to tell, according to you. You

said you have to have another meeting with Lethal Littleton before anything firm emerges.'

I had to stop myself ticking her off for calling the Head of HR Lethal. How attitudes can change in one day.

'I'm not asking you about the bank stuff. What did you tell Paula about getting your hair done?'

Everything, was the short answer – if Sullivan did short answers, which she didn't. It sounded as if Paula had got a ten-minute download on Newtownmountkennedy, Mr Bloomie, the cost of ashy lowlights and how Jen, Angie and Drew coped with the pressures of the fame they now shared with Sullivan Spencer.

I put my head in my hands.

'Paula would never talk to the media,' Sullivan stated with the absolute certainty of the pig-ignorant.

'Someone will,' I said.

I was right. The next day *The Irish Sun* had Mr Bloomie, oozing sympathy and self-promotion, and that night, Mrs Hugo (or perhaps it should be ex-Mrs Hugo) was on radio again, implying – no, *saying* – that Sullivan got money from gobshite men and that was why she was able to afford to spend gross amounts of cash on her hair.

'I'm going to sue her,' Sullivan said. 'I am. I'll get millions. She's implying I'm a prostitute.'

'Sex worker.'

'That's a prostitute. And I can prove her miserable ex never gave me anything. She's destroying my reputation. Now, I know by the look on your face you're going to say that I have no reputation, but my mother and father are destroyed about this with people telling them and it doesn't matter that it's only in the tabloids and everybody says they don't read them, they really do and then they tell other people and when it ends up on radio it sounds like a confirmation and if I don't immediately slap in solicitors' letters, it'll just go on and on and the next thing they'll say I'm pregnant.'

'Why would they say you were pregnant?'

'That's always the next thing they do,' Sullivan said wisely. 'They get a photograph of you that makes your tummy look bulgy and then they say you're pregnant. D'you not remember poor Katie after she had Suri? I'm going to ring that lawyer, Mike Kearns.'

'He's a barrister.'

'Well?'

I was about to explain that barristers., by their nature, don't tend to issue solicitors' letters to tabloid newspapers, when the phone rang and Mike announced himself.

'The very man,' I said ironically.

'I wish my partner said that more often,' he replied.

'Sullivan was just going to ring you to get you to send a solicitor's letter to the *Star* to stop them saying she's pregnant.'

'Is she?'

'He wants to know if you *are* pregnant?' I asked Sullivan.

'Who does?'

'Mike Kearns.'

'Tell him he has a bloody nerve and no I'm not, I'm already bloated and headachy.'

'I heard that,' Mike said. 'Tell her to take evening primrose oil and go for a long walk. Infallible for PMS.'

'Anyway,' Sullivan said, red in the face with generalised rage, 'the *Star* hasn't said anything yet.'

'No, but if this pass-the-parcel continues, they're next in line,' I pointed out.

'I'm not a parcel.'

'Gorgeous really does have PMS,' Mike observed quietly. 'Ask her if she's crampy.'

'I will not,' I said. 'You're a shit-hot lawyer, not a wannabe actor auditioning for the role of Cameron Diaz's gay best friend.'

'Not Cameron Diaz,' he said. 'Don't like those pale eyes. She should wear dark Prussian blue contacts.'

'Oh, Jesus, how did I land on this planet?'

'And another thing,' Sullivan said. 'Tell him my employment prospects are fucked, too.'

'Tell her that's true only if she wishes to end up getting a gold watch from the bank when she hits seventy,' he told me. I relayed this.

'Why would I have to wait until I'm seventy?' Sullivan wanted to know.

'Because the pensions situation in this country is so ropy, the pension age is going to be put back and we'll all have to work longer. The question is, does she want to work for the bank for more years than she has lived up to now?'

I did a shorter version of this to Sullivan while fiddling for the button that broadcasts a conversation all around the room.

'Jaysus, no.'

'Well, then.'

'What d'ya mean, "well then", you supercilious prick?' Sullivan yelled at the kitchen table, where the phone was now sitting. I was quite impressed by the 'supercilious.' I was used to 'prick' from Sullivan.

'I put you on speaker phone,' I told the table.

'No challenge is beyond you, Patricia.'

'See, he's a supercilious prick even to you and he's supposed to be your friend.'

'Jaysus, Sullivan, we only met Mike two weeks ago.'

'You saying I'm *not* your friend, Patricia?'

Sullivan's mobile phone rang and she stalked out of the kitchen to take the call.

'She's left the room,' I told him.

'Right,' he said briskly. 'Don't let her talk to any solicitor. Tell her I'm reading her file and considering the implications.'

'Are you?'

'Patricia? Earth to Patricia? What file?'

'Oh, there's no file.'

'And no implications, either. But it'll bring her down to a simmer and by the time her period has arrived, she'll have forgotten about it. You do not go to a solicitor on something like this.'

'That Mrs ex-Hugo is a bitch, though.'

'Add a dash of pity. Here's this old model – what? Fifty-five? Older? Humiliated in front of all her upmarket friends by this beautiful young girl. Marriage at an end. Reinvention of career a long shot but possible. Best of all, willing slaverers slopping hypocritical sympathy all over her in public. How could she miss such an opportunity?'

I filled him in on the bit of the conversation with Lucy Littleton that I was allowed to share. It met with such a long silence, I thought maybe the call had dropped. Just as Sullivan walked back in, her face even redder as a result of whatever her caller had told her, he spoke.

'Interested to hear you calling her Lucy.'

'We got into other stuff and I ended up liking her a lot.'

'Oh, good. Lucy's a love-boat just waiting for someone to break a bottle of champagne over her prow.'

I might have liked her in the pub over carrot+coriander+tears, but this far I couldn't go.

'Hmm,' I said. 'Hope nobody hits her with a bottle before I get to see her again this afternoon.'

'What time you meeting her?'

'Four. Starbucks at College Green.'

'Excellent.'

'Meeting her or the location?'

'Both.'

'Tell *him* my mother's crying on the phone to me,' Sullivan said, tossing the new coif in a way that would have been fetching to anybody who hadn't known her since first holy communion. (And yes, she was by a mile the most adorable of all the snow princesses on that day. I was in cream. My mother wanted to make an individual out of me. You can see why I was never close to my mother.)

'She's not *on* the phone to you,' I pointed out.

'No, but when she was, she was.'

'Such syntax,' Mike murmured.

'She says she's devastated and distraught.'

'Talent for alliteration, that girl.'

'What's he saying?'

'Tell her,' he said, loud enough to carry right across the kitchen to her, 'tell her she deserves better than a mother who is so self-absorbed that all she can think about is the non-existent effect Sullivan's real miseries are having on her.'

Sullivan stood at the sink, pondering this.

'Tell her that in the Mother Lotto, she got the wrong numbers.'

'Oh, and I suppose he got the right ones?'

'Too right, I did. And the bonus, too. Nothing anybody ever said about me – and you can imagine, they've said plenty – ever mattered to her. She'd cut people off at the knees if they tried to pass on stinky stuff about me and she'd never even mention it to me. I might discover years later by accident. But never from my mother.'

'Could we do a swap?' Sullivan asked and burst into tears.

'Gorgeous, my beautiful mother went to her reward three years ago and it better be *some* reward, is all I can say.'

I handed Sullivan a tissue. From a new packet. The illustration on these tissues was of a zebra with his stripes unravelling over the caption *Stress!* My serendipity with cute tissues was awesome, I thought.

'Go to bed,' I told her. 'I'll bring you a hot-water bottle. Just go to bed, right now, all right?'

She nodded miserably, twinkled her fingers at the phone, and left.

'God love her,' I told Mike, taking the phone off speaker, 'She's so confused, she waved goodbye at you as if you could see her.'

'How's the new hairdo going?'

'Really well. Mr Bloomie may be a bastard, but he cuts and colours beautifully.'

'It's perms you have to be wary of,' Mike said thoughtfully. 'When I was devilling, I got a perm and the very memory of it makes me shudder. I was as tall as I am now, but much skinnier and it made me look like a stalk of broccoli. However. Enough. Suggestion. Daragh Gibbons. Write down the name. Daragh Gibbons looks like Mephistopheles. Same height as me, dark, bearded.'

'No offence, but why am I getting all this information? Am I going to have to do a Missing Persons report to the guards?'

'My, aren't we snippy today. I've always thought it a fascinating fact that when you put women working together or living together, their menstrual cycles tend to coincide…'

Which of course implied my period was on its way, just like Sullivan's, and put it up to me. I could yell at him that it wasn't. Or yell at him that it was none of his business, which would be accurate, but then he'd know he'd got it right. I maintained a dignified silence.

'Daragh you will, courtesy of my splendid description, recognise when you meet him at three in the College Green Starbucks.'

'Why wou –'

'Patience, Patricia. Patience. Young Daragh is a tax genius. I happened to mention to him that a friend of mine had inherited a Martello tower that might need renovation, and he gushed like a tap about special tax schemes to benefit anybody who restores such a building.'

'I need to meet this guy.'

'Indeed.'

'Thank you.'

'Pleasure. In the meantime, I'd suggest a hot-water bottle apiece for you and Gorgeous and a quick nap.'

CHAPTER TWELVE

Tax Reliefs and Exit Signs

I began to laugh the minute he walked in from the Dame Street entrance, thus making it easy for him to work out that I was the person he was due to meet. Starbucks had maybe four coffee-drinkers not involved in couples or groups, and I was the only one not glued to *The Irish Times,* with the exception of an earnest corduroy-wearing old money type in the corner who was reading the *Village* and looking as if he was sure to be outraged at any moment, as *Village* readers tend to want to be.

The bearded guy gave me one of those slow smiles that crawls up one side of a face and then takes over, including the eyes, which were the darkest brown I'd ever seen.

'Patricia?'

'Mephistopheles?'

He laughed and tossed his coat over the empty armchair.

'More of that?' he asked, nodding towards my cappuccino.

I shook my head and he went up to the counter, coming back with one of those tiny cups of espresso. He set it down and reached into his overcoat pocket, emerging with documentation.

'Mike made me easy to identify, I gather,' he said, unfolding the papers.

'Well, let's face it, Mephistopheles is not much of a reach.'

'You seen any of Mike's sketches of people?'

Another head shake from me.

'He captures the essence. Like a good cartoon. But not unkindly. Anyway, go ahead, tell me about your tower.'

That one tiny word 'your' gave me a jolt. I tended to talk and think of it as 'the' tower. But it was mine. My personal piece of history. My link to the Little Corporal who had lost at Waterloo…

I showed him the pictures we'd run off from Sullivan's camera. That girl may not have the wit to keep herself out of the tabloids, but she was the only one of the three of us who'd taken photographs on that first visit. They weren't the greatest photographs, but they gave a sense of scale and situation which evoked an appreciative low whistle from Daragh as he went through them.

'I can see why Mike's so taken,' he muttered. 'Ooof.'

I leaned over to see what had drawn the exclamation. In front of him was a shot of the floor of the Martello, cluttered with great damp dusty broken masonry and boulders.

'There will certainly be physical work involved,' I said. 'But that would probably be a good thing for me and Sullivan. Sullivan Spencer is my closest friend. Oh, and she's a girl,' I said, automatically clearing up potential misunderstandings based on Sullivan's name.

'I know her, don't I?'

'Do you?'

'Well, not *personally*,' he said, reddening. 'But she – she shares herself through media, doesn't she?'

'When photographers lie in wait to catch a glimpse of your arse-cleavage, it's not hard to end up being shared,' I said furiously.

He did this slow double take, kind of mouthing some of the words I'd just said: *arse-cleavage...* 'I've lost you,' he said politely.

I growled the story of the lost-phone picture at him and he listened sadly, sipping from his tiny cup. It should have looked ridiculous.

'Oh dear,' he said when I finished.

The comment was a lot more neutral than the glances I was getting from the three girls at one of the high tables.

'Bugger,' I hissed. 'I've been talking too loud.'

He shrugged, which annoyed me even more, since I had planned for him to say, 'Nonsense, don't worry, they couldn't have heard a word.' I opened my mouth to sell him Sullivan Spencer, Misunderstood Very Best Friend, and then closed it again. The priority in the immediate future had to be to *un*sell Sullivan, not enmesh her in a new set of appreciative/exploitative men friends. Fortunately, he seemed to have lost interest in her and moved on to the documentation he'd brought with him.

'I have two items here,' he said. 'One's an application form which we can leave to one side for the moment. This more important one is a leaflet from the Revenue Commissioners.'

I picked it up, expecting to see pictures of Martello towers. The leaflet had no pictures of anything. And there's me, believing the Revenue Commissioners had gone all soft and cuddly in recent years. Maybe they have, but their dense prose doesn't get broken up by pretty pictures of Napoleonic towers.

Daragh Gibbons began to explain Approved Building Tax Relief to me. This relief apparently applies to a building the Revenue Commissioners decide is 'intrinsically of significant historical, architectural or aesthetic interest.' So far so good, I thought. *My* tower was indubitably all of the above. He stroked his beard as he talked. I wouldn't mind doing that, I thought. Concentrate, you moron, I told myself. I *am* concentrating, the mad little voice inside my head responded. Yeah, but on the wrong thing, I told it.

'I'm sorry,' I said to him. 'My concentration lapsed there. Would you mind starting again?'

'No problem.'

Any expenses incurred on the repair, maintenance or restoration of a building that had significant historical, architectural or aesthetic interest would be deducted from the tax payable on the owner's other income.

'How do you mean "other income"?' I asked. 'I only have my salary.'

'What I mean is that if you spend, say, €50,000 on restoring the building, you will save up to €21,000 in income tax. Assuming you pay tax at 42%.'

I admitted to 42%. I wasn't long in that bracket, but I was quite proud of myself for getting there.

'This sounds great,' I said. 'Up to now, everybody's been bringing me bad news about this tower, telling me An Taisce and the Planning Board are going to make my life hell if I want to change the smallest thing in it. But are we sure it qualifies for this relief?'

He rifled through his papers and found some handwritten notes.

'I talked to a woman in the Department of the Environment who was very helpful. She gave me examples of the kind of information that would be required to prove that the building is of "historical interest".'

He pointed with his bic at a line in the notes. Isn't he a lovely, unpretentious man, my mad internal voice commented, he doesn't have a showy pen. *Shut up, little voice.* OK. But he has beautiful hands, too, had you noticed?

'What did the DOE woman say was the kind of evidence needed?'

'Well, it might include famous people who might have stayed there, and evidence from books and newspapers to support this.'

My heart plummeted. Nobody had ever stayed there, as far as we knew. Certainly nobody historic. Nobody famous.

'Now, I don't know about you,' he went on, unaware of my sudden onset of despair. 'But I would have thought that a 200-year-old fortified gun tower built to repel a Napoleonic invasion qualifies automatically as both "historical" and "interesting". Definitely more so than a Victorian two-up two-down where Yeats once had a cup of tea.'

'You're absolutely right,' I said. Un-plummet, my heart.

'So her choice of example could mean one of two things. Number one would be that the bar has been set pretty low, and the tower is guaranteed to get the nod as being of "historical interest", or, number two, the people who make these decisions have a very different understanding of what constitutes "historical interest" compared to the rest of us.'

My heart did a half-plummet.

'Or maybe it means nothing at all,' he finished, inappropriately happy about the imprecision. 'I should warn you, this is all virgin territory for me (that's what makes it interesting), and I can't help throwing in a health warning every so often.'

Bugger health warnings, I thought, but didn't say. The three girls on the high stools left. Either they found income tax relief less interesting than Sullivan's rear-cleavage, or they couldn't hear Daragh's quiet husky voice.

'You a smoker?' I asked.

He nodded, sadly. We did a joint silent consideration of his habit – and, on my side, on how attractive it made his voice – before he moved on.

'The sticking point,' he began and paused.

'Oh, shit,' I blurted. My heart was running out of enthusiasm for plummet-and-recovery.

'The sticking point is that in order to qualify for the relief, "reasonable access" must be afforded to the public.'

'You're kidding me.'

He shook his head.

'So I'd have to let ten busloads of American tourists into my tower every day?'

This made him laugh, and to prevent myself from hitting him, I got up and went to the counter and ordered repeat coffees, watching him from the place where you wait for your work of caffeined art. For an accountant, he had surprisingly Byronic hair.

When I got back with another teeny cup of espresso for him and a cappuccino for me, he got technical in a big way.

'The question of what constitutes reasonable access is decided in each individual case, but the absolute minimum requirement is that access is allowed to the public for an average of four hours a day for at least 60 days a year.'

I did the mental math. That could mean opening the place each morning at nine for the entire three months of the summer.

'Or,' I said slowly, being evil, 'It could mean opening the place each morning at 5 a.m., for the three worst months of the winter.'

He smiled at me and shook his head.

'The access must be in a reasonable manner and at reasonable times, and details of opening hours must be provided in advance to Fáilte Ireland.'

'What's unreasonable about early winter mornings?'

He smiled at me and didn't even bother to shake his head.

'Bugger, bugger, balls shite and feck,' I said.

'Do I get the impression you're not much into people? Or is it just American tourists you draw the line at?'

I started to answer that and couldn't work out what would impress him most, me as a people-loathing recluse, a sort of Martello version of J. D. Salinger or whoever that poet was who never met anybody and never published anything until after he was long dead, or me as a social animal who just drew the line at busloads of blue-hairs.

'That's the first sticking point,' he said gently. 'Whether or not you would consider the burden of public access tolerable for the sake of the relief. Now, I really must have a cigarette. Would you excuse me for five minutes?'

I nodded, restraining myself from offering to go out into the sunshine to keep him company. We were in the window at Dame Street. And, as always when I'm there on my own, I became enmeshed and entranced by the variety of people and walking styles Dublin presents.

Across the road, I could see a woman and a man bent over examining something in the Pen Corner window. As I watched, she gave him an ecstatic little hug – the two of them still bent over – as if she'd spotted something that solved a problem. They walked into the shop and I immediately thought I must pop over there after my meeting with Lucy Littleton. It's one of my favourite places in Dublin, with its old fashioned wooden pen cases. Even if I only buy a cheapie fountain pen there, rather than a Mont Blanc, I get a kick out of it.

I finished my coffee.

'Did you know it's considered naff, in Italy, to drink cappuccino after noon?' I asked Daragh when he came back, all nicotined up.

'Really? Did some Italian tick you off for doing it?'

'No, it was in this book.'

I lifted up a paperback of *Echo Park*.

'Oh, the *Lincoln Lawyer* author,' he said enthusiastically.

I promised to give him *Echo Park* as soon as I was done with it, and my mad little voice whispered that this would be a great reason to meet him again. *Why would I want to meet him again, for Chrissakes? All he does is depress me about my tower.*

'Busloads of blue-haired Americans,' I prompted.

He looked taken aback.

'Nothing against them,' I promised him. 'Just the thought is a bit offputting.'

He suggested, mildly, that my problem would not come from elderly American visitors, whose tours didn't tend to lower themselves to anything as recent as a Martello tower, instead visiting the Neanderthal Tomb at Newgrange, the Book of Kells in Trinity and Dublin Castle when they were on the east coast. The kind of visitors who were more likely to want to go through a Martello were Europeans who were readers or walkers or students. Which would make them bad news if I was running a souvenir shop, because that kind of tourist doesn't spend a lot of money. I couldn't see myself running a souvenir shop, though.

'I may be wrong, but I am assuming that you would like the access to the public to be at the bare minimum level necessary to qualify for the tax relief?'

'You're not wrong, Daragh. You're not wrong.'

'The key definitions, then, lie in the Revenue Commissioners' requirement that "conditions, if any, in regard to that access are such that they do not act as a disincentive to the public from seeking such access."'

One approach to this, he speculated, might be that access would be provided on the basis of pre-booked appointment only. In other words, a person could book a tour at any time during the 4 hours of any of the 60 days a year that access must be granted according to the legislation, but nobody would be able to drop in on a whim while I was watching *Big Brother*, which I don't.

'And insisting on pre-booking wouldn't be seen as a disincentive?'

'Dunno.'

'I wonder how difficult it would be to administer that kind of a pre-booking system?'

'Mobile phone and a notebook would cover it, I'd have

thought. I don't honestly think you'd be getting dozens of calls in any one day. Another possibility would be that you could lay down an additional requirement that bookings would be made by credit card only.'

'Hang on. You saying I could charge people to come in?'

'You need good banking advice,' a female voice said, startling Daragh, who instinctively got to his feet.

'This is my friend Lucy Littleton,' I said, overstating things a bit. 'Lucy, this is Daragh Gibbons, tax genius.'

'May I join you or would you rather I lurked over there? I know I'm a bit early.'

'Oh, join us by all means.'

Daragh waited until she was seated before he sat back down. See, he has lovely manners, said the mad voice. *Shut the hell up, you immature asshole.*

I gave Lucy Littleton a quick rundown on my new inheritance.

'Wow. Fantastic. Congratulations. Is it beautiful?'

I thought about that for a minute.

'No, it's not beautiful in the way that a ruined Norman castle is beautiful,' I said honestly. 'It's squat and solid and sort of planted there, impregnable.'

Like you, Lucy, the mad voice said in my head.

'But it's so different to everything else. Even being circular. And to just touch the rough stones and go up the narrow stone staircase and see the view from the roof. It's quite ridiculous, but it's taken me over. So yes, in a weird way, it *is* beautiful. To me, at any rate.'

'But it may need renovation?'

'That's putting it mildly,' I said.

'Mike says you're looking at a million, minimum,' Daragh offered.

Never mind my heart plummeting. My stomach, spleen and appendix plummeted along with my ticker. Mass plummet.

'Who's Mike?' Lucy wanted to know.

'Mike Kearns, he's – '

'The barrister?'

'Yeah.'

Lucy sat back and smiled across at me.

'Well, isn't Dublin a *very* small place,' she observed.

Daragh looked uncomfortably from her to me and back again.

'A million,' I said. 'Jaysus. There'd better be an awful lot of tax relief or this tower's going to stay exactly the way it is or get sold.'

'Part of the legislation also refers to an "easily visible and legible sign in a conspicuous location at or near the place where the public can gain entrance to the building concerned",' Daragh read, glancing up at me to see how I was taking it.

'That would seem to indicate that the spirit of the relief is to actively encourage – '

'Casual tourist traffic,' Lucy interrupted.

'Frig casual tourist traffic,' I said.

'Why? You were enthusiastic enough about it, talking to me. Would you not like to have the opportunity to show it off to other people?'

'Me? A tour guide? In my own home?'

'Does it have a garden?' Daragh asked.

'It sits on half an acre. Why?'

He handed me a sheet and pointed to a paragraph beside which he had put a couple of Xs.

'If the building is approved,' it read, 'then money spent on the maintenance or restoration of the building's "garden or grounds of an ornamental nature" will also qualify for relief.'

'In other words,' Lucy hazarded, 'if the building qualifies, the garden automatically does too. I'd love to see the Martello, by the way.'

'Me too,' Daragh said, gathering all his paperwork into a folder and presenting it to me.

'Oh, sometime you both can come and have a look.'

'Why not now?'

'*Now?*' I looked at Lucy to see if she was joking. She wasn't.

'OK,' I said.

'You coming?' she asked Daragh, who shook his head.

'I really can't,' he said regretfully.

I started to put his folder into my bag.

'Feck it, why not?' Daragh asked nobody in particular.

So we all piled into my car and headed for Sloe Point.

CHAPTER THIRTEEN

Paddling and Planning

*D*on't ask me how it came about that me and the bank's Head of Human Resources ended up paddling in the shallows of my nearly private beach on a sunny summer afternoon. I couldn't get over it. This forbidding woman stood on the sand, yanked up her skirt and tucked it into her knickers like a child and walked out until she couldn't go any further without wrecking everything she was wearing. If Daragh had rolled up his trouser legs he could have gone out even further, given the length of his legs, but he went climbing on the rocks instead, promising to rescue us if we got swept away by a freak wave.

The breeze was blowing the hair off Lucy's face and – as always, control-freak me – I wanted to suggest she think about having her hairline raised by laser treatment. Of course, I've never had laser treatment myself, but I read all Sullivan's magazines, so I know everything from how to make your eyelashes look longer than they are to how to minimise the pain of a Brazilian. If I was going to have a Brazilian, which I never will.

The great advantage about being unattached is that you don't have to give serious consideration to torturing the hell out of yourself at enormous cost in order to prevent your new guy being traumatised by the sight of an errant pubic hair or two.

Splashing around in the shallows that day, I found myself wondering about the briquette-brown Lego helmet. It was sort of the opposite to fuck-me boots, I thought. It was fuck-off hair: the sure-fire way, thirty or more years ago, to remove all the attractiveness of the lithe blonde tennis player and turn her into a formidable sexless corporate apparatchik.

She had wandered about a hundred yards away from me in the sea, so I was getting her back view, which was quite ridiculous, between the brown hair planted down on the top of the roundy little head on the roundy little torso atop the roundy bundle of skirt-in-pants. At that distance, because no legs were showing, she looked like a dressed-up thatched rubber duck floating on the sea.

The weird thing about growing to like someone is how you can observe all the things about them you'd describe as ugly when you didn't like them, and find them at most unpretty and maybe even endearing. The dread, of course, is that it most often goes the other way. Couples accept a bunch of habits, rituals, deficits and miseries in their loved one, glossing over them all with the sugar-glaze of initial affection, and, three or four years later, it's precisely those traits that make their hands tighten with the desire to clasp and tighten around the other's neck and choke them until they are dead.

Lucy waded back towards me. I was standing in one of those streams of particularly warm water, imagining swimming on my own there in winter. Running down from the tower, across the tiny beach through whistling cold air so that the water, breasted in one gasping dive, would seem not so shockingly cold.

'Can you imagine facing that tower if you were one of Napoleon's soldiers who'd just been ordered onto the beach?' Lucy asked.

'Assuming they ever got near the beach,' I said, looking out at the bay.

The two of us stood in the water looking at the tower. Imagining what it would have been like to be a Frenchman, exhausted from a sea battle, boots waterlogged, musket held overhead, making the run up the steep slope of the beach towards this apparently impregnable fortress.

'You know something?' Daragh called from the black rocks he was standing on. 'From the road, it looks big, but not threatening. By Jesus, from down here, it looks pretty bloody threatening. It *looms*.'

'Can you imagine trying to scale it?' Lucy asked him, and he shook his head.

'With all the lads inside boiling water and pitch and getting ready to pour it down on you? No.'

The two of us came into the shallow water and she undid her skirt so that it fell, crumpled, around her legs. Then she walked briskly back and forth on the hard sand, presumably to dry her feet off before she jammed them back in those shoes that are called classic, not because they're always stylish, but because they were never stylish. Daragh clambered down beside me.

'For its time, this must have been as formidable a defence system as Iwo Jima.'

'I'm sure you're right.'

What the frig, I thought, was Iwo Jima?

'During the Second World War, the Americans landed on an island that looked uninhabited. Except that every square inch of it had been tunnelled out and there were secret shooting places at points in each tunnel so the marines were mown down by a hundred sub-machine guns the minute they hit the sand.'

Lucy came up to listen.

'The guys were slipping in each other's blood and guts and the tanks that were supposed to protect them hadn't been disembarked and it was a godawful merciless massacre.'

'Did they retreat?'

'The marines don't retreat. They kept coming in waves and they eventually won the island. But you had to have overwhelming numbers, overwhelming determination and no alternative. And it seems to me that much the same would have applied here. If Napoleon had wanted to get an army ashore, he'd have had to come in –'

'With a flotilla,' Lucy said, her arm sweeping in the direction of the sea, conjuring up dozens of warships.

I'm going to have to sell the bloody tower, I thought, but for the moment, this is fun. Fun with the sun slanting into our faces and throwing a great tower shadow over the beach. I started to get into my shoes, wobbling one-legged. Daragh extended a bent elbow for support. I laughed, grasped it and slid the other shoe on.

'How do you know all that Iwo Whatsit stuff?'

'My father's a Professor of History in DCU.'

'Why didn't you do history rather than accountancy?'

'I just loved the figures. I could tell you how many battalions Napoleon's generals had at the battle of Waterloo, but the social significance of the battle would elude me. Plus,' he said, scuffing the sand at the edge of the shadow cast by the top of the tower, 'my father casts a long shadow. He's the best there is. Which reminds me; if you want to go for that tax relief, the Department of the Environment said you might need to get a historian or a guy from the Office of Public Works to visit the site and evaluate its historical importance. My father would be a credible authority and he'd love to do it.'

I told him that would be wonderful, and led the way to the tower.

'That's a godawful ugly garage door thing,' Lucy observed.

'That may look like a godawful garage door thing to you,' I told her, 'but that godawful garage door has two great benefits, I'm told. One is that because somebody broke out the wall in such a big way a long time ago, we'll be able to extend the tower in a way An Taisce wouldn't have let us if we were starting with an intact tower.'

Who's this 'we', Tonto? I wondered to myself. You're on your own in this, Patricia, and you haven't a hope in hell of doing anything but selling it and paying off some of your mortgage. Which is not what your grandfather wanted. The combative bollix was putting it up to you: be a weakling and take the money or fight to own a bit of history. Well, Grandad, you know where you can stick your posthumous challenges.

'And the second great benefit?' Daragh asked courteously.

Although, Grandad, I might try to play it out for a while if playing it out meant Mephistopheles here hung around for a bit.

'Once we pull that big lump of timber out, we've got one hell of a workable space through which to remove the seventy-eight tons of rubble whoever broke out the gap left on the floor of the tower.'

'Seventy-eight tons? You're sure?'

Daragh looked horrified.

'Don't get numbers-focused,' Lucy reproved him with, I kid you not, a twinkly little smile. Twinkly little smile? Lethal Littleton? 'She's speaking figuratively. What puzzles me is why anybody would break *in* a space like that and leave the rubble inside.'

'Don't get logic-focused,' he told her, laughing. 'People do dumb things all the time for no reason.'

'Not usually with seventy-eight tons of rubble.'

'It's only figurative rubble.'

'Right. Even *I* could be illogical with figurative rubble.'

When the two of them were standing on the platform inside the door of the tower, though, Daragh expelled a longer breath than a smoker deserved to be able to expel in an awed whistle.

'That's an awful lot of rubble,' he acknowledged.

It was very handy, our respective sizes, I thought. She and I could stand at the front and he could see over the two of us without even going on tiptoe.

'And it's an awful lot of work,' he added.

'To what?'

'To make this as beautiful and as— as— *authentic* as it could be,' Lucy said.

I didn't tell her she was stroking the rough stones the same way Sullivan had. Somehow I didn't feel the comparison would appeal to her.

'I wonder if there's any rule against removing those stones,' Daragh said, half to himself.

'Oh, let's not go looking for any more bloody rules,' I said in a snarl. 'Come on.'

I let the two of them go past me and then banged the door closed. Even *that* wouldn't work for me and Daragh had to reach past me and bang it a couple of times before he could force the bolts in place for me to padlock. I dropped the heavy old keys in my jacket pocket and clinked like a jailer as I led the way down the metal stairs and got into the car. I had it revving before they could even get the passenger doors open.

'What's eating you?' asked Lucy, belting herself in ostentatiously as if she was appearing in a TV commercial for road safety.

'Realism.'

'Meaning?'

'I'm coming to terms with the impossibility of tackling that bloody tower.'

Daragh, who didn't seem to have belted himself in at the back of the car, leaned on the back of my seat to hear us.

'I wouldn't have thought it impossible,' he murmured.

'Yeah, well, we've already established that you're not good at seeing the significance of figures. You said yourself. Mike Kearns, may his arse fester and fall off, is quite right. It *is* going to take a million euro if not more to get that bloody thing workable.'

'Why?'

'Because, before anything could be done, there would have to be massive removal of shite – once we had begged some benighted bureaucrat to let us get rid of our own shite.'

I could feel the back of the seat shaking and took my eye off the road long enough to see that Daragh was in stitches but trying not to make a noise. He made an apologetic face at me.

'What's so effing funny?'

'Well, it's actually *not* our own shite. It's two hundred year old shite belonging to someone else.'

'It's not shite at all,' Lucy said and I did a forehead smack.

'I'm *so* sorry for using bad language.'

'That's not what I meant,' she said coolly. 'I meant it isn't throwaway stuff. It's stuff that will allow you to link whatever you construct on the outside visually to the rest of the tower. No bureaucrat's going to get in the way of that.'

'And what, pray, am I going to construct on the outside?'

'Whatever you want. Kitchen, dining room, sun room, conservatory.'

I could feel myself being seduced all over again by the possibilities of this monstrosity.

'So let's say two hundred thousand euro for a dining room and a sun room. OK?'

'OK,' said Daragh, earning himself a filthy look from Lucy.

'What,' he said defensively, 'you think it could be cheaper?'

'Of course it could be cheaper.'

'It could be dearer, too, just as easily,' I said, cutting through this pointless debate between two non-experts.

'True,' she said and the old curt Lethal was back in force, from the tone of the single word.

'Then the whole thing would have to be plumbed and wired. That would be another two hundred thousand. What are we up to now, figures-man?'

'Four hundred thousand.'

'A floor put in halfway up,' I added, having seen it somewhere on the web. 'Because otherwise you have the ground floor and a ceiling six miles up and the roof and that amounts to loads of space but not *living* space. Putting in another floor is going to cost a quarter of a million, if you take in having a stairs.'

'Six fifty,' Daragh said.

'Wind turbines and solar panels, another hundred.'

'Seven fifty.'

'Showers, sinks, stoves, fireplaces, beds, tables, chairs.'

'Fifty thousand,' he suggested.

'Have you ever equipped even a modest kitchen, never mind a bedroom?' I demanded.

'No, my girlfriend did all that kind of thing.'

My heart had obviously got fed up with this plummeting lark, because it stayed put and all I experienced was a grim sense of confirmation: sure, had to be. No doubt she's as tall as you are and built.

'Well, the current costs would be such that you're not going to get a super kitchen and built-in wardrobes and all the space-saving carpentry you'd have to have tailor-made because of the circular shape without a budget of about a hundred and fifty if not more,' Lucy said.

Even though she was agreeing with me, or maybe because she was agreeing with me, I wanted to lean across her roundy shape to the door handle, open it up and turf her straight out into the path of oncoming traffic. My father used to quote G.K. Chesterton as saying that if men knew what women did when men weren't around, they'd never marry them. My own take is that if men knew what women *think*, they'd never marry them. And if women knew what other women think about *them*, they'd never stay on the same planet with them. Except poor oul Sullivan. Every time she has an evil thought about anybody, she wants to make it up to them.

'You haven't done anything to the walls,' Lucy said, unaware of my plans to defenestrate her. No, that'd be putting her out the window, I thought nastily, and she wouldn't effing *fit* if we tried to.

'Like what?'

'Waterproof them from the outside. Whitewash them on the inside.'

'See, there's more expense.'

'You're up there near the million, all right,' Daragh conceded.

'See?'

'There or thereabouts.'

'Where would I get a million? I've only four years of my bloody mortgage paid off and, as it is, I have to bloody effing budget for everything.'

Neither of them had a suggestion to solve that problem, which was extremely depressing in its confirmation of a grim reality I had *so* hoped not to have confirmed.

'And to get any tax relief, I'd have to do it bit by bit over twenty years. This year the whitewashing. Next year the wardrobe. I mean, for Chrissake I don't know how I could have been so naïve as to think this shagging tower was anything but a bloody oversized white elephant. And it's not even white.'

'I'm not sure you'd get the relief if the place was not in a condition meriting visits by tourists,' Daragh said helpfully.

'So to get some of the money back, I have to do it all at once with money I don't have? This must be what they call the nanny state. With a nanny that's barking mad. Where am I dropping you two, anyway?'

Daragh started to do extreme courtesy, indicating that anywhere was fine. Whatever was handiest. He gave the impression that if it suited me to fling him out the door without warning into the middle of a convocation of Hell's Angels, that would be fine by him. I cut through it and asked him where he bloody worked or lived, for Chrissakes, and to stop wasting my time, which implied I had a bunch of really interesting and urgent things to do that night when in fact all I had to do was go home, turn Sullivan on and pretend to listen to her as she went through the latest instalment in *Sullivan's Exciting Life*.

Lucy told me crisply where I was to leave her and Daragh said, with some relief, that would suit him grand and when I pulled in, I thanked them for their time with the formal civility my mother used to prove she was a lady and wouldn't bring herself to be rude when members of the travelling community called to her door. Politeness with extreme prejudice.

As I drove off, I could see them in the rear-view mirror. Mephistopheles towering over the Lego Lady. I wished I could laugh, but it was all I could do not to cry.

And then I cried anyway.

CHAPTER FOURTEEN

Secret Meeting in the Jervis Shopping Centre

*T*he really annoying thing about being a rude bitch is that part-timing it doesn't work. If you don't mind being hated, you can be a consistent, unfailing unremorseful bitch.

But if, like me, you just become a bitch under extreme pressure and hate yourself afterwards, it's rotten time management. You spend a ridiculous amount of time digging yourself back out of the hole you dug yourself into.

The following morning, I had to craft and then send an apologetic e-mail to Lucy Littleton. (Who got her own back mechanically: one of those maddening little automatic responses that says the recipient is out of the office at the moment but will attend to whatever crap you've sent them when they get back, ergo, in their own sweet time.)

Then I had to text Mike Kearns, asking him if he had an e-mail address for Daragh Gibbons and of course Mike Kearns rang, full of the joys, if not of spring, certainly of early August, warbling on about what a delightful person Daragh was, was he not, and how helpful had he been and what were the next steps in my excellent Napoleonic adventure. Arse.

I took a deep breath and told him the adventure was over. Done. Finito. Kaput. I was going to have to sell the tower and smartish. Even as I was telling him, it struck me that if I knew within eight days of inheriting it that I was going to have to unload it, nobody in their sane senses would pay any worthwhile money for it. It probably wouldn't even cover inheritance tax or whatever that thing is called.

I wouldn't call myself paranoid, but lurking at the back of my mind was the temptation to ring cousin Goretti and tell her I was ready to give the bloody thing away at this stage, because it was now clear to me that our unbeloved mutual grandfather had died as he had lived, taking pleasure in putting gobshites between a rock and a hard place, me being the gobshite and the tower being the hard place.

Mike Kearns didn't present any arguments to dissuade me, just promised to text me the e-mail address and duly did. I wrote and rewrote a letter which tried to say thank you to Daragh Gibbons for being an all-round nice guy and expert as hell while at the same time indicating that he should not waste another moment of his valuable time on the complex issues around the tower and would he please send me a bill for what he had done thus far?

The letter ended with a clumsy attempt to indicate that I really wasn't the bitch he undoubtedly and on good evidence now believed me to be, it was just that a confluence (I know, it crept in there) of circumstances had caused me to become preoccupied. All of which must have confirmed his view of me as a bitch but added a perception of me as a complete obnoxious headbanger into the bargain. Which, since it was accurate, I couldn't fight with.

If I could have, I would have, though. I'm lucky I don't have a cat. No. It's lucky for cats as a species that I don't own any of them. Because I would have kicked that cat squarely in the crotch, although for all I know four-pawed animals don't have crotches. Crotches, all the better for kicking you in, my dear, may be the preserve of two-footed upright animals. And if you don't mind, I really don't want to get into a discussion about crotches at this time.

The other thing that was really maddening was that Sullivan had decided to clean the house and was singing at the top of her voice so that I could hear her even over the Hoover. That woman's lungs are as enviable as the rest of her. She was consistently the soloist in the school choir. I was always in the front row of said choir, but only because of being short, not because of being able to do anything more than hold a note.

I called up to her that I had to go and get the paper, which of course I didn't, and I called out just loud enough to assuage what we might at a stretch call my conscience, but not loud enough for her to actually hear me.

Of course it was the day the Property Supplement was in *The Irish Times* and of course I couldn't resist furthering the downward slope of my humour by reading all it had to say about houses not selling at auctions at the moment, and the price of houses going 'soft', whatever the hell that meant. I sat listening to Sullivan doing a great version of the unfortunately appropriate 'I Will go Down With this Ship' while the message sank in.

Not only did I have a tower I no longer wanted, I had a tower it was unlikely anybody else would want. Assuming Ireland held a potential buyer who would overlook the small matter of seventy four tons of rubble on the ground floor of their bijou military pillar-box (plumbing and electricity extra), if *The Irish Times* property pages were talking about the property market coming in for a soft landing, given their dependence on advertising from every real-estate company in the country, what that translated into was an absolute dearth of spare money to be spent on a defensive tower misconceived from its daft beginnings, which wasn't at this point in inviting condition. That phrase appearing in the small print under some of the colour pictures in front of me didn't quite match the reality of what I was setting out to sell: *May need renovation*.

May need renovation to the tune of a million, I thought, before you could swing a cat in it, and you wouldn't want a big cat, either, with or without a crotch, because them walls, them walls, them wet walls are so thick they leave only a little tubular space inside for cat-swinging or other pursuits congruent with the integrity of the building, and you'd better keep all your pursuits congruent with the integrity of that bloody building or An Taisce will come and kick *you* in the crotch.

It was at that moment that I turned a page of the supplement and found myself staring at a big colour picture of a Martello tower for sale. Set in terraced gardens which (the text told me) exploded with daffodils in the springtime. On an acre of its own land with another building within the curtelage (I'll raise you a confluence, I thought), this latter building called a rocket house because back in the old days of the steam ships, didn't they fire ropes out to people who might otherwise drown when their ship hit the rocks.

This tower, it was clear, wasn't going to pose any planning problems at all, because the owners had already broken out through the walls wherever they wanted to back in the 1930s and so it had every mod bloody con you could think of.

'Fantastic,' I said aloud as Sullivan came into the room, wearing a bandana to testify to her transient domesticity. 'The first and only time in my life I'm ever going to need to sell a Martello tower and there's another on the market at the same time.'

'You're not going to sell your Martello,' Sullivan said, with such horror you'd think I'd announced my intention to become a full-time professional cat crotch-kicker.

'No choice,' I said, folding up the paper.

'There are always ways,' she said solemnly and I didn't ask her what ways she had found, after twenty-nine years on the earth, to stop her mother manipulating her and making her feel like a slapper. Instead I announced I was going to the supermarket. Specifically, I was going to go into the Jervo and do a massive grocery shopping expedition to fill up the freezer. She was welcome to come with me, I told her, in a tone that promised to kneecap her if she tried. She said no, she'd continue with her cleaning blitz.

I got parked as near as possible to the 'Collect by Car' signs at the back of M&S and was halfway down in the lift when I remembered: shopping bags. The plastic bag levy I approve of, but never remember. So it was back up to the car park to retrieve the stored folded-flat green bags from the boot. One of them started to slide as I reached to push the elevator button and that's when my phone rang. I sorted the bags (turfed them onto the tiled floor, actually) and opened the phone.

'Yes,' I snarled.

'Where are you?' It was Lucy Littleton.

Oh, puhlease, don't start. Don't start this effing call as if we were two teenage VBFs. What does it matter to you where the hell I am?

'In the Jervis Shopping Centre, actually.'

'Oh, good.'

Oh, bad.

'I'll meet you in the coffee place – you know, under the stairs.'

No, you bloody well won't.

'I'll be there in ten minutes.'

'Lucy, I –'

Click.

I stood in the space between the elevators in front of a puddle of my green bags and I literally jumped up and down with rage. Shoppers coming out of the lifts thought it was great. I gave them a filthy look, picked up my bags and headed down to the ground floor in an empty lift.

'I could simply not turn up,' I told my own reflection in the mirror at the back of the lift.

'But I won't. Why won't I?'

Because, you gobshite, you're inquisitive. You're egging to know why she'd want to meet you so suddenly in such a place.

'Doesn't give a shit what I might be planning, of course,' I told the mirror bitterly. 'Doesn't care that I have to postpone doing my shopping until after she's given me her time, which is, I'm sure, the way she thinks of it. Frig her time.'

As the lift settled on the ground floor, I realised I'd forgotten to bring my parking card with me and that I *had* brought the green bags with me, so was going to be stuck with them in the café, where I arrived first, of course. I ordered a pesto chicken panino and a cappuccino and sat down against a wall, where I could hide my bags and spot her a mile off when she hoved to.

Which, to give her credit, she did within three minutes, nodding at me under the unmoving helmet. Watching her, I wondered what would happen if she stopped dyeing the hair. It probably wouldn't go back to being blonde. If she wasn't already good and grey, the blonde would have darkened. Talk about painting yourself into a corner…

'Here we are,' she said, sitting down on a bentwood chair, not quite opposite me but at a slight angle.

'True,' I said sourly.

As in: Lethal, you've never done meaningless small talk, so don't effing start now. You don't have – as you'd say yourself in HR-speak – the competence for it. My monosyllabic answer did not have the desired effect on her. In fact, it had shag-all effect on her.

She was pulling a folder out of her briefcase. Lethal's brief-case was a baggy close-at-the-top job like you'd expect a nine-teenth-century doctor to bring with him when he went off to save a child from diphtheria. It was so old, its leather was natu-rally distressed. As opposed to half the leather things Sullivan wears, which are artificially distressed. Sullivan pays out a for-tune to look like she scavenged her wardrobe in a Vincent de Paul charity shop. When I borrow her stuff, other women look closely at the leather or even finger it, to indicate to me that it's had an accident of some kind. When she wears it, they ask her where she bought it.

'I want to talk to you first about Sullivan.'

I did a *what*ever shrug and bit into my panino, which stuck green tongues out the side and dripped olive oil on my trousers. I put it down and sat there, not even able to chew, I was so annoyed.

'Not your day?'

It sounded like a question, but it wasn't. Not really. It was 'I can see you're being screwed up by life, but I've got an agenda here, so we'll put your life on hold until we get to Matters Arising.'

I didn't answer.

'Here's the situation. Sullivan Spencer is a competent staff member who has put herself in a position – a public position – which is likely to have negative effects on the perception of the bank. She isn't a banker born. She has no major ambitions within our corporate structure.'

I wanted to fight with all of this, but it was true. I just didn't like where it seemed to be heading.

'There is no issue of termination.'

You might sing that if you had an air to it, I thought.

'What we're looking for is a win-win.'

Before I could stop myself, a snort issued from me. Her eyes narrowed and she went silent for at least a minute.

'Patricia. D'you see the couple at the table three away on the left?'

I glanced and nodded.

'Where do you think they're from?'

'Mongolia, probably.'

'So if we talked to them and they had accented English, what would be your reaction?'

'What the f –'

'No, what would be your reaction?'

'None. I'd expect it. I mean, bloody hell.'

'Precisely. No, I come from a country called Human Resources, where I have to speak a particular patois all the time. You will bear with me if it seeps across occasionally into our conversations.'

Yes'm. Except I hadn't noticed that this was much of a conversation.

'Now, the elements in a win-win might look like this. Sullivan Spencer would be able to leave a job she's not crazy about, carrying no negatives into whatever she chooses to do next.'

'That'd be good.'

'With enough money to give her time to choose whatever that's going to be.'

'Like?'

'I beg your pardon?'

'How much money?'

'I'll come back to that. No, don't sulk at me, it has to come in this sequence.'

Sulk? I licked some of the pesto sauce off the side of the panino in as insouciant a way as I could. Who's sulking? *Moi?*

'Now if that were to happen, it would have a downside. Sullivan Spencer would be missed in a general way by the people in her division, but would be missed in a specific way by her lifelong friend: you. Because the combination of you two adds up to more than the sum of its parts. It isn't just that you make Sullivan competent: she brings out the best in you, too.'

That surprised me. Even back in school, teachers used to think that I was the responsible one, minding that moronic, talkative Spencer girl. All the credits came my way. None of them realised how much I depended on Sullivan for knowing where things were, for recalling details I had forgotten because I'd decided they were irrelevant, and for creating a constant background noise that helped me think. I couldn't get over Lucy Littleton spotting that, especially given how infrequently she'd seen the two of us in action within the bank.

'Turning that downside into an upside would require that Patricia Gogarty was enabled to break free from her job, too. With the same benefits.'

I thought about that. Leaving a job I'd been in for more than six years, a situation where I was comfortable and where, even if the work wasn't startling on a daily basis, it wasn't as dull as outsiders tended to believe.

'You've been out of the office on leave for the last seven working days. How much have you missed it?'

Not at all, was the answer. But then, when you're dealing with inherited white elephants and friends on the front pages, the normal routine of your life can pall, just a tad, by comparison.

'You don't seem to me to have much in the way of withdrawal symptoms.'

She had me down pat. I could walk out of that job tomorrow, no bad feelings, but no trailing wires of nostalgia, either. Any of the colleagues I really liked I would stay in touch with, but probably not for long. No matter how much you believe yourself to be the exception to office rules, you never are, and so the gossip that's satisfying when two people are observing the same third party on a daily basis is less rewarding when one of them is out of the building. The observed grow smaller and smaller, their accidents and errors of less significance, until the spider web of one-liners and compliments and snideries becomes too fragile to sustain a relationship. For a couple of years thereafter, the two people refer to each other as friends, then used-to-be friends, and then just as 'I knew her a while back' acquaintances. Either could lift the phone and ask a favour. But neither is a shovel friend, who'd come around at ten minutes' notice and help you bury a body, no questions asked, whereas however ostensibly unmatched Sullivan and me are, we're shovel friends, sure as hell.

'It has not been announced, but the bank will shortly be embarking on a restructuring strategy.'

'A redundancy programme. Getting the numbers down.'

'If you want to put it that way. Packages will be offered for those who would wish to opt for early severance.'

'Great, for old farts who've worked for the bank for the last twenty-five years.'

'Like me, you mean?'

'Oh, Jaysus, Lucy, you know I didn't mean you. I mean the people who stopped really working years ago but still turn up and still draw a salary.'

'I'm so relieved.'

That pulled a laugh out of the two of us.

'Have a look at this.'

She slid across the table a two-page document, headed *Sullivan Spencer*. I took it and looked over the top of it at her.

'I'm not reading this, right?'

'How could you be? Would Lethal Littleton ever breach confidentiality in such an egregious way?'

'Never. For someone with her level of seniority, it would be a fireable offence.'

'If anybody ever heard about it.'

'But how could they hear about it when it's definitely not happening?'

It took me three readings of the document to understand that, by clever interpretations and smart tweakings of every available possibility, the Head of HR was able to offer Sullivan a package that – because so much of it was tax-free – amounted to just under three years' salary.

'God, you're good,' I said, putting it down.

She silently slid another two pages across. Me, this time. The basic sum, because I was on a higher grade to Sullivan, was even better, and the document carried a suggestion of some kind of ongoing consultancy which improved it further. I looked from one document to the other.

'They're not going to wear this.'

'Who aren't?'

'The bank.'

'The bank will wear anything that will close down the whole Hugo–Sullivan issue. For good.'

'So even if his barking-mad wife keeps barking, it's no longer a matter that involves the bank in any way?'

'How could it? None of the people work for the bank any more. She never did. That would be the standard response.'

'It could even be good PR. After all, if people were helped to draw the conclusion that the bank had booted out these sleazeballs and their pals, would that do the bank any harm? Not a bit of it.'

She ignored that.

'So,' I said, getting back to the point. Her point. 'This isn't a theoretical package?'

'This is the package I will formally offer you and Sullivan

163

tomorrow if I get the nod from you today in this meeting we're not having.'

'Well, I can't speak for Sullivan – '

'Course you can.'

Don't mess with me, the tone said. You two move and speak as one, and you're the one.

'I *think* she'll grab it with both hands,' I allowed. 'But say if I'm wrong?'

'Text me in the unlikely event that she has some insuperable objection to an offer no sane person would refuse. Just be clear, and make it abundantly clear to your friend, this isn't up for negotiation. I've pulled every string I can legitimately pull and a few that I *can't* legitimately pull, so neither of you should imagine for a second you could screw anything more than this out of the bank.'

'Listen, I can see by the look of this the strings you've pulled. And I'm certainly bought in. But why? Why're you moving heaven and earth for two people you hardly know?'

She handed me a folder to secrete the two documents in and I resolved to put them in the boot of my car before I did any shopping. I further resolved to buy a bottle of champagne, since a) we now, me and Sullivan, had something to celebrate, and b) I could afford it. Or soon would be, when the package came through.

For one brief darkening moment, the spectre of the tower, trying to suck the financial life out of me, loomed in the background, but I shut it out. Having considered my question, Lucy Littleton pursed her lips.

'I know you shit on all of our feedback systems,' she said coolly, 'but if you read them very carefully, as I make it my business to do in all cases, interesting insights surface.'

I had a fleeting image of her, bringing home the question-naires and going through them on her own at night, probably under a green banker's lamp, concentrating on every quotation in the hope of working out what comments had really been made by me and by Sullivan, and what had been said *about* us. God, she really did have no life. Or maybe, as she'd put it herself, she'd had a half-life since that Stapleton guy stood her up all those years ago. She had started to talk again.

'And I always enjoyed the atmosphere the two of you cre-ated on the third floor. I would often go up there just to hear Sullivan in full spate and you giving the odd noise in response or telling her to belt up when you couldn't concentrate.'

Something really peculiar, I thought, about two pals behav-ing with each other as they've always behaved since they were seven, representing something warm and likeable to an out-sider they never even noticed. It said something, but I wasn't sure whether it said it about me and Sullivan or about Lucy Littleton.

'And of course, it fits into the bank strategy and my wider plans,' she said briskly, heaving herself to her feet. 'You will be careful with those?'

'Going straight up to put them in my car. In the boot.'

'Excellent.'

'We can't shake hands in a place like this.'

'Not when we haven't met.'

'Consider your hand shaken.'

She nodded and pulled her coat on.

'No, on second thoughts,' I said. 'Consider yourself hugged.'

She laughed and then went suddenly serious. I stood up so she could say whatever she was going to say quietly.

'That's the single worst thing about being single, for me,' she said. 'You get very few hugs. Formal embraces and airkisses. Not many hugs.'

I pushed the bentwood chair out of the way and gave her the hug of a lifetime. The fact that the chair screeched loudly enough to attract every eye in the restaurant and the attention of everybody on each of the two staircases was beside the point. Sometimes a hug is the only answer. And hump the begrudgers.

CHAPTER FIFTEEN

Just Another Friday

*I*t was Tuesday and I was due back at work next day anyway. I was expecting Sullivan to make some gesture at coming with me, although in theory her gardening leave was still in operation. But she just asked a few questions and then leaped at the offer outlined in the two pages, scribbled a note on personal notepaper to Lucy Littleton, accepting the terms as offered, and handed it to me.

'You have personal notepaper?'

'My mother gave it to me at Christmas.'

'How thoughtful of her.'

'It was because she discovered I was using pink paper with flowers on it. Apparently it's very low class to use colourdy paper and it's worse if you have decorations on it. My mother would feel it reflected on her if people got letters from me on the wrong kind of paper. She gave out hell to me the year we went to France as au pairs because I put 'Dear Mam' on the postcards when you're not supposed to put any greeting on a postcard. Of course, she was mad at me anyway when we were away in France because she said postcards are what you send to distant acquaintances, not to your mother, and I know it was because she thought I should be telling her more of what we were up to, but can you imagine if I'd told her what we were really up to? Not that you were up to as much as I was up to, but still.'

We were lucky to get out of Paris alive, when the wife in the house Sullivan was in walked in one day to find her husband kissing Sullivan in a way that transcended mere friendship. Sullivan was surprised by Mme Bouchard's rage, having been led to believe that a) all Frenchmen had mistresses, and b) their wives were complaisant about it. She learned the truth and a lot more interesting French than she had expected, and I ended up begging my family to let her stay in my room for the final two weeks of our stay.

She sent me off to work that morning like a mother hen, making sure I had a packed lunch ('because you should eat at your desk to show you're not skiving off, now you have the package'), instructing me about the disposal of her property ('make sure Denise gets the little travel desk clock, she's always looking out for one like it') and entrusting me with a raft of handwritten notes to friends within the bank, sealed in envelopes matching the notepaper her mother had given her ('I must tell my mother how useful her pressie turned out to be').

I kept the notes in my desk drawer and kept the drawer locked with the key in my wallet. I sure as hell wasn't going to give them out before my own last day. Indeed, I wasn't going to say anything to anybody about Friday *being* my last day. Partly because the availability of the package wasn't going to be announced until the following week, but also because I needed like a hole in the head all the questions I would get inside the bank and *nobody* needed media to put two and two together and work out that if I was going, Sullivan was going, too.

The way Lucy worked it out, Sullivan's gardening leave was going to last another three weeks, after which she could take the annual leave that was due to her, and by the time that was over, it would be late October. At which stage, when people in the bank missed her, it would be easy for someone like Lucy to say 'Oh, she took the package that was on offer in the summer, I thought everybody knew that.'

Yesterday's news. Because I didn't have gardening leave (for which you qualify by bonking top management and burning down your apartment while standing semi-naked on a balcony for the benefit of passing photographers, none of which I'd be good at) I would take my annual leave and then send everybody a note saying 'Byeee!'.

This complicated the final three days, because I had to be careful not to commit myself to meetings or projects a month down the line, when I would no longer be a bank employee, while not giving anybody cause to ask why I wouldn't be available on that date. In addition, I had to work late, because if I was trailing up to Human Resources every five minutes, it would give people furiously to think, and neither Sullivan, me nor Lucy Littleton wanted to cause furious thinking. So we met in the evenings to sort out pension and superannuation and shifting my VHI over to a personal direct debit.

On the Thursday, she and I and Daragh Gibbons had met, because I had followed up my awkward apology with a request for him to advise me on the tax implications of the package, although Lucy had wrung as much as I thought anybody could from the system. However, Daragh found all sorts of extra cunning devices, all of them legal and proper, to save me money, and didn't seem at all bothered by me being rude to him on the way back from the tower.

'We are so *good*,' he said, delightedly, when all the details were done, dusted and about to be signed up to.

'Give me your autograph here and on the same place on the following page,' Lucy instructed. 'Incidentally, did you know that a person's autograph when asked for doesn't necessarily mean a name? At one of those book signings in Easons, a writer asked for an autograph could, technically, write "Jesus, who told you you could pull off red polyester at your age?" and be well within their rights. Strictly speaking, he or she should ask for the writer's signature. I just know you both needed to know that.'

'Every contact with you is an education,' Daragh told her, rising and – believe it or not – bowing to her.

'You can sit right back down there,' she responded. 'I need to pick your brains about another case. Patricia, we're done with you. You'll slide out on Friday evening as if it was any other Friday evening. Well,' she amended, 'any Friday evening other than the Jaguar-crumpling Friday evening. That was something of an exception to the normal run of the banking week.'

'It was an exception, which, when you come to think of it, hasn't had bad results, really,' I remarked.

'I wouldn't think Hugo or his ex would agree.'

'Frig Hugo. Never had the decency to lift up the phone and even ask if Sullivan was OK after the fire. And frig Ex-Mrs Hugo, too. She's doing knock-off Twiggy ads for some clothes shop.'

Daragh looked bewildered. Either he wasn't in the loop about Hugo or he didn't know Marks & Sparks ads for older women featuring Twiggy looking like no older woman ever looks without extensive help from a plastic surgeon, an air-brusher or both. He seemed to enjoy the general tone, though. I told him to invoice me and that I'd see him sometime, which was not likely to be true, since selling the tower – and I was going to have to sell the tower – I'd have no further excuse to see him.

Excuse? What a sad life. Wanting excuses to meet a guy who hadn't shown the smallest interest in me. Time to get a cat. Definitely.

I walked out the revolving door on the Friday evening with-out an emotional backward glance. Quite proud of myself that I'd taken home satchel-loads of personal property (mine and Sullivan's) on the two previous evenings so that nobody would wonder why I was weighed down with so many items.

I was just another employee leaving for the weekend. Probably the least noticeable of any of them. Certainly the only one to give a slightly damaged lamp post a friendly pat in memory of Hugo's Jag.

CHAPTER SIXTEEN

Sullivan Takes Control

I had to get petrol and when I stepped into the shop to pay for it, there was Mike Kearns on the front page of the *Evening Herald*. A huge picture of him, in full court regalia, looking, if it were possible, even more handsome with a wig on, talking to a young woman, looking deeply into her eyes, his hand reassuringly on her shoulder. I picked up the paper and the cashier silently added it to my bill.

The fact that I was still admiring Mike every time I got a chance to glance down at the paper on the passenger seat is probably the reason I failed to notice all the strange cars lined up in the parking places near my house. I drew in to my paved garden, took out the paper and my bag, clicked the central lock and stood there for a moment, reading the story about Killer Kearns the SC winning some *ginormous* compensation figure for this girl from the company that had employed her.

It wasn't the only thing they'd done to her, according to the *Herald*. They'd also sexually harassed, bullied and excluded her. Not as a corporate strategy, you understand. Although that was where Kearns had struck the killer blows, according to the inside analysis piece. He had established beyond reasonable doubt that the culture of this organisation (you'd know the name, so I won't give it) was one of mutual disrespect and intimidation. This culture, he had stated, came right from the top. From the high-profile managing director of the company.

The analysis piece ended with a quote from the managing director indicating that he'd pay any money to get rid of the woman involved and that the other accusations were the kind of bullshit you expect from a politically correct Senior Council with f**k all experience of the commercial world. (The *Evening Herald* had supplied the **.) Any a***hole who earned his living dressed up like a pantomime dame should keep his opinions about the real world to himself, the quotation concluded.

'D'you think I should sue him?'

I leaped as if he'd stabbed me. Kearns was behind me, in jeans and a white t-shirt. I looked at the picture and looked at him.

'No matter what you wear, you look fantastic,' I said.

He shrugged as if this was a given and not terribly important.

'But d'you think I should sue him?'

'You'd be able to get great legal advice free.'

'You greatly overestimate the mutual support system of the Law Library.'

'Which bit would you like to sue him for?'

'I might start with "dressed up like a pantomime dame". That's the sort of line that won't quickly go away.'

I began to giggle.

'You mean lawyers on the opposition benches will say "my learned colleague, the one who dresses like a pantomime dame"?'

'We don't have opposition benches, but your general thrust I go along with.'

'You don't mind being called an arsehole.'

'He didn't. Well, according to the *Herald*, he called me an A***hole. Is that what he meant? You shock me to my foundations.'

'Which are cool in jeans.'

'Why thank you, my dear. I do hope Eric continues to share that view.'

I assumed Eric to be his partner.

'I should leak that comment to the guy here who's attacking you. It would prove you're not politically correct.'

'But because he's probably homophobic as well as a chauvinist pig, it would undoubtedly confirm to him that I'm an A*** —'

'I *really* wouldn't go there,' I advised him, doubled up with laughter.

'No. There's a time and a place. Many, some of us hope.'

'Could you sue? I mean, I know you won't, but could you?'

'Be very foolish. What he's said comes under the heading of vulgar abuse.'

'Seems to me everything that guy says comes under the heading of vulgar abuse.'

'And you might be surprised at how many other businessmen love it every time he utters a word.'

I folded the *Herald* lengthways so that his picture wasn't cut in half.

'Why're you here, anyway?'

'That's why I like you so much, Patricia. No warm and fuzzy stuff. No "as you're passing, why don't you come in for a drink?" No "explain yourself and then get your admirable foundations out of my front garden."'

'Perish the thought, b –'

'Are ye planning to stay there for the night?'

Sullivan was hanging out of the front door and if she'd had much in the way of boobs, they'd have been hanging out of a dress that was equal parts spangle, gauze and satin ribbons but not much in the way of body coverage. Barbwire fashion: protect the property, but don't spoil the view.

Mike Kearns advanced on her and kissed her hand, then produced a bouquet from behind his back and presented it to her. I stood, filled with sudden dread. It was her birthday and I'd forgotten.

'Not my birthday,' she said, laughing at me over the flowers.

Then the door filled up with faces and Mike pulled me up the step and into the house and someone pressed a glass of champagne into my hand. Lucy Littleton was the champagne-giver. Mephistopheles, directly behind her, gave me one of his so-slow gentle smiles. Bryan (*Bryan?*) advanced and, careful not to jolt me in a way that might spill the champagne flute, gave me a hug and murmured that it was really nice to see me again. A few strangers I didn't know introduced themselves and shook hands and of course I didn't get their names. Sullivan's father waved at me from the kitchen.

'Now,' said Sullivan, all business. 'Here's where we're at.'

'Before you tell me where we're at, thanks a bunch for giving me the time to shower and change,' I said, gesturing at my creased black suit.

'If you think about it,' Lucy Littleton said, 'it's pretty clear nobody but Sullivan is dressed as if they were planning to invade Anabel's tonight. Not that some of us have ever been inside Anabel's.'

'We must correct that,' Mike Kearns told her. 'Not so that you can enjoy Anabel's, but so that Anabel's may enjoy you.'

'I know where you got that,' she told him crossly. 'Some poet telling some girl to come into his garden so the flowers could enjoy her.'

'Literate, too,' he smiled. 'There is simply no end to your wonders, Lucy.'

'My arse,' she replied.

'We do keep looping back to that part,' he murmured. 'But how bad is that, I ask myself?'

Sullivan ran halfway up the stairs, which distracted everybody, and used the height she'd gained to reassert her control.

'Tonight is two things. It's a celebration of freedom for me and Patricia with *big* thanks to Lucy. And to Daragh. And it's a meeting.'

Somebody groaned.

'One of those things with an agenda?'

'Absolutely.'

'Slight problem,' I said, generating a gratifying silence. Sullivan looked so stricken, I had to wink at her. I'm no good at winking. The top of my face does a kind of grimace. But she's used to it.

'Someone with fuck-all experience of the commercial world will never be able to cope with a meeting and agenda.'

'Who has fuck-all experience of the commercial world?' Sullivan's father wanted to know, looking from face to face and not finding an immediate candidate.

I held up the *Evening Herald* to admiring comments about the picture and a stinkeye glare from Mike, then flipped to the analysis page and handed it to Lucy.

'Read out the last paragraph.'

She did so, to howls of laughter and thumps on the back for Mike.

'Food,' Sullivan announced, and led the way into the dining room, where my modest table had been extended under a table cloth, it wasn't obvious how, where starters of Ogen melon slices and parma ham were already laid out.

'Who's chairing this meeting?' I asked, as Mr Spencer came behind me and poured wine into my glass. Such a lovely man, I thought. How did he ever get stuck with Sanctimammy?

'I am,' said Sullivan.

'Did the bank ever send you on a chairing skills course?' I said.

Daragh, sitting beside me, introduced me to the curly haired woman two chairs down.

'Clare Younge. Indie TV Producer. She used my house in one of her programmes about interior design.'

Yeah, and I know why, I thought. The girlfriend who takes care of your interior design needs dragged you to it. For her own glory. Frig her.

Now that we had all been served, Sullivan sat down at the head of the table again and banged a dessert spoon for silence. Her father handed sheets of paper to each one of us, just as he had handed out the wine.

I started to read.

MEETING RE MARTELLO
AGENDA

#1   History and Importance – Professor Gibbons.

#2   The Scale of the Project – Sullivan Spencer, Project Manager

#3   Finance and Administration – Lucy Littleton and Daragh Gibbons

#4   TV Production – Clare Younge and Mark O'Connor

Daragh leaned over to me again, this time to give me salt. Sea salt, I noticed, in a screw-your-own salt container. When Sullivan decides to take charge, she misses no detail.

'Mark O'Connor is a former OPW guy who knows everybody who has anything to do with conservation architecture or planning,' Daragh explained.

'What's conservation architecture?'

'I haven't a clue.'

'Oh, hang on,' I said, getting distracted. 'I've just realised that's your dad up at the other end. He's like a photographic negative of you.'

Daragh looked up the table at the white-haired, white-bearded man who was eating his food with elegant expedition, and then looked back at me.

'Never struck me before. You're *so* right.'

I began to eat and at the same time try to work out a way to prevent this going any further. I now knew I had to sell the bloody tower. But I hadn't told anybody. So the fact that Sullivan and friends had now involved a wider group of people to bark up what was decidedly a wrong tree could be embarrassing. Daragh's father started to talk before I could halt him.

'In 1794, Britain was at war with revolutionary France,' he began. 'The French had occupied Corsica, and the Corsicans sought British help. The Royal Navy set out to take a reinforced tower at a place called Martello Point. My own view is that the battle at Martello Point had such an impact on the British that the term probably does derive from it, rather than from the "hammer towers".'

'Because it wasn't easy to take?'

'Because it was – at least at the first foray, *impossible* to take. What happened was that the Navy bombarded the tower and were initially repulsed. The cannons on the tower inflicted sixty casualties, and the Navy had to withdraw. They returned, however, and eventually took the tower, largely because of a lucky shot that set fire to some flammable materials on the roof.'

By now, everybody had finished their main course, but were content to drink their wine or water (or in Sullivan's case, Diet Coke) and listen.

'Having captured it, they destroyed it, which, because of the way it was constructed, was not easy either. Their difficulty in capturing it and in eventually razing it caused their Commander-in-Chief in the Mediterranean, Admiral Sir John Jervis, to announce that he "hoped to see such works erected on every part of the coast likely for an enemy to make a descent on".'

'Was he the guy the shopping centre is named after?' Sullivan asked.

'Who?'

'Sir John Jervis.'

'The shopping centre was named after a hospital,' somebody said.

'No, it wasn't,' Mike said. 'The hospital was named after the street it was built on. Jervis Street.'

'Oh, that's right. Well, was the street named after this admiral?'

All faces turned to Daragh's father, who looked discomfited.

'I do wish I had anticipated that question,' he smiled.

'You can't be expected to know everything,' Sullivan told him warmly.

'You don't know my Dad,' Daragh said with great affection. 'My Dad expects himself to know everything. Not for display purposes. Just in case he's asked.'

'We'll google it,' Lucy said impatiently, uninterested in father/son amity. 'Go on.'

'Towers were built around the English coast in response to the Martello Point experience. What they had in common was that they were round, virtually impregnable, had two small windows, a magazine on the ground floor and a cistern to store fresh water, and a series of rooms on the middle floor in which twenty-four soldiers and one officer lived. When I say "ground floor", it's confusing, because the entry point was to the middle floor. In Britain, twenty-four of the towers still stand.'

'Only twenty-four?' Lucy demanded.

'Even though Napoleon never arrived?' Clare Younge asked.

'I may be proved wrong; indeed, I'd love to be proved wrong, but that's what my mathematics say. Property development did away with some of them, and some of them were washed away by rising sea levels.'

He nodded at Clare.

'Even though Napoleon didn't arrive, the remaining towers were utilised during the Second World War, when it was feared that the Germans might invade. I cannot, however, find any evidence that they were either useful or damaged during the second world war.'

'White elephants,' I said despairingly.

'Lack of challenge to a defensive mechanism does not, *ipso facto*, render that defensive mechanism worthless,' Mike Kearns observed. I decided not to argue with him. Who argues with a guy who argues for a living?

'At least a dozen Martello towers were built around Dublin Bay,' Professor Gibbons went on.

'That many? That couldn't be right.'

'Well, you must remember that in the eighteenth century, Dublin was the second city of the British Empire.'

'As opposed to the stag party capital of Europe,' Daragh muttered.

'Others were built around the coast. All to the same basic design, none of them precisely the same as the next, all constructed from local stone.

'The one at Sandycove's converted to the Joyce Museum, isn't it?' Daragh prompted his father.

'I'm sorry, I should have mentioned that. Different uses have been found for them. One in Howth was used to house the trans-Atlantic cable. Sorry. I mean the telegraph/telephone cable between Ireland and Britain. I think it may be open to the public. Let me think what the others are. Oh, yes, the Geneological Society of Ireland is doing up one of them to serve as a people's archive. That's the one at Seapoint. Then the one at Sandymount was restored to serve as a restaurant.'

'I remember that,' the OPW man nodded. 'But it didn't last. It closed again shortly after opening, isn't that right?'

Several people seemed to know about this one.

'I wonder why?' Sullivan said, and then got people's choices for dessert and coffee.

'And, of course, a lot of them passed into private hands and are used as homes. I saw a story on that RTÉ programme, *Nationwide*, about a couple who restored one in Cork to live in. It looked very comfortable.'

'If you don't mind living in a circle.'

'The Inuit have no problem with living in a circle.'

'They've no problem living on whale blubber, either.'

'It's interesting, though,' the OPW man said. 'So many societies leave evidence of having lived in circular buildings, yet as space becomes more limited, they do tend to move to the rectangle as the shape of choice.'

'Now that we're all up to speed on what Martello towers are,' Sullivan said, 'let me show you – any of you who haven't seen Patricia's tower – what it looks like.'

She had a computer in front of her and someone had turned on the flatscreen TV. A few keystrokes and the tower was there, in the room, with us. Indrawn breaths all around, including from me. Because the pictures were no shots taken randomly from a mobile phone. These were crystal clear, detailed, studied shots, angled to show the tower and the blue sea behind it, to show the tower and its great shadow, to show the view from the roof, which caused several people to call on Sullivan to 'leave that one up there for a minute or two'.

'I wanted Patricia to put a Jacuzzi on the roof, but she wouldn't hear of it,' she told them.

'That Ireland's Eye?' someone asked.

'Lambay.'

'Named by the Danes,' Daragh's father said, helpfully. 'Lamb Island.'

'Where they now have a small herd of wallabies,' Sullivan said, her steeltrap memory in play, 'because in the 1980s Dublin Zoo ran out of space and fecked them over there.'

'Interesting challenge to the local flora and fauna,' the OPW man said disapprovingly.

Mike Kearns looked at him amusedly.

'If a wallaby challenged a sheep, my money would be on the sheep winning.'

'Wallabies are very intelligent.'

'And sheep aren't?'

'Have you ever been close to a sheep?'

'No, thank God.'

'Well, a dormouse has more intelligence than a sheep.'

Sullivan ran through the rest of the shots, including pictures of the rubble piled on the Martello tower floor. Then Mike turned the TV off and she closed down her computer.

'You've seen the tower at its worst.'

Not true, honey, I thought. I don't know who you got to take those wonderful photographs, but you found someone who could convey all of the bleak magic of the tower.

'In the sense that it has never been occupied. Never been developed. We can't be sure what the hell they thought they were at when they created that big gap you saw with the wooden door, but whatever they were at they didn't complete it. So, effectively, the tower is as close as it can be to what it was when first built. Patricia's grandfather bought it back in the 1930s. Most of the Martellos were sold off by the state around that time. He left it to her in his will. And the purpose of this meeting is to establish that selling such a chunk of history would be a tragedy.'

'Nobody told me that was the purpose of the meeting,' I said, bridling. Not that there's much point in bridling when you're as small as I am. 'And I'm sorry, but I have to tell you all – and thank you for all the trouble you've gone to – I have to tell you all that I've gone into the figures in great detail, helped by Daragh, here, and no matter which way you slice it, restoring the tower is simply beyond my finances.'

'We knew *that*,' Lucy said dismissively. '*That's* not the issue.'

'Well, what *is* the issue, then?'

'Going beyond your finances.'

The simplicity of it floored me. I looked from one to another. They all seemed delighted with themselves. Even the ones I didn't know.

'Stand up, the consortium,' Sullivan ordered, standing up herself.

Beside me, Daragh stood up, almost hiding Lucy, who'd come up off the chair beside him. Mike Kearns eased himself to his feet and jammed his hands in the back pockets of his jeans.

'You've got a choice, Patricia,' Sullivan told me, craning to see around Daragh, who was leaning on the table beside me and laughing at how red in the face I was getting. 'You can sell the tower at a knock-down price, because Martellos are such odd-ball buildings, they don't fit in the normal property market at all, really. Or you can have a controlling interest in it. 51%. And sell 49% of it to this consortium. Use the money to restore it to being the most beautiful Martello in Ireland –'

'Even nicer than the one in Baginbun,' the OPW man said, which went straight over my head.

'– and use the combined expertise within the consortium and among the brilliant people the consortium has found – ' she gestured at the newcomers '– to become the greatest living expert (along with me) on Martellos and maybe make a living out of *that*, down the line. OK, consortium, take your seats.'

'Would anybody care to enlighten me as to what this group has decided, behind my back, constitutes the cost of 49% of my Martello?'

Mike Kearns looked across at Daragh.

'Give that woman a cup of coffee,' he told him. 'It's the only way to prevent her doing her trainee-bitch performance.'

'I would have thought it was better than trainee,' Lucy said, shoving a jug of cream towards me.

'Nah,' Daragh said. 'She just rants and gets sorry afterwards.'

Under the laughter, he leaned towards me again and murmured again.

'And the rant is worth it for the apologetic e-mail afterwards.'

'It was a *shite* apologetic e-mail.'

'But very funny,' he said.

Lucy leaned out past him. 'You want to know what we value 49% of the tower at?'

'Yes.'

'Three hundred thousand.'

'If I sold it, I'd get more than six hundred thousand for it?'

'Possibly.'

'So why would you people put up money you know I wouldn't get on the open market?'

'Because I'm rich,' Mike said with a shrug. 'I can afford to have interests other than dressing up as a pantomime dame.'

Clare Younge looked startled at this, as did several of the others. He favoured them all with an uncommunicative smile and tapped the side of his nose: Don't ask.

'Because for the first time in my life I've a bit of money and there's nothing I'd rather put it into than something as – as – as *romantic* as the tower. I mean, look at that Jeremy Irons thing,' Sullivan said. 'And his was pink.'

'Because it would be fun,' Daragh told me, ignoring whatever pink thing Jeremy Irons owned. 'And I'd hate to see you lose it.'

'Because now I've left the bank, I want to do something completely different and I have the money to do it,' Lucy finished.

Now, that was a show-stopper. Well, it was a show-stopper to me and Sullivan. The strangers didn't react at all. Mike, Sullivan and I all turned to her as if she'd been transformed into a horse or a wallaby. It was that unexpected. It was that improbable. Daragh, in contrast, continued to drink his coffee without turning a Byronic hair.

'And your issue is?' Lucy demanded. Jesus, if I had bridled earlier, I hadn't done a bridle that was in the same league as the one she was doing now. Never mind playing tennis for Ireland. At that moment, Lucy could have bridled for Ireland.

'You're leaving the bank?' Sullivan wobbled.

'Have. Left. The. Bank.'

'Why?'

'Why did *you* leave?' Lucy demanded.

'I'm not sure it's safe to intervene,' Mike said softly, 'but, with great respect, Lucy, I can't figure you've been having affairs, posing naked on balconies and causing perfectly pleasant fellas – ' he gestured elaborately at Bryan, who looked as if he didn't know whether to laugh or break a champagne bottle over him '– to wreck other fellas' Porsches.'

'Jaguars,' Bryan corrected, furiously.

He was sitting beside Clare Younge, and this rabid statement was the first thing he'd said since introducing himself at the outset. She looked unsurprised, though. Must, I thought, have made the connections to the newspaper stories.

'Jaguars, *plural*?' Mike asked, as if he was twice as impressed.

'There were no affairs,' Sullivan said, looking as if she was going to cry.

'I don't know why *you're* all getting offended,' Lucy said, cutting across the emotional build-up. '*I'm* the one he's implying couldn't get laid if I was a carpet.'

'Dad, I'm not sure you're old enough to listen to this kind of talk,' Daragh said out of the side of his mouth.

'I left the bank because I was finished with the bank,' Lucy Littleton stated. 'And also because it was at a time when a decent package was on offer, particularly to people who'd worked a lifetime in the bank, and because I suddenly realised there were new possibilities out there, involving new friends and an old tower.'

Daragh patted her on the back.

'Oh, *now* I know why you held Daragh back the day you and he sorted out my package,' I said. 'You were getting him to help you with *your* package.'

'This place has so many packages, it could be FedEx,' Clare

Younge observed to nobody in particular. 'That's the great disadvantage to working for yourself. You can *never* get a package except at Christmas.'

I was still stunned by Lucy's abandonment of the bank, but for some reason pleased. Personally pleased. I couldn't help but wonder if talking to me about Whatshisname Stapleton the footballer had been a catalyst, sparking her out of her half-life, no matter how successful and well-remunerated that half-life might be.

Another thought struck me: if Lucy Littleton was sticking some of her end-of-career dosh into it, the tower *must* hold some promise.

'But what would any of you get out of it? When would you get your money back?' I demanded.

'When you have it fixed, you can rent it to rich tourists. Or you can sell it for much more than it's worth right now,' Mike Kearns said tranquilly. 'We'd get our cut either way.'

'Say if I decided to live in it?'

'You'd sell your own house and buy us out. It's only 75K each.'

'Now, time is moving on,' Sullivan said, 'and members of the consortium have agreed to a working session out at the tower tomorrow afternoon, so the minutiae can be sorted through then. My Dad will introduce you to a guy who used to work for him in Britain who's going to supervise the task – he knows old buildings. Paddy's his name. Clare? Will you talk about item 4?'

The woman with the cascade of dark curly hair smiled around at the group.

'I make television programmes. I'm a partner in an independent production company. We make a wide range of programmes.

I've been persuaded by Sullivan that a series on the restoration of a Martello would be worth pitching to RTÉ and possibly to the Discovery Channel also. There's no guarantee that either will pick it up, but I would rate the chances as pretty good. Especially with a new face like Sullivan's.'

Sullivan's father, passing behind her to get rid of two empty bottles, gave his daughter's shoulder a squeeze.

'And especially with the level of expertise represented by Professor Gibbons, who would be the history advisor to the series, Tomás Rafter,' she acknowledged the man directly across the table from her, 'who as a former OPW officer, specialised in works like Martello towers, and Jim Redmond here beside me, whose company as done more work on towers and similar structures in England than any other comparable company. We'd work out a deal whereby the consortium got some money – quite apart from the publicity for the tower – if we sold it to RTÉ.'

Then it was coats and scarves and forgotten items and everybody kissing everybody else and the sound of cars revving on the Ranelagh Road. I found myself at the front door with Lucy Littleton.

'Selling the tower on the open market is the proper thing to do,' she said. 'Uncomplicated. Money it would take you a long time to earn.'

This didn't seem consistent with what she had said earlier, and I frowned, puzzled.

'Cheap at the price,' she said briskly, putting on a pair of black leather gloves and flexing her fingers in them. 'All you have to do is abandon a dream. The only thing I'll say to you is this. The pain of an abandoned dream never goes away. Never fully.'

She stomped off down the garden, flagged a taxi and was gone. I realised Daragh was standing patiently behind me, waiting to leave. If he backs her up, I thought, I'll hit him. He said absolutely nothing, just gave me the kind of forehead kiss you'd give a good child, and strode away to his car.

CHAPTER SEVENTEEN

Let Battle Commence

Some day someone will explain to me why it is, when someone hands you a ready-made solution to a problem, you still want to kick the solution in the goolies and continue to clutch the problem close to your bosom. I kept thanking Sullivan conditionally. I was grateful, very grateful for what she'd done. It was truly generous of her to have pulled all those people together on my behalf and they had obviously been incredibly generous in their response, generous with their time and generous with their money, but...

The third time I hit the 'but' over breakfast on Saturday, she stood up and rinsed out her coffee mug with such vigour, you could tell it was standing in for me and that it was really me she believed deserved a fast sluice with boiling water, and then said she was going to get the papers. On foot.

For Sullivan to go anywhere on foot is a breakthrough. Back when we were in school and she used to argue with teachers, I remember her advancing a thesis that God had made one serious error when he finished us off with feet. In the first place, feet were just not easy to improve. If you were born with bad feet or had bunions in your DNA, you were buggered. (She didn't put it quite that way, but we all got the message.) In addition, they were subject to all kinds of annoying problems like blisters and corns and that awful thing every girl in the class got the year before from the swimming pool. A verruca. And the smell of them. Essentially, feet had no virtues. (This was before Sullivan discovered how a good pedicure gives you peace of mind, improves your self-esteem and allows you to wear the sexiest sandals Brown Thomas can come up with.) If God had his wits about him when he was creating the world, he would have finished off our legs with those wheels good luggage has, that spin in all directions.

One of the other girls, who was into hill-walking, delivered herself of the snidery that it might have been just a tad difficult for Sir Edmund Hillary and Sherpa Tenzing to make it up Everest if their legs had ended in luggage wheels. Which Sullivan squelched by saying there was no limit to the adaptability of human beings. Which the other girl double-squelched by pointing out that if humans were that adaptable, God might have put feet on us to see what we would do with them. Sullivan's last offering on the topic was a classic Sullivan non sequitur: 'Well, I think walking is even more boring than swimming lengths.' This was not a good opinion to express in front of the Religious Knowledge teacher, who was also our Physical Education teacher and a former champion swimmer.

Against that background, for Sullivan Spencer to go trudging off to the local shop to get the Saturday papers, in which she had less than no interest, indicated her amiable desire to get away from me lest she be persuaded to throw something at me. Now and then, down through the years, she has been over-come by the throwing instinct, which never does me any harm, because her aim is so lousy.

By the time Sullivan returned, she had, unbeknownst to her-self, walked her way back into good humour and immediately got launched on a monologue.

'I have three guys coming over from the company Jim Redmond works with on Wednesday, including their top guy who's originally from Ireland; he's old but Jim says he's very nice and really good on old buildings and how to restore them and get them perfect.'

'And who's paying for their time?'

'If necessary, I will pay for their time out of my own account,' she answered, refusing to let me rain on the parade she was creating. 'I've arranged for the local authority woman and someone from An Taisce and the man you met who used to work for the OPW all to be there at the same time, so they can make a complete list of the things that need to be done and the permissions that would have to be sought, plus Daragh because of the tax relief.'

All the while, she was putting flasks of coffee, wrapped-up packages, plastic cups and spoons and tetrapaks of milk – skimmed and full fat – into one of those plastic crates that collapses flat when you're done with it.

'Do you want me to put that in the boot of my car?' I asked humbly. Resentfully, but humbly.

'No, the boot of your car is full of picnic chairs.'

Picnic chairs? Sullivan had been buying picnic chairs?

'And tables. But you could put it on the back seat.'

I obediently followed instructions, muttering that she should set herself up as a caterer. She might very well do that, she told me airily, but for the moment she was happy being project manager on the tower. Either she had picked up some of Lucy Littleton's bossiness, or she was instinctively adapting to the project-manager role, because when she gestured me into the driving seat of my own car, I couldn't think of an alternative to complying with the gesture.

'I was glad to see Bryan there, last night,' I said, as the car moved through the Saturday shopper crowds in Ranelagh.

'His brother Derek gave him a lot of grief for his behaviour,' she said. 'Told him he should attend anger management classes that this was just the latest in a series of outbursts that weren't doing either Bryan or the people around him any good. I didn't get all of the details, but Bryan is very influenced by his big brother. Derek told him he mustn't love me if he'd just take what some stranger in a pub said about me as gospel and that he should have sat down with me and discussed it before doing anything, or even better, not paid any attention to that kind of rumour-mongering in the first place, because if you have a decent relationship with someone, what some asshole in a pub says shouldn't bother you and that really all Bryan had done was prove he *didn't* love or trust me and was only thinking about himself and how damaged he was if the pub thing was true, although it was neither here nor there as far as Derek was concerned. Bryan said he did so love me and felt completely betrayed and Derek told him not only did he not love me, he probably didn't even really know me at all, and that he should at least apologise to me and that at least would be a decent way to end things.'

'But Bryan obviously doesn't want to end things?'

'No, but his brother said that the only thing to do was stop the dysfunctional relationship and start somewhere else.'

'With someone else or with you in some other country?'

'Neither. Derek said that if Bryan was that keen on me he should start all over again if I was mad enough to go along with it, and Bryan said he would like to do that, so Derek set up a meeting between Bryan and me and he facilitated it because he's a psychologist although he mainly deals with autism and Asperger's Syndrome. We talked for three hours and it was really interesting.'

'I'm sure it was.'

She looked at me to see if this was a sneer, then went on, satisfied that it wasn't.

'Then we met the following day again and Derek had drawn up a compact.'

'A what?' I asked, associating 'compact' with my mother and face powder.

'A compact for going forward. Like a contract, you know? The things we would promise to do, each of us. And the things each of us would promise not to do.'

Pity the three of you didn't call on the services of Lucy Littleton, I thought but didn't say. Then you could have introduced six-monthly performance reviews and 360-degree feedback with a guaranteed bonus into this process.

'We each promised that we will not telephone each other, except in emergencies, more than once a day, and we will not see each other more than twice a week. During the first six months, we both accept that the other may go out with other people but we're not allowed to ask about that or listen to anything anybody else says if they see us somewhere together, whichever of us might be with someone else, you follow me?'

'Just about.'

'No sex with each other for six months, either. No sleepovers.'

That I quite liked. Nothing against Sullivan and her relationships, but the Ranelagh house is not big enough. Or maybe too big. If two couples were living in it, fine. But one singleton and a couple is invasion of privacy – both ways – no matter how hard everybody tries. It's all averted eyes and tiptoeing and earphones in bed (on me) so as to preclude the possibility of overhearing. Yeuch.

'Derek thought all this up?'

'Yes and Bryan taking anger management courses, too. And going back to the gym and giving up the drink.'

'You or Bryan?'

She had to think about that before deciding that this stricture applied more to Bryan than to herself, on the basis that Derek said Bryan had a lot of energy he needed to work off in healthier ways than full frontal assaults on parked Jaguars.

'What did Bryan say to all this?'

'"For fucksake, this is like joining a fucking seminary."'

He had a point, I thought. This 'compact' had an element of Victorian regimentation in it. The only thing missing was cold showers and saltpeter.

'So he's not buying?'

'Oh, he is.'

'Really? Why?'

'I don't know. Maybe he really loves me?'

I reached out and patted her on the leg.

'Some of it was very hard,' she said, sniffling into a tissue which, thanks be to God, she had brought herself and consequently it had no cheery little messages on it like mine do. 'D'you know what Derek got out of me?'

'No. What?'

'That I've never enjoyed sex. I told him what you said about Marilyn Monroe.'

This is going to make any casual meeting I ever have with Bryan's psychologist brother very interesting, I thought.

'I thought Bryan would die, he was so hurt. And then he said I must have been pretending, that I was pretending to enjoy sex all the time. I asked him what he expected me to do, did he want me to tell him that I'd just like to get a hug while I went to sleep? And he asked me if it was just him or other lovers and Derek told him it was none of his business and I said if he ever said "lovers" again about me or "slapper", even if he was quoting someone else, I'd never ever speak to him again.'

Not sure, I thought, that Derek should have got involved in a process participated in by his own sibling, but his ethical boundaries were his own problem.

'Anyway at the end we both signed.'

I drove the car into the space beside the tower, which was bathed in autumn sunshine. Suddenly, she was all business, working out where the sun would be an hour hence and what location would be best to set up the picnic chairs and tables, to capture the afternoon rays while sheltering the sitters. I let her at it, leaning on the car absorbing the warmth through my windcheater. When she reached a conclusion, I took orders, carrying tables and chairs, unfolding them and finding rocks to secure the legs of the more wobbly ones. She carried the crate over.

'Here's Mike and Daragh,' she said, waving up at the Lexus as it cruised in behind my car, making the latter look like it was made out of tinfoil and given away free with a packet of cornflakes.

'And Bryan,' I added, making no comment on the fact that the bull-bar front of the SUV had been meticulously mended. Or replaced.

'You know nothing,' she hissed.

'Oh, *Sullivan,*' I said reproachfully.

'I know, I know you'd never,' she whispered. 'I'm sorry. All right?'

'All right.'

The guys were all dressed casually, in jeans or cords and boots.

'So you can dress up as a working stiff as well as a panto-mime dame?' was my greeting to Mike.

'We all had our instructions,' he said, nodding at Sullivan.

'The first thing you guys need to do is get inside the tower – Patricia has the keys – and clamber over the rubble to that big wooden door and see if you can get it open. It has a million bolts and bars on it, so you'll need to take Patricia's keys.'

'And this,' Bryan said, holding up a can of WD-40.

'Good for arthritis,' I confirmed.

'WD-40?'

'Some people spray it on aching joints and claim it works wonders.'

'Now, *that* would be a seductive smell to get off your lover's skin,' Mike said.

Careful with that word 'lover,' my mad little voice said. And if you feel the urge to say 'slapper', restrain yourself. We need really neutral boring language today.

When I reached the top of the metal stairs, I spotted Lucy's car in the middle distance. An arm waved at me from its window. I waved back, then got the tower door open. Mike stepped past me and put down two lanterns. Once he had them switched on, they did a good job of attacking the dark inside the tower.

Daragh was already scrambling down to the rubble-covered floor, followed by Bryan. Mike handed down a torch and scrambled down after them. The three of them climbed – literally – across huge boulders and rocks, some of them wobbling unexpectedly, fetching up at the heavy wooden door, which dwarfed the three of them. Bryan sprayed every bolt and bar with WD-40.

'Anybody lights a match, we blow this place apart,' Mike said, starting to try the big gaoler's keys in one lock after another, grunting with the effort to turn the old mechanisms, frozen with time. Two of them gave in to pressure. The third would not.

'Give it another lash of that stuff,' he told Bryan, who obliged.

The three of them stood back to let the fumes clear, then Daragh took over at the lock. No luck. Bryan sprayed it again.

'We sure we're using the right key?'

They tried all of the keys without any success. Bryan put down the WD-40 disconsolately, and, losing his footing, fell between two boulders.

'You all right?'

'Bloody boot's trapped.'

He struggled fiercely with his boot but stayed trapped.

'Let me get at it from the other side,' Daragh said, and freed it so suddenly that Bryan went shooting up and knocked

Mike off *his* perch. The torch and the can of WD40 disappeared down between mountains of rubble. I laughed and was favoured with a tripartite glare. Daragh got himself up out of the pit and left the other two where they were in order to have another go at the lock.

'Now, I can't see the frigging thing,' he announced. 'Oh, hey, I've got it.'

He pulled out the key and – two-handed – turned the curved section of the old padlock so that it could be unhooked from the massive iron bolt it secured. The other two got themselves level with him and started to pull at the bars, now free from mechanical constraint. They didn't seem to be free from rust constraint, though.

'Hit it with something,' Bryan suggested.

'Like what?' Mike politely asked him. 'My flute?'

Daragh lost his balance laughing at this and disappeared down a crevasse so that none of him showed above the rubble at all. The other two started instructing each other as to how best to bring him back to the surface. I went back out into the sunshine to find Lucy coming up the stairs with a torch. She was dressed in a sweater, canvas trousers and Wellington boots. Lego Labouring Lady.

'Nice timing,' I told her. 'You might go up there and shine it across on the lads. They're trying to disinter Daragh who fell down a hole laughing at Mike's flute.'

Making no comment, she let herself into the tower and I climbed down to find Sullivan talking to Clare Younge, who was clutching a clipboard and making notes. I hadn't realised she was so short. The tower project seemed to attract nobody of average size. Only giants like Daragh and dwarfs like me.

'How's it going?' the curly-haired TV producer asked.

'Not great, right now. One of the consortium has disappeared beneath a mass of rubble on the floor of the tower.'

'Who?'

'Daragh. And perhaps I should say "between" rather than "beneath". It's just he can't be seen or reached.'

Clare looked more upset than I would have expected.

'This *always* happens,' she said crossly. 'Really good disasters occur before I can get a camera in position. If the inside of that tower is so dangerous, I wonder if we should have a camera running all the time…?'

'Is he hurt?' Sullivan asked me.

'I don't think so. He didn't scream or anything.'

By now I was beginning to realise that this could be a lot more serious than I'd thought. I climbed back up the metal stairs, followed by the blonde and the brunette. Bloody stairs wobbled as much as if half a battalion was climbing up them.

Inside the door, Lucy Littleton was standing, directing a steady stream of light onto Mike and Bryan, who were now lying across some of the rocks, their arms extended into the gap down which Daragh had fallen. Nothing could be seen of the bearded accountant.

'Is he OK?'

Lucy never took her eyes off the two men.

'He says he doesn't think he broke anything, but his ankle is iffy.'

'Why is he still down there?'

The patent idiocy of this question made Lucy turn – briefly – to favour me with a look that would have shattered glass.

'Because he hasn't been able to get back up.'

201

'Fuck,' Bryan said, over the ominous sound of shifting stones. From below, we could hear Daragh moaning. The two men stretched over the rubble, took their arms out of the hole and looked at each other.

'We need to think about this,' Bryan said.

Sullivan nudged me, presumably to make me note Bryan's new-found commitment to reflection. The nudge was a mistake, because I was trying to shake sand out of my shoe at the time and standing on one foot. I lurched into Lucy, who fell down the stairs into the rubble, taking her torch with her. The two men, plunged into semi-darkness, looked over crossly. Sullivan went past me like a rocket and yanked Lucy to her feet.

'Did you do any damage to yourself?' I asked.

'Shouldn't you be asking did you do any damage to me? No is the answer. But the torch is now ten feet down under the rubble.'

Daragh's voice came faintly from below.

'Thanks for the extra light, whoever's responsible.'

Lucy shrugged. The torch must be still on and pointed his direction.

'Houston, we got a problem,' Daragh added.

'We had noticed,' Bryan said patiently. *Very* patiently.

'No, we've got a worse problem than you can see from where you are. Some of the bigger blocks have shifted and hemmed me in. You're never going to be able to pull me out. You're going to have to shift the rubble above me.'

'He'll go into shock,' I said to Sullivan.

'We'll get hot sweet tea down to him,' she said, and disappeared.

Bryan pulled himself into a sitting position.

'Do we have a hammer?'

Now *there's* a guy question. It ranks right up there with 'where are my clean socks?'

'Yes,' Lucy said, surprisingly, and went out of the tower at a sprint.

'D'you know what I really need?' Daragh's muffled voice inquired.

'What do you really need?' Mike responded.

'Frozen peas.'

He's already gone into shock, I thought. He's delirious.

'I'm not sure I heard you correctly,' Mike told him.

'Frozen peas!' Daragh yelled.

'Why would you need frozen peas?'

'Because my ankle is swelling like a hoor and I need to get something icy around it.'

'I'll get them,' I said, turning and colliding with Lucy, who dropped the lump hammer she was carrying on my foot. For one split second, nothing registered, and then the pain hit. The yell that came out of me could have been heard in Lambay.

'What's wrong? What's happened?' Daragh's voice asked.

Sparking lights lit up at the back of my eyes and my head filled with static.

'Sit down,' Lucy told me, forcing me onto the cold stone. 'Put your head between your knees. Bend over.'

In waves through the static, I could hear Mike telling Daragh that they didn't know exactly what had happened, but that I was hurt.

'I'm all right,' I whimpered to Lucy. 'Tell him I'm all right.'

'Tell Daragh I dropped a lump hammer on Patricia's foot, but she's getting over it,' Lucy told Mike, who relayed it to

Mephistopheles in the underworld. Someone rubbed the back of my neck. Clare, the producer lady. I flexed my toes inside my shoe. They seemed to work. The stars were fading from behind my eyes. I started to try to get up.

'Stay put,' Lucy ordered me, and I did.

'What the hell are you all sitting around for, doing nothing?' a new voice demanded. Sullivan's.

'You don't want to know,' Lucy assured her. 'And be careful making your way over there, the rubble shifts. We've already had one in-house rockslide.'

I straightened up a bit and in the semi-darkness could see Sullivan, one hand locked around a beaker with a lid on it, making her way slowly across the rubble to the two men.

'I asked for a hammer,' Bryan told her.

'I don't give a shit what you asked for, find a way to get this down to Daragh.'

I slowly got to my feet and tried the one the hammer had fallen on. It was tender, but seemed in working order. I bent over to undo the laces.

'Leave them tied,' Lucy told me. 'Your shoe will keep the swelling down.'

She clambered down onto the rubble and, stretching out, handed the hammer to Sullivan, handle first. Sullivan went back and delivered it to Bryan, who stood up carefully and gave the recalcitrant iron bolt the mother and father of a blow.

'Jesus, what was that?' Daragh's voice asked.

'That,' said Mike, coming back up from the crevasse, 'was Bryan filling my hair with iron filings.'

'Tell whoever sent the tea I'm very grateful. Is Patricia all right?'

'Fine,' I croaked, pathetically pleased that he cared. 'Daragh needs frozen peas to keep his ankle from swelling any more,' I told Sullivan.

'No problem,' she said. 'Be back as soon as I find a shop selling them.'

'I really am desperately sorry for dropping the hammer on you,' Lucy said.

'No worries. It was an interesting experience.'

Mike and Bryan were now doing a coordinated pushing manoeuvre on the stuck bolt, while Daragh wanted to know who had made the tea. I considered lying and saying that I had.

'Sullivan,' Clare called out to him. 'She's gone for the peas.'

'She's gone for a pee?'

'Yessss!' Bryan shouted, as the bolt shifted.

The two of them talked to each other for a couple of seconds, then Mike moved nearer to Bryan and, on a count of one, two and three, the two of them hurled themselves, shoulders first, at the great wooden door. Sunlight flooded into the tower. It opened only about six inches, but the two of them worked on it until Mike could squeeze out through the gap and match Bryan's pushes with pulls from the other side. Grinding on the shell-scattered pavement outside, the door opened in slow increments.

The two of them kept at it until it was fully open: a great square about twelve feet across and roughly the same in height. The tower was now filled with so much brightness, Lucy's torch, wherever it had got to, was irrelevant. Bryan and Mike, now on the outside, were dwarfed by the rubble facing them. We could barely see them over it. Lucy patted me on the back and went down the metal stairs at a run. Clare took her place beside me.

'This would have made a great opening programme,' I said, probing my foot.

'As long as Daragh's OK, that doesn't matter.'

The two guys were now in a crouch, talking to him from the outside, Mike saying that no, Sullivan hadn't come back yet, it might take her some time. Lucy arrived beside them, holding out tough working gloves.

'My God, you think of everything, Lucy,' Mike said, pulling the cardboard publicity material off a pair and pulling them on to his hands.

'No, the project manager thinks of everything. Sullivan told me to buy the lump hammer and the gloves. And a shitload of other stuff, too.'

'Sullivan is a great woman,' Bryan said quietly.

'Takes an awful long time to have a pee, though,' Daragh opined.

Bryan bristled.

'How would *you* know?'

'How would I know what?'

'That it takes Sullivan a long time to pee?'

'Well, no offence, but she left here at least ten minutes ago.'

'Daragh?'

'Yeah? Who's that?'

'Patricia. Sullivan didn't go for a pee. She went to buy you frozen peas.'

'Oh.'

'Patricia,' Mike called across the rubble. 'We're gonna need every hand to the pump over here.'

'Be there,' I shouted, and enthusiastically made my way down the metal staircase. Or started to. Because it was then that the fire-escape steps pulled away from the wall in a great slow-motion arc, depositing me and Clare and her clipboard in the garden and coming down on top of us like a metal dinosaur skeleton. I was so winded and stunned, I just lay there. Then a hand groped through the metal and pulled at my jumper. I reached down and patted it.

'Oooof,' Clare said.

'You. Break. Anything?'

'How the hell. Would I know?'

In the distance, we could hear Bryan bellowing a question. What the hell was keeping us?

'Fuck. Off. Bryan,' I gasped.

'Seconded,' said Clare.

We could hear a car drawing up and the sound of running feet.

'Oh, Jesus, Oh, Sacred Heart, Oh, Mother of God, Oh, fuck,' Sullivan said.

I twisted my head to look at Clare. She twisted her head to look at me.

'You know. What I think?'

'No.'

'I think. Maybe selling. This tower. Wasn't such. A bad idea.'

'Are you all right?' Sullivan asked, crawling under the metal skeleton until she was facing the two of us.

'How the hell would we know?' Clare asked.

Within seconds, it seemed, Bryan, Mike, Lucy and Sullivan were in front of the latest setback. Or setdown, which was what it felt like.

'Sorry for delaying you, Bryan,' I couldn't resist telling him.

'Fucking thing came away at the top but is still attached to the wall lower down,' Mike said. 'We're going to have to get it completely free before we can lift it. '

Their feet disappeared out of our line of sight. I tried to move, but the thing weighed a ton.

'I'll be back in a minute,' Sullivan announced.

'Godalmighty, Sullivan, don't go away now,' Bryan's voice said.

'These petit pois are melting,' she told him. 'I'm getting them to Daragh while they can still be of use to him.'

We listened to the disappearing footsteps and I'm convinced I heard Bryan muttering 'petit fucking pois'. Then there was a ten-minute period filled with hammering, every stroke of which vibrated through the metal structure into Clare and me. Every now and then we could hear Mike and Bryan giving each other instructions. Suddenly, metal screeched and what was pinning us to the grass got markedly heavier. I could hear the breath coming out of Clare in a whoosh. When I tried to inhale, I couldn't.

Three sets of feet appeared in front of us. No, four. Through a rising tide of real terror, I could hear someone calling out numbers and on 'three' I could breathe. Don't lower that thing on me again, please, I will die, I thought but didn't have the breath to say. Someone's knee came in beside my face.

'You're not going to be able to hold that,' Mike's voice said.

'So get something to brace it,' Bryan grunted.

A rock came rolling in beside me and was forced into place. The knee cautiously withdrew. The heavy metal staircase tilted slightly towards me, but did not sink back to where it had exerted fierce pressure on my capacity to breathe.

'Going to have to do the same on the other side,' Bryan said.

Sullivan crawled in towards the two of us.

'Mike says they'll have you both out in five minutes.'

She stretched her hand out and stroked my face gently.

'Will I call ambulances?'

'I'm not in agony,' I said. 'I may be just bruised.'

'Same here,' Clare said. 'I can't move my lower legs, but I can feel my toes, so it's probably just pressure from this bloody staircase rather than anything broken.'

'When they lift the staircase, if there's any problem, we'll take care of it,' Sullivan promised and reverse-slid her way away from us. We could hear her telling Lucy Littleton to stay with us while she went to check on Daragh. Then another rock was rolled across the grass, a plank that looked like the size of a railway sleeper was introduced and used as a lever, and – oh joy, oh bliss – I was free. Wriggling forward was painful, but possible. The two of us inched our way out from under the arch of twisted metal. When we were good and safe, I rolled over on my back. Mike's worried face appeared from one side, Lucy's from the other.

'Lift me into a sitting position very gently.'

They did. This gave me an interesting vantage point. Clare, four feet away from me, had gone the other way and was now on hands and knees, flexing her back up and down. I pulled my legs in under me and shakily stood up. Bryan lifted Clare to her feet and unceremoniously pulled up her sweater at the back.

'You're not cut, but the bruising is already coming up. You're going to be black and blue from head to toe.'

'Bruises never killed anybody,' she said, pointing to her scattered papers and clipboard on the grass. Lucy gathered them up for her. 'But I think I'll go home before I stiffen up too much to drive. You wouldn't mind?'

Lucy swept her in front of her, got her into the car, fastened her seat belt for her and patted the roof: off you go.

I tried to walk. The foot the lump hammer had fallen on was throbbing like hell and I had the sense that every muscle in my back had been strained. I hobbled like a ninety-year old, holding on to Mike's arm for stability.

'Would you like to go to your car and drive home? Or would you prefer Sullivan to drive you home?'

'I'm not going anywhere until we get Daragh out.'

'Dear darling Patricia,' Mike said. 'You're not going to be able to provide much assistance to Daragh, and you'd be better at home in bed with a hot-water bottle. Or maybe a massage.'

'You out of your mind? I've never had a massage in my life and if any human being did that drumming side-of-the-hand thing down my back right now, I would swing for them.'

'I appreciate that, but why cause yourself more discomfort when you can't actually help –'

'Mike.'

'Yes, dear.'

'Shut up and just help me walk.'

'Petal, it's a pleasure.'

When we came around to the side of the tower where the big, now open, wooden door was, I could see Sullivan coming at a run from the other side, clutching a picnic chair which she planked down and then covered with two coats. Tears started to my eyes at the kindness of the coats. I was not going to have to lean a brutally bruised back against the hard structure of the plastic chair. I sat down with great difficulty and did shooing gestures at Mike and Bryan: get on, get on.

The two of them tackled the pile of rubble like lumberjacks, sometimes pulling the big blocks towards them, sometimes climbing in behind them and pushing them outward. One after another, blocks as big as chest freezers came away from the mountain of stone and were rolled with enormous effort past me by the two men assisted (mainly when it came to steering and darting in to get the smaller stones) by Lucy.

Sullivan disappeared into the gathering dusk and came back with hot sweet tea. One beaker for me, one to be handed in to Daragh.

'Where are you making the tea?'

'Not making it. Made it this morning. The Thermos has kept it fantastically hot.'

I buried my face in the warm steam and drank the entire beaker in seconds. Sullivan climbed over the rubble sideways. They were now paranoid that they would either weigh Daragh down further by standing on a stone that was already pressing on him, or cause a landslide that would entomb him worse than he was at the moment. She lay across some of the rubble to talk to Daragh, whose voice, although tired, was coming through louder and louder as the obstacles were removed.

Mike stopped beside me, tore off his glove and back-handed the sweat off his face.

'He'll be out in less than ten minutes,' he said, half to himself.

'He'll need to be,' I answered. 'It's beginning to get dark.'

Lucy handed Mike a water bottle and he drank, drank, drank, sucking on the spout so hard that the plastic bottle went almost flat in his hands. Then he pulled the gloves back on and went to help Bryan with a block the size and shape of a fire hydrant. When it rolled away, we could see Daragh's face. He blinked as if he had dust in his eyes and smiled tiredly. Sullivan came to my side and handed me a cup of water that was fizzing. I looked a question.

'Solpadeine. The pain is going to get worse and it's the only painkiller I have.'

Her apologetic tone referred to rants I'd made in the past about the addictiveness of Solpadeine. One of the girls in the office took Solpadeine every three and a half hours, every day, because of her terror of the rebound headaches that would follow going cold turkey. I looked at the fizzy water and drank it without a qualm.

Sullivan knelt down and pushed a matching fizzy cup through to Daragh.

'Awright,' said Bryan, as he, Mike, Sullivan and Lucy went at the remaining stone pile between me and Daragh until he was sitting in a kind of cave.

'Don't move,' Sullivan told him and ran away, returning with a length of the kind of plastic sheeting you lay on a floor when you plan to paint the ceiling. She scrambled in close to him and started to push sheeting under him.

'Tilt towards me,' she told him and slid him very gently into a prone position on the sheeting. Then she slid out and Mike crawled in where she had been and, with him at one end of the plastic rug and Bryan at the other, they slid Daragh out through the open door of the tower. He pulled himself into a sitting position and winced.

'Where does it hurt?' I asked.

'Everywhere,' he said frankly. 'But it's probably cramp more than injury – being bent over for a couple of hours is kind of surprise to the spinal cord. The ankle's in a bad way, though. The Solpadeine helped, but whoo!'

'I'm taking you to Beaumont Casualty,' Bryan told him.

I half expected Daragh to resist this but instead, he nodded, gratefully. Mike and Bryan 'fireman-lifted' him out of my sight. I thought about getting up to say goodbye to him, but the Solpadeine was delivering such a pleasurable euphoria of diminished pain, I couldn't summon up the resolution to make the move. Bryan's car started up and I could hear Daragh calling out that he'd see us later. Then Mike and Sullivan were back.

'Without the staircase, it's not possible to reach and lock the door,' I said, having had time to think about this.

'True,' Mike said, crouching down on one side of my chair. 'I hope you have the tower insured against the possibility of mad burglars coming tonight and stealing stones from inside it, because there's no way either of the doors is going to be closed.'

He and Sullivan joined hands under the chair and carried me, chair and all, to my car. Mike lifted me into it and I was grateful – for once – for being small as he tucked my legs in after me like extras. He leaned in and kissed me.

'I do apologise for reeking like a ripe peasant,' he murmured.

'Mike, you can reek at me any time.'

'I'll hold you to that, darling.'

Sullivan ran around the car and got into the driver's seat, flinging some plastic bags into the back seat as she did. The car started and she spun it in a half circle. I caught a glimpse of Lucy and Mike waving.

'That's the first time I realised there was a sort of speedbump at the exit,' I muttered, as the car, moving over the bump, made every bruised tissue protest.

'I'm really sorry,' Sullivan said. 'I'll drive as smoothly as I possibly can.'

She did, too. Fogged with codeine, I closed my eyes and began to drift, jolted back to wakefulness by every bump and turn the car had to make. When we drew into the front garden of the Ranelagh house, she turned it so that the car door on the passenger side was set to decant me virtually on to my own front doorstep.

I was moving in such slow motion that I only had the door open when she was beside me, undoing my seatbelt and gently pulling my legs out in a way that pivoted me on the seat and allowed me to get out in one creaky movement. I couldn't straighten up when I got out of the car. All I could do was move forwards in a crippled crouch. Sullivan was everywhere – opening the front door, helping me up the steps, turning on the hall light, steering me towards the stairs and helping me up their endless length. At the top, she turned me in to the bathroom and I realised I needed very badly to pee. She reversed me towards the loo and before I could stop her, pulled down my trousers and pants and sat me on it like a toddler.

She turned away and started to fill the bath. I sat watching her, reminding myself to go and shoot Ex-Mrs Hugo when I could walk again for all the bad things she had said about my shovel friend. I staggered to my feet and in some Sullivan-managed co-operative chaos, ended in a seethe of agonising, infinitely pleasurable, deep, deep hot water, foaming with bubbles.

I hung on to the sides of the bath and let the hot water punish and pleasure me while Sullivan gathered up my dirty (and, I noticed torn) clothes, ran downstairs (I could hear the car door banging and the tweet of the electronic central locking) got the kettle on (we have a whistler) and kept running back upstairs to check that I hadn't slipped under the surface and drowned.

At some point she used the hand shower to wash my hair and rinse the soap off me and enveloped me in a cloud of Turkish towelling robe – hers, bought during a visit to the hot-stone spa – instructed me to slide my feet forwards into spa slippers, and staggered me across the landing and into a bed toasty with the comfort of electric-blanket heat.

'Have to take robe off,' I said, feebly resisting the descent over me of a duvet. 'Can't go to sleep in your robe.'

"Course you can. Drink this.'

'"This" turned out to be some kind of cream soup that warmed me so much, I'm sure I developed an external glow. She held the mug for me between sips and when I was done, put it on the bedside table and slid me down in the bed, covered me up, turned out the light and put the palm of her hand on my forehead so gently, I hiccupped with gratitude.

'You'll be asleep in two shakes of a lamb's tail,' she told me.

'You'll make a great mother.'

'I sincerely hope so. But not right now.'

'You know all the words. And the tune.'

'Good night,' she said and closed the bedroom door.

Sleep tight, I thought. That's the next line. Sleep tight.

CHAPTER EIGHTEEN

Triage of the Wounded

*S*leeping tight, paradoxically, requires that you're also able to sleep loose. So that you're able, without thinking about it, to turn over in the bed in your sleep. I couldn't do that. I woke up in the middle of the night and realised I wanted to go to the loo. I lay there thinking about it and the next thing the door opened and Sullivan surveyed me, illuminated as I must have been by the shaft of light coming in from the landing.

She padded to the side of the bed and moved the duvet off me, then gently shifted my legs so my feet were on the floor and offered me her hands to pull myself up, rather than putting her arm around me, which was a good choice, because when I looked at my back in the bathroom mirror, using my make-up mirror, I could see why I was so tender. I opened the bathroom door.

'Look,' I said, turning around, my t-shirt still pulled up at the back.

I could hear her breathing in through clenched teeth. My entire back (and, for all I knew, my arse, also) was blue, black and purple. Halfway down my back was a straight line, about an inch deep and eight in length, of pure black, probably where a step of the staircase had pressed. No, *certainly* where a step of the staircase had come down, the time I couldn't draw a breath and had been terrified.

'We should have brought Clare home with us,' I said, as Sullivan reverently lowered the back of my t-shirt.

'She promised me she had someone who would take very good care of her.'

I got back into bed and lay on my front. I never lie on my front. It felt peculiar, but better than trying to lie on the bed of nails that was my back.

'D'you need painkillers?'

'Why are you whispering?'

She giggled.

'You have to whisper when it's dark. It's a natural law.'

'No, I don't need painkillers, thank you. It doesn't hurt except when I move. And it's lovely when I stop moving. Like knocking your head off a stone wall, it's pleasurable when you quit.'

'You're a masochist.'

'Possibly.'

'That's another reason why it's good you decided to hang on to the tower. You have all the stone walls you could ever need, if you want to knock your head off them.'

'I don't remember deciding to hang on to the tower. I have this impression the decision was sort of made for me.'

'Is anything inside hurting you?'

'Inside me?'

'Yes, organs.'

I considered this, remembering once when I had a kidney infection, the unpleasantness of internal pain.

'No.'

'Good.'

She patted the duvet around me and padded away. I think. Because sleep descended on me as abruptly as the staircase had, only more softly.

In the morning, she got me into the shower and got me out of it, wrapped me in a bathtowel (the robe was obviously headed for the washing machine) and propped me in the bed using pillows borrowed from her bed. I sat there, considering my next move, listening to her clattering around the kitchen, until she came back with a tray.

'Room service,' she said, putting it gently down on my lap.

'No single flower in a tiny vase? Tsk tsk.'

I ate every bit of the scrambled eggs and toast and drank four cups of coffee.

'You really should be a caterer.'

'Bryan says that, too.'

'Oh, Jesus, Bryan took Daragh to the hospital. I'm a selfish pig, I never thought of Daragh.'

'He's fine. Very bad sprain. They taped his ankle up and gave him anti-inflammatories and lent him crutches. Bryan took him home with him.'

'Where's "home" for Bryan at the moment?'

'His brother's house. Derek's wife is lovely.'

'And Daragh'll be able to get therapy for any mental stress being buried alive caused him.'

'Of course, you're right.' I wanted to know why Bryan hadn't delivered Daragh into the loving care of his girlfriend, feck her, but I wasn't going to ask.

'They were six hours in A&E.'

'A bad sprain is low on the totem pole in A&E.'

'Bryan said it was OK, actually, because they found they have a lot of interests in common.'

'Starting with sport?'

'No, cars, actually. Bryan's going to get rid of the SUV and Daragh apparently knows everything about cars. And not for the reason you think.'

That threw me. I hadn't assumed anything about Daragh's knowledge of car mechanics.

'Bryan's fed up of people writing messages on the car when it's dirty: "asshole, stop wrecking the environment" and stuff like that.

'Do they?'

'Oh yes. This last year, a lot. A kid of about twelve gave out to the two of us one day, out the window of his own car, with his mother driving and she looked thrilled that he was giving out to us.'

Her mobile phone rang in her own room and she sprinted to get it. When she came back, she handed me two little tablets. I held them and looked doubtfully at them.

'Arnica.'

'Homeopathic shite,' I said, swallowing them.

'Clinically proven,' she said loftily, taking away the tray.

'To do what, pray?'

'Reduce bruising,' she called from the stairs.

My arse, I thought, but didn't say. No point. Her phone was going off again. I sat there and listened to what seemed to be an endless sequence of calls on the landline and her mobile. After about fifteen minutes, she came back.

'Now,' she said, all business. 'Here's what's happening today. Lucy's going to Wexford to see the Baginbun tower.'

219

'They don't mind showing it to a total stranger?'

'Why should they?'

I was silent, thinking about my reluctance to have tourists marching through my tower.

'That's an interesting thing,' Sullivan observed. 'It's like there's a kind of family of tower-owners and they're all delighted to be helpful and to show you what they've done. Lucy's also going to see the one in Dundalk they've turned into a museum.'

'I thought it was Drogheda.'

Sullivan did a 'don't bother me with the details' face. Towns in county Louth were all much the same, to her.

'So Lucy's chief researcher?'

'Well, not exclusively. Paddy Thingummy, the guy who owns Jim Redmond's company, will be at the tower today and you and me will meet him afterwards to hear what he has to say about it, having worked on other towers. I've arranged for the ex-OPW man and the woman from the local authority to meet him out there.'

'How are they going to get in, now the staircase is buggered?'

'They're bringing a cherry picker. Daragh's girlfriend is collecting him and taking care of him.'

It fell on me like the tower staircase. Like a fool, I had convinced myself that because he never mentioned her, she was past tense. History. Gone.

'What's wrong?' Sullivan was clearly convinced one of my organs had failed. My heart, I thought.

'Nothing. I'm fine.'

'Bryan said Daragh was very good on the crutches.'

To hell with him and his crutches and his girlfriend and her interior-design skills.

She disappeared and came back with my laptop. I looked at it and looked at her.

'I thought you'd want to check your e-mails?'

I powered the thing up and noticed that she had plugged my mobile phone into the mains within reach.

'I'm going to the shower and then I've a few things to do, but shout if you have a problem.'

I nodded, already concentrating on removing the offers of drugs, airline flights and online degree courses. Although I noticed that the volume of e-mails had dropped slightly, now that people connected to the bank were encountering an automatic blocker redirecting them to someone else. One of the e-mails was from Mike. All gentle queries about how I was feeling and how much fun the first day's work had been, even though the casualty rate had been high.

'No doubt Gorgeous, our inestimable project manager, will institute health and safety regulations for us all to obey in order to obviate a repeat of Saturday's drama,' the e-mail went on. 'Otherwise the frozen-pea costs might be excessive.'

He apologised for the fact that he was going to be totally unavailable in person for the next two weeks, as a major case was starting, but said he'd e-mail and text whenever he could.

'I've asked Eric to come up with something for the tower,' the e-mail finished.

'What does Mike Kearns' partner do?' I asked Sullivan when she came back and finished the call she was on.

'Painter.'

'House or art?'

'Art. He had a painting in the RHA this year. He's really good. He started to paint in prison.'

'Who had he killed?'

'Nobody. He was never violent. He was got for prostitution. Mike got his sentence reduced and paid for him to go into the Rutland. But that was two or three years ago. It's only in the last year they've been together. Eric's mother just abandoned him and his sister when he was four and went to England with some guy and he was left with his father. He's barely literate. Mike gave me his mobile number because he's really organised and always knows where Mike is. Very helpful in the beginning, when I'd talk to him or leave voice-mails. It was only when I left texts I realised he couldn't read that well. Voice-mail him and you get instant help. Text him and he has to wait until Mike comes home to find out what you said.'

A senior counsel living with a former male prostitute. Only in modern Ireland, I thought.

'The folks have met out at the tower,' she said, waving the mobile phone.

'Who's texting you?'

'Paddy. Really nice guy. He says they got in, no bother, and that he's getting a bunch of lads up there tomorrow to clear the rest of the rubble, because that'll give access to the interior before rigging up a safe temporary staircase and no planning permission is required for shifting the boulders – the local authority woman said go ahead.'

My phone made its text message noise. I clicked on the message.

U still in bed? D.

My fingers flew, inputting the answer.

None of your business

Small pause before the phone beeped.

No solidarity among the wounded? D.

Busy right now

Sullivan announced that the alternative energy people had visited the tower and found it to be surrounded by 'really useful wind'. She sounded so proud of our wind, I had to laugh. The implication seemed to be that other places had inferior wind that you wouldn't insult a wind turbine with.

My phone beeped again.

Anything wrong? D

TOLD you was busy

Meaning: go talk to your bloody girlfriend. Or is she so boring that you have to fill in the saggy bits by texting me? Well, shove it.

'Paddy says the local authority woman told him if a sensitive enough design is done on the extension, planning permission should go through very quickly.'

'The extension being whatever we might put where they broke out the wall?'

'I'm thinking a ring of glass all around the bottom of the tower,' Sullivan said, looking out the window as if the tower was in view. 'So no matter what side you're on, from the outside you can still see the full shape of the tower. Triple-glazed, probably.'

'*Glass*? In a place where the wind comes like a tornado up from the sea?'

'Glass is deceptively strong,' she informed me.

My phone vibrated.

I'd send you an icon of a sad face, but I know they annoy you. D.

No you don't, I thought. Well, maybe you do. Maybe I said something you listened to. Because I really do hate effing smiley faces stuck onto messages. Why do I care that you listened to something I said? I'm sore and drugged. That's the only reason I'm obsessing about you.

CHAPTER NINETEEN

Lower the Resistance, Raise the Scaffolding

*I*t's been so long since I had a really good bruise, I'd forgotten how they mutate from one colour to another over a week. Clare and I exchanged reports. Hers went from blue to purple to reddish/black. Mine went from blue to a greeny yellow. Sullivan claimed this was because of the arnica, and that mine would be gone long before Clare's would be. The great thing was that the pain and stiffness were gone by day three, and I was able to take a spin out to the tower.

It was surrounded by scaffolding. Startling, the difference scaffolding makes to a building. It made the tower look oddly vulnerable, like a patient in one of those frames they put onto the heads of people who've had a spinal injury. I couldn't get my car close to it, either. All over the forecourt area were cars, vans, a forklift (why?) and the cherry picker. The latter seemed to be redundant, because a solid wooden staircase now led up to the raised entrance, which was closed. Hard-hatted workmen were going in and out of the big front entrance, carrying loads of small stones and muck and dumping them beside a monumental pile of rubble. A big workman in steel-reinforced boots and a yellow hard hat stood watching the arrival of my car. After a few minutes, he came towards me, stripping off work gloves, in the kind of comfortable limp you know isn't a recent infliction. I rolled down my window.

'Can I help you?'

'No, I'm happy just to take a walk around and look.'

'Sorry,' he told me, not sounding a bit sorry. 'This is a work-site. Health and safety regulations exclude casual visitors. I'm afraid I'm going to have to ask you to leave.'

He had such authority that for one brief idiot moment, I bloody nearly obeyed him. Then the incongruity of it struck me and I began to laugh. He stood back and pushed the hard hat up a bit on his head. I could see he had completely white hair. White like it had gone snowy in his twenties. I controlled myself and stuck my hand out the window for an introductory shake.

'I'm sorry,' I said. 'I'm Patricia. I own this place.'

'Identification?'

'You're not serious.'

'I couldn't be more serious. I'm in charge here and I have a duty of care to anybody who steps on to this site.'

I groped in my handbag and found my driver's licence. He looked at the picture, looked at me, and smiled.

'You should sue whoever took that picture.'

'I took it myself, in one of those supermarket booths.'

Now it was his turn to extend a hand.

'Paddy Stapleton.'

My hand felt like it was being embraced by half a bear.

'You going to let me out of my car?'

'As long as you put on a jacket and a hard hat, yes of course.'

I thought about this.

'Are your guys working on the roof?'

'No.'

'Then why do I need a hard hat? Nothing's going to fall on me.'

'The regulations say you must wear a hard hat.'

'Frig the regulations.'

'With respect, don't frig the regulations. I've been in the building trade for thirty-five years, and I've seen dead men that would have lived if the regulations had existed at the time or been observed. Nobody's going to die or be maimed on my watch.'

I could feel the rage beginning to boil up in me. He took his hard hat off and stood there, looking at me.

'Forgive me if I'm missing something,' I said softly. 'But am I not your customer?'

'You are that.'

I raised an eyebrow: think it through, mate.

'And if you were the customer of a surgeon, d'you think he'd let you walk all over his operating theatre whatever way you liked?'

'Or she.'

'Yes. He or she.'

'No.'

'You see what I mean.'

'So everybody on site has to wear a hard hat?'

'Yes.'

'Well, why aren't you wearing one, then?'

He laughed, clapped his yellow helmet back on his head and opened the car door for me before calling on one of the lads with the wheelbarrows to find me the smallest size of helmet and a reflective jacket. I looked at myself in the side mirror of the car. I looked kind of cute. Small has disadvantages, but sometimes it can work. The big man lumbered towards the building, advising me to watch my step, and I followed him to the big open entrance. The last time I'd seen it, the floor had been piled ten-feet high with broken boulders, rocks and blocks. Now it was almost clear and the impact was unbelievable. The tower seemed huge inside.

The men came over to be introduced. When I'd pulled in, I'd had the impression that dozens of them were at work, but in fact there were only three, including Jim, who I'd met before.

'You told me Paddy knew all about old buildings,' I said to Jim. 'You didn't tell me he was a pain-in-the-arse pedant about rules and bloody regulations.'

One of the other men, named Máirtín, although he had an English accent, who wasn't sure whether I was joking or serious, told me firmly that Paddy's safety record was unequalled. The company had won awards. I nodded a bit more respectfully than I intended, glancing sideways at the big boss man.

'So now, so,' he said in a countrified way and a tone that conveyed a gotcha.

The third guy, who looked Mongolian and whose name was Togso, simply smiled. At everything and everybody.

'This tower is in marvellous condition,' the big man said.

I'm standing in the entrance someone in the twentieth century chewed out of a tower built in the nineteenth century, looking at a floor covered in filth and stones and rough-hewn interior walls with weeds growing out of them and this man is telling me it's in marvellous condition.

'Jesus. I'd hate to see one in bad condition.'

'It wouldn't be hard. Some of them have been bowdlerised by builders before the regulations stopped them. Some of them have been vandalised. Some of them have structural problems. This one is sound as a pound.'

'Except we've moved to euros.'

'More's the pity. I always loved Lady Lavery on the old pound note.'

'When you say "bowdlerised", what do you mean, exactly?'

'We've been in towers where they've bricked up the fireplaces and put in pretend coal fires fuelled with Calor Gas.'

'The condensation,' Jim said reprovingly. 'The *damp* it created inside the tower.'

'Seems to me this place is pretty damp without any gas heaters,' I said, gesturing at the fern fronds growing a few feet overhead.

'You're right,' the big boss man said. 'But you get the two fireplaces going and you leave them going for a couple of years, it'll dry the whole thing out.'

'A couple of *years*?'

'Well, when you have walls six or eight feet thick, you're not going to get rid of two centuries of damp with a hairdryer.'

Never, I thought, had I met someone who felt such little need to be liked. This big man dealt in data and truth and if you didn't like it, tough. Which, of course, made him totally likeable.

'Look at that vaulted ceiling, though,' he said, pushing the hard hat to the back of his head so he could see it. 'Must have taken them several years to complete this and Jaysus they knew their business. There are apartment blocks going up in this city at the moment and they'll be torn down before fifty years is out.'

'Not to mention buildings so ugly they should never have been built, like Hawkins House.'

'That the one behind the old Dublin Gas Company? Where the Department of Health is? Living disgrace. That's why Jim and me decided, about ten years back, to specialise in old buildings and wherever possible, in Martellos. Buildings that were made to last. That had a bit of workmanship in them. Bit of pride. Instead of bloody glass and steel.'

'Sullivan says we should clad the bottom of this tower with glass.'

'That would be all right because you'd still see the shape of it. You could put a low wall around, made of the bricks they took out. There must be how much in that pile, Jim?'

'Hundred and forty-four cubic feet. Minimum. Good stuff, too. They shouldn't have taken it out at all, but they didn't hack it out.'

Togso had given up his silent smiling and gone back to his shovel. The floor was coated in pitch-black mud. Paddy said he wasn't sure if it had been tracked in when the place was being built or had been deliberately laid down as some kind of rough flooring, but one way or the other, it had to go.

'Have to get to the good stone floor,' he told me.

'Is it solid or is there a cistern underneath?'

'We'll know that the week after next,' he said, looking, I hoped, a bit impressed with me knowing about cisterns.

'How are the pigeons up above taking all this activity?'

'No problem. They come and go as if they owned the place. We checked to see if there were any bats, but there's no sign.'

'You sound as if you'd like me to have bats in my belfry.'

'Bats are fascinating,' he said. 'But they're an endangered species. So there's all kinds of – '

'Don't tell me,' I said. 'Regulations.'

He laughed and nodded.

'Your friend Sullivan is drawing up a work plan with us,' he went on. 'At least taking care of bats won't delay us. We have to treat this place as if we were building from scratch, because of plumbing and heating, light and power, while preserving everything that's here.'

'How're you doing with Sullivan?'

The Stapleton man looked at me sideways.

'Great for short-term projects.'

'Meaning?'

'She'll lose interest and concentration before the task is done.'

You're right, I thought, but you bloody well shouldn't be saying this to me.

'Event management,' he said.

'Sorry?'

'She'd be great at that. Concentrated work for three weeks, then on to something else.'

'You may be right,' I told him. 'The great thing is we also have a woman on the team who was known as Lethal Littleton in the bank, she was so tough. But she's really very nice,' I hastened to add, realising I was setting Lucy up to be loathed before she ever appeared onsite and had this big man insist on her wearing a yellow helmet over her personal brown helmet. Lucy the Lego Lady with as many variations as any of the toys.

'The TV producer lady brought a camera out here yesterday and filmed everything we were doing,' Paddy said.

'Was that OK with you?'

'I'll be honest with you, Patricia. In my lifetime, I'm never going to get another job like this. In fact,' he went on, looking to Jim for confirmation, 'we've never really had a job like this before. We've gone in and done work, yes, and good work. In the process, we've built up an unparalleled understanding of Martello towers and how to restore them. But this – this is the capstone. This is the ultimate. It should be recorded, every step of the way.'

And, I thought but didn't say, it may be the last you'll ever do. They don't come on the market that often (despite the one for sale – still for sale – in the newspapers at the moment) and you look as if you're pushing sixty. Although you're one big impressive fit man, that limp suggests a brutal leg injury that's going to go arthritic on you if it hasn't already. So this is the swansong. The job that pulls together all your pride, your skill, your knowledge. I put my hand on his arm.

'This means a lot to you, doesn't it?'

He looked down at me for a long time in silence.

'You have no idea how much, Patricia. No idea how much.'

I was slightly taken aback by the undiluted, unprotected quiet passion of him.

'It's only a building,' I said.

He wiped his huge right hand over his face a couple of times.

'It's a lot more than a building.'

I waited, but nothing more came out of him and it was clear nothing more was going to come out of him.

'Are you all going to be here tomorrow?'

He nodded.

'All right, I'll head off and come back then. I won't get in your way.'

'Might be better if you came the day after,' he replied, leaving me in no doubt that this was more than a suggestion. 'We'll have cleaned off the roof by then and there'll be something to see.'

I thought about giving him an argument. And thought better of it.

'I really like the wooden staircase,' I said.

The two of us were walking back to my car, me not having made the decision to walk back towards my car. I just found myself doing it.

'Temporary. Solid, though,' he said, looking at it approvingly.

I got into my car, still a bit cautious because every now and again the bruising indicated that it wanted to be taken more seriously than I was taking it.

'The metal staircase fell on you, I hear,' he said.

I nodded.

'All of that should have been checked out before any amateurs were allowed to wander around the site.'

'Amateurs?'

'Amateurs.'

I belted myself in and got ready to roll up the window.

'Amateurs and bystanders,' he said thoughtfully, looking at the tower. 'I hate the fuckers.'

'Thank you,' I said stiffly.

'You were bloody lucky you didn't get a ruptured spleen out of that accident,' he said, looking at me in a brook-no-argument glare. 'It wasn't unimportant. It wasn't funny.'

'Listen, I know rather better than you, with great respect, that it wasn't funny.'

'Remember how it felt when you were underneath it. As long as I'm in charge of this site, that's not going to happen to anybody else. Now, turn slowly, because the mud that's been tracked out is slippy.'

Slippery, I mentally told him, and did the first two bits of a three-point turn while he watched as if he knew I was going to make a balls of it.

'Hey,' I called as he started to limp away.

He turned, awkwardly.

'I'm really glad you're in charge.'

'You should be,' he told me.

CHAPTER TWENTY

The Interflora Girl

*Y*ou don't invite the florist into your house. Nothing against the florist, but it works like this. The little van draws up. The guy gets out. Goes to the back of the van. Takes out the bouquet, brings it up to the door. Knocks. You open the door, get an armful of flowers, beam at him over the top of it. He goes away. You go indoors and gloat.

Right? Wrong. Wrong this time. This time, when I arrive home, there's this tall, *tall* woman at the door of my house, clutching flowers and looking lost.

'No answer?' I asked, getting out.

She shook her head, advancing, flowers shifting into her left arm, right hand extended.

'You must be Patricia. I'm Tracy.'

I shook hands with her and got the door open. Dumped my bag halfway down the hall, turned to take the flowers at the door. Except the door was closed and she was on the inside of it.

Now, you can't say to the Interflora girl 'You're supposed to stay outside.' So I kind of dithered my way into the kitchen and she followed me.

The other thing you can't say to the Interflora girl is 'You have no idea how tired I am of receiving flowers for Sullivan.'

So I offered her a cup of coffee, knowing she'd refuse it. She accepted immediately, and sat down. This, I thought, is one relationship too many.

'You're exactly as Daragh described you,' she said.

Now, you will think I'd be insulted that Daragh was describing me to the Interflora girl, but I wasn't. I was chuffed. How pathetic is that? I'd have been chuffed if he'd been discussing me with the Dyno-Rod man.

'How did he describe me?'

'Positively,' she said, and giggled.

I handed her the coffee and shoved a plate of biscuits at her.

'I told him I wanted to go and see the tower and he said you'd growl first but then you'd let me because you're always letting on to be tough but you're marshmallow, really.'

'What florist do you work for?' I asked.

If I'd asked her what brothel retained her services, she couldn't have been more surprised.

'Florist?'

'You brought me flowers.'

'From Daragh.'

'Yes?'

She looked at me, mystified. I looked at her, equally mystified. And then the light came on: The Girlfriend. Omigod, The Girlfriend.

The light came on for her, too, and a blush like an outbreak of scarlet fever rose up out of the v-neck of her t-shirt, surged over her neck and settled on her cheeks.

'I'm sorry,' she said, looking miserable.

'For what? Impersonating the Interflora girl to get a cup of instant coffee out of me?'

She laughed.

'My fault,' I said. 'It just didn't strike me Daragh would have his very own flower-delivery service.'

'I only offered so I'd get to see the tower,' she said.

Never was I so glad to hear the doorbell. I excused myself, closing the kitchen door and opened the hall door. Lucy Littleton ploughed past me at speed. I hauled her back.

'Daragh's girlfriend is in there.'

'So?'

Good question, I thought, and released her. She flung her coat at me, opened the door into the kitchen, introduced herself and got into a monologue about all the towers she had visited around the country. Tracy quietly made another cup of coffee and asked questions.

I hate you, I thought. I hate you because you are un-hateable. You are precisely the girlfriend I would want Daragh to have if I was just interested in his happiness.

'How did you meet Daragh?' I asked, when Lucy ground to a halt.

'In college. I used to beg him for his notes when I'd miss a tutorial. Which I did constantly, because I was having a great social life. And then I realised this guy was much more interesting than the others – you know the way he sits like Rodin's *Thinker* when he's working out something?'

I nodded.

'Seven years ago.'

Seven years is a long, long time, I thought.

'Of course, then I lost interest in accountancy.'

'You do interior design?'

'Which bores Daragh stiff,' she told me.

Doesn't stop him quoting your expertise, I thought.

'Are you going to do some work on the tower?' Lucy wanted to know.

Over my dead body, I thought. This is one nice woman, but do I need the two of them around all the time as a unit? No, I sure as hell do not.

'Oh, no, I just said to Daragh that I was going to beg to get a look today, because I've a flight tomorrow.'

'I can drop you up there, but I can't go in with you,' Lucy said. 'Haven't the time, today.'

'Wouldn't dream of dragging you out of your way,' Tracy assured her. 'Just tell me how to get there and I'll introduce myself to whoever's there.'

Stapleton, I thought, you're going to *love* the opportunity to put a hard hat on a girl taller than you are.

'You chose my favourite flowers,' I said. 'Freesias.'

'Sorry, but no credit to me. Daragh told me exactly what I was to buy.'

Lucy retrieved her coat and guided the tall girl ahead of her, giving her directions to the tower as she went. At the front door, Tracy turned and hugged me.

'I hope the tower brings you all the happiness it should,' she told me.

I watched the two cars take off (no, her car wasn't a van, I hadn't been paying attention when I assumed she was the

Interflora girl) and went back to the flowers. On a plastic lolli-pop stick in the middle was a card. I opened it.

Trish,

Hope you're feeling better.

Much love, D.

Much love? And he sends it via his girlfriend? And she's a sweetheart?

'I should put you straight in the bin,' I told the flowers.

But of course I didn't.

CHAPTER TWENTY-ONE

Comfort Food

'*P*atricia?'

I looked up from my newspaper to see Sullivan looking bothered.

'What's wrong?'

'Nothing. Just, you know Bryan's brother?'

'The anger management guru?'

'Yes. I was – me and Bryan were – in his house earlier for a session, you know?'

'Mmmm?'

'I noticed something. Derek doesn't listen to his own wife.'

This threw me.

'The carpenters' children never have any shoes,' she told me.

This threw me even more.

'D'you remember when we went on the personal growth weekend?'

'When you dragged me to the personal growth weekend, you mean. I'll never forget it. What was the name of that group-leader guy? The one who sat there all humble, letting on to be one of us while just waiting for one of us to say something unguarded?'

I'd hated him on sight and of course he spotted it and kept asking me why I was so defensive.

When I shut up and stared at him, he had invited everybody to find my defensiveness interesting. At which point I told him to stick it and walked out. I was calling a taxi, because I didn't want to leave Sullivan without transport, when she arrived beside me, said he'd given her the creeps from the moment she'd walked in the door, that she wouldn't trust him as far as she could throw him and dragged me off to the swimming pool. We ended up having a great weekend, except that one of the personal growthers kept shoving love-notes under our bedroom door. Addressed to Sullivan.

'Is Derek like the guy at the personal growth weekend?' I asked now.

'He's nothing like as bad. But he has this air they all have of knowing stuff you don't know and being wiser than you, you know? He loves you when you're crying in front of him or agreeing with what he says, but you can see him stiffening up but pretending not to if you don't go along with everything. It's like you own the failure you've been up to now, but he'll own the success you'll be if you do everything he tells you to do. I'd say a lot of people are delighted to have someone to listen to them and look out for them. People like to be bossed around, I think. As long as…'

She struggled for a moment in silence and I restrained myself from telling her what she thought.

'It's like you qualify by being unhappy and you buy the attention to your unhappiness, but you kind of have to continue to be a bit unhappy. I know what it is. It's like you've a project that's never going to end. It's like he would be a bit lost if you suddenly said to him "look, you've been great, but I'm cured, I know what to do now".'

'Is Bryan cured?'

Please answer no, I willed her. I could not bear it if you told me you want him to move in with you in this little house in Ranelagh and I don't think I could bear the fights. Because you're bored with the six months of celibacy even though you're only two months into it.

'He's different.'

'Not what I asked you. Is he cured?'

'He's working very hard at it.'

'Is he cured?'

'Derek doesn't think so.'

'Derek is so focused on his personal ownership of an inter-esting problem process that he sure as hell doesn't want Bryan buggering off and showing independence of spirit and free will. He wants him kept in the deep freeze like a biopsy.'

She looked at me with enormous relief. The fact that I had said it, rather than Sullivan saying it for herself, absolved her from viciousness, but she wanted it said. No, that's unfair. Sullivan doesn't plan her life around what will make her feel good or bad. It's just that sometimes her sunny-side-of-the-street niceness makes her subservient to circumstances.

'I always know what I think after you've said it,' she said.

I looked at her sharply to see if she was sending me up, but no. She meant it.

'Well, if you want Bryan to move out of Derek's house and he can't move into Daragh's house, does that mean he's coming back here?'

'No. We did a deal and we're sticking to it. In fact, I might never go back to sex.'

'Like a nun?'

'*You*'re not a nun and *you* have no sex.'

'I don't rule it out as a possibility in the future,' I said calmly. 'I have never set my face against a good sex life. I just have this peculiar prerequisite that it should be part of something else.'

'Like love,' she said, all doe-eyed.

I closed my eyes and did some deep-breathing.

'I really liked Daragh's girlfriend when I met her at the tower last night,' she added.

'Lovely girl,' I said briskly. 'Perfectly suited to him.'

'I'm not as clever as you,' Sullivan said, standing up and going into the kitchen. 'But I'm not stupid, either.'

I considered that truth. She came back to the door of the sitting room.

'And sometimes you being cleverer than me is not good for you. It makes you pretend to me when I don't pretend to you.'

She was back in the kitchen, clattering around, before I could think of a good answer to that. Other than saying 'You're perfectly right, Sullivan.' So I sat, a clever moron, looking at a fading bruise on my arm, and did nothing. Ten minutes later she came back with a tray of what looked like freshly baked scones, butter, jam and a pot of tea. Comfort food. I poured the tea and handed her a mug.

'I didn't bake the scones,' she said huffily, as if I'd accused her of fraud. 'They're those ones you get in Tesco, you just put them in the oven for ten minutes.'

We buttered and jammed our scones in silence. They tasted wonderful.

'Sullivan?'

'Mmm?' Mouth pursed to prevent scone-crumb escape.

'You're perfectly right and you're a lot cleverer than I am. You know that thing they say about houses in the property pages, "May need renovation"? Well, I'm beginning to realise it's true of me, too. I didn't know I needed renovation, but I did. I do. And it may not be on your task list for the tower, but I think it's happening as part of that project. You've gathered maybe the best personal development group in the world. Good people.'

'I didn't gather Daragh.'

'No, Mike gave us Daragh.'

'But he's OK, isn't he?'

'He's a lot better than OK. He may be everything I ever wanted in a man.'

'Tall.'

That made me laugh, even though it was probably true.

'Tall. Gentle. Funny. Generous. Clever. Unpretentious. I feel so totally comfortable in his company – even in e-mails and texts. I love to see his name in my inbox.'

'Well, then,' she said, splitting another scone and sliding one half of it over to me. We know each other that well: one and a half is our capacity, not two.

'Sullivan, he has a girlfriend. I don't make moves when someone has a girlfriend. Even if I thought I'd succeed. Which I wouldn't. You've met Tracy.'

The two of us concentrated on the scones and a second mug of tea apiece.

'There's a thing,' Sullivan said. 'Sometimes it's like the way you can be with Mike.'

'I don't follow you.'

'You know how you can be as open with Mike as if he was one of us because he's gay and he has Eric and you know he's really interested in you, not trying to get you into bed with him? Well, Daragh having a girlfriend could be the same. You can be really friends with him, closer than if he was your *boyfriend*.'

I told her she was quite right and she went off, delighted, to do the washing up. While I tried to understand why the freedom she had just handed me was such a sad, unwelcome freedom.

CHAPTER TWENTY-TWO

Stepping into the Same River Twice

*M*ike was in the papers again for the major case he was arguing in court and which prevented him coming near the tower or meeting Paddy, Jim, Togso and Máirtín. It was one of those cases where four or five friends start a business in the hope of creating a reasonable income for themselves, luck into something much bigger, and end up, ten years later, putting each other through the legal hoops and accusing each other of everything short of budgie-buggery.

I e-mailed him the following morning.

Mike,
We miss you. The new head bottle-washer out at the tower is a big old guy named Paddy, with a limp and one of those accents lightly dusted with English inflections after a lifetime in the building trade over there. You'd like him. You must not like him too much though, because I might have to take a bullying case against him. He forces me to wear helmets and boots

with reinforced toes. (He does the same to Sullivan, who accedes to each request as if it was no problem.)

Bloody rules. Bloody regulations.

Everybody in that court case you're doing sounds a total shit. Does it not depress you, always having to deal with wankers who are fighting/divorcing/generally shitting on each other? Because nobody ever goes to court for good reasons and nobody is improved by going to court, even if they win. (Personal opinion, strength undiminished by ignorance.) How d'you wind down at the end of the day?

Having minimised my e-mail programme, I was looking at glass staircases on the web (Sullivan's suggestion as a way of making the most of the space within the tower by illusion: if you can see through it, it's not really there) when I heard the blip noise indicating I had mail. It turned out to be an almost instant reply.

Patricia, dear, your most welcome reminder of reality reaches me just before I set off to dress up as a pantomime dame and seek to persuade the uninvolved that the involved are pure, filled with integrity and altruism and have made life errors which you might call crimes only in the same harmlessly delightful way a Labrador pup will chew your slippers.

I know you will not be offended if I state that Gorgeous is the only woman on the planet who can make reinforced toe boots as sexy as four-inch heeled strappy sandals. Keep every scrap of evidence on this guy Paddy and we'll decide how best to punish him for bullying my friend Patricia.

In answer to your question, I wind down, first of all, by cooking for the two of us. Then, when he lets me, by watching Eric paint. That happens only when he has reached a particular point in the composition of a painting. If steam is coming out his ears, I curl in a corner and read. Currently on the go: Paul Auster. Always to hand, poets like Heaney. I keep telling Eric he's ready for his Heaney phase: the harsh-textured lichen-crisped greys and browns.

Dear Mike,

I'm sure you're gone off to court by now, but feckit, I'll respond now because I have the time and you can look at this later, when you have the time.

What kind of cooking do you do? I bet you do effing towers with red streaks drizzled over them. I bought myself 6 metal yokes for cutting things into circles for delightful display on the dish and the whole six are gathering dust (and, for all I know, lichen) on the top of a press somewhere. I can't be arsed with food as a work of art. Just cook it and sling it at me.

I'm keeping Easons in profit at the moment. First time in my life I really had the space to read. I know, I know, every half-literate plonker in the world says 'I used to read a lot, but I'm soooo busy, I can't find the time'. Well, as a package-recipient, I'm here to tell you that 'I used not to read a lot, but I'm soooo idle, I'm enjoying a promiscuity of literary input like you

wouldn't believe.' Must now include Paul Auster and
don't hit me for not knowing who he is. Before now,
I mean.

Is Eric listening to you about a Heaney phase?
Would a visit to our lichen-covered tower help? And
how do you pronounce 'lichen' anyway? I've heard two
versions since we got started on the tower.

Hope you have a great day with the villains.
Patricia.

Even after fifteen minutes with the glass staircases, nothing
happened, so I closed down the computer, just as my phone
beeped.

Trish, I hear Sullivan's been displaced as the power figure, at least out at the tower, by Paddy with the Limp.
How's she taking it? D.

I'll give you 'Trish', I thought, looking at the clock. Coffee-
break time. It had to be. Or lunch time. Or home-on-the-
LUAS tine. Daragh tried, as far as possible, not to do personal
texting or calling during office hours. Partly because he said
he felt he was grossly overpaid for what he did anyway, and he
therefore owed it to the partnership to work when at work, and
partly because he was afraid the inattention caused by enjoy-
able chats with friends would lead him to make a mistake on
client work. This boy is going places. You can see managing
partner all over him. Ten years down the line, he'll be charming
the knickers off government ministers, appearing on the odd
TV programme to defend accountancy when someone does

an Enron, and making big decisions like will the partners pay themselves two million in salary next year or two and a half.

Daragh, you don't understand. Sullivan's been promoted to Man Director + Paddy is Gen Manager w/out Portfolio. He's an old partner of her father's, remember? She knows him from childhood. How's ur limp? P

Trish, hv 2 meet this guy. Does he wk Sat? U still black+bl? D

D, believe it r not, he does. Go figr. Am a sickly yellow with prple accents. YR ANKL? P

Akl prfct. Crutch rtrned to hosp. Any public viewings? D

Of what?

The prpl accents?

Shag off. Thanks again for the flowers. Tracy is lovely. U @ twr Sat?

Yes.

CU

I was just about to put the phone away when it vibrated again.

Bring u lunch? Lucy

God, yes. Sullivan will be back @ 2. Food 4 her too?

OK.

Because there was a knock at the door immediately thereafter, for a split second I thought Lucy was bringing efficiency to an unprecedented level. But it turned out to be our postwoman with a parcel from Amazon.

'Oh, great,' I told her. 'You're brill.'

She seemed pleased to have delivered something so welcome. I made myself a coffee and curled up on the sofa to read the book – an account of Martello towers, long out of print. I had it finished by the time Lucy arrived with an armful of bags from Donnybrook Fair.

'Plates?' I asked tentatively.

'Not at all. Eat from the containers. Saves washing up.'

'You bought enough for the Red Army.'

'Always do. Why do you think I'm the size I am?'

I waited for the usual question about how I'm so slim. Short answer: genetics. My mother and father were commendably thin, as were my grandparents. None of them survived to be sixty, but they were thin. I can eat any bloody thing and not gain more than three pounds. Whenever I *do* gain three pounds, they seem to go in their entirety to my boobs. Now, can you get over that and still love me?

Lucy sat down and addressed something with a lot of noodles in it.

'You are so lucky,' she told me, 'that you didn't abandon that tower. It's the best thing that ever happened any of us.'

'Tell me that after you've met the new gaffer on site. Paddy with the Limp.'

'What's wrong with him?'

'He'll make you wear a helmet and jacket and boots and quote health and safety rules at you.'

'Right and proper. Like the sound of him.'

'I didn't expect a building boss to make like everybody's mother.'

A sudden rare memory of my own mother floored me. The first time I got a bike, she limited her instructions to one: if you see the bus, get off. It worked for me, as a seven-year-old. Anything else I could cope with, but a double-decker bus, no.

'Somebody should do a study into the pointless instinctive resistance otherwise quite reasonable people bring to health and safety rules,' Lucy said, finishing one container and starting another. I couldn't work out whether the first had been a starter or if she ate lunch in an unplanned sequence and stopped when the containers ran out.

'Before your time,' she said, waving a plastic spoon red-stained with tomato at me, 'I brought in a health and safety inspector, a retired guy, to do an audit before we could get caught with our trousers down by the real thing. I brought him in to the head of corporate banking, who was barely civil to him while making all the usual noises about the bank's commitment to health and safety, and the inspector, bless him, told him that his desk was in the wrong place, making access to the fire extinguishers virtually impossible. The head of corporate banking got tetchy and told the inspector that at least he could give us credit for having the two different kinds, and the inspector invited him to tell him which was which and what each was used for.'

'Which, of course, he couldn't do, right?'

She nodded and then laughed.

'The best thing was when I brought him to the kitchen on the third floor – you know the small staff kitchen? He reached to the top of the fridge – outside the fridge, I mean, not inside – and took down this huge round tin – the kind you get Cadbury's Roses in when you want to give a Christmas present to a family. He took the lid off it and found it was filled with packets of Panadol. He stared at them and then demanded to know why they were there. "For headaches," someone said. "They're Panadol, for Godsake, what's the problem?" "Suicide," he said. I didn't like to tell him we were too busy to get around to suicide in the office, no matter how unhappy we were. I just took the Panadol out of there and spent the next six weeks devising a health and safety code for the bank.'

'That code, in common with all the others you devised, was part of the reason why you were less than popular with the troops on the ground.'

'If it saved someone getting burned, scalded or worse, what do I care about popularity?'

'You're going to *love* Paddy with the Limp. The two of you can drink in the pub after work sessions at the tower and discuss great health and safety protocols you have known.'

As I tidied away the empty food containers and started a pot of coffee, Sullivan arrived, hair flying, made up as if for a photo opportunity, dressed to the nines if not the tens. She hugged Lucy as if Lucy was her VBF, and hugged her all over again when she learned that Lucy had brought Donnybrook Fair food. Lucy bore this onslaught of affection with equanimity.

'You were doing some sort of training course?' she asked.

Sullivan took the plastic lid off a container of goat's cheese salad and removed the smaller container of dressing. It would go in the fridge, to be used later by me on some other salad. Sullivan's salads always stay naked. But pure. Untouched. Virginal, even.

She gave us a rundown on her morning, standing up all the time so she could eat and do action replays of her great moments reading SpeechQue, that device where they put words rolling up in front of the camera while the presenter pretends to have those words pouring fluently from a well-stocked brain. Now, a well-stocked brain, whatever else she has, is not one of Sullivan's strengths. Stocked, yes. Stocked to overflowing with good things, indubitably. But stocked as randomly as an old person's attic or a metropolitan landfill.

'The guy who runs the SpeechQue is just the loveliest fellow you'd ever meet,' Sullivan told us, and my heart sank. It must have sunk visibly, although quite how that might work I don't know, because she immediately told me – to ease my fears that she was off on another instant bonding-and-bonking sequence – that the SpeechQue operator was *way* too young for her but a total darling. Diarmuid, she told us carefully, as if we were both going to have to go on Irish language radio and would need to be able to pronounce his name.

Diarmuid had run her though a sample script a number of times while she was filmed doing it, and then they'd sat down with the trainer.

'I was watching it, and I knew it was awful, but I didn't know why,' she said, catching an escaping shard of lettuce with a plastic fork. 'But once the trainer explained, it was like a break-through, you know?'

'Only *like* a breakthrough, not a real breakthrough?' Lucy asked.

Pedantry is difficult to extirpate. You can dilute it with good-will, but it's always there, ready to make a cameo appearance.

'It was like suddenly I was free. It was always going to be there, you know? I'd been doing it like this –'

She froze in position, holding her head rigidly on her neck and moving only her eyes from side to side. Because only one bit of her moved, she looked like one of those amateur animations you see on websites where Hillary Clinton and Barack Obama stand perfectly still while a song plays in the background, but their mouths go up and down.

'But then I learned – hey – that's not the way I'd talk to *you*.'

'It's the way you always talked to me in the bank,' Lucy said, concerned as always for accuracy.

'Yeah, but that was because I was shit-scared of you. Jesus, whenever I was summoned to your floor, never mind to you, I started shitting planks. Sideways.'

Always the felicitious phrase, our Sullier.

'But I wouldn't talk to you that way now. So why would I talk to someone at home like that?'

'Who at home?' I asked, confused as always by her style of communication.

'Anybody. People. Whoever. Viewers.'

'Oh, right.'

'Because talking to a camera is really talking to people in their own sitting room. You're just visiting them, you're not making a speech to a big audience.'

'I assume, if Clare sells this series, she will be hoping for a very big audience,' Lucy said, puzzled.

'No, but yes, of course,' Sullivan clarified. 'The thing is that they're big but not joined up. Thousands of them. Hundreds of thousands of them. But they're all in different places.'

By now, Lucy was looking seriously dazed.

'Sullivan means that although collectively the viewers would constitute a big audience, each of them watches as an individual, in their own home, unaware of the others watching at the same time,' I told her.

'That's what I mean,' Sullivan acknowledged. 'Once I had that, I was away. I really was. I was so brilliant, I couldn't believe it. I'd have done it all day if I could. I began even to do it like this –'

She turned sideways, so she was talking to us over her right shoulder in a very fetching way.

'– or like this.'

She embraced herself – always a pleasing activity – and did a studied thoughtful hesitation.

'I can just be myself,' she said, plumping down on the sofa beside Lucy.

Lucy and I forebore to tell her that when she was being herself, studied thoughtful hesitations didn't play much of a part in her natural gait.

'Even if the Martello tower series doesn't make it, you will,' Lucy said.

'Do you really think so?'

'I know so. But I told you that in the bank, when I was offering you the package. Anybody could see that there was some career out there just waiting to happen for you. It sure as hell wasn't banking, though.'

Sullivan finished the salad and took a cup of coffee from me with disproportionate cries of gratitude.

'Now the next thing is,' Lucy said. 'You're going to need an agent-cum-manager.'

'I can manage things,' Sullivan said, looking hurt. 'I'm doing a good job project-managing the tower. Oh, wait till you meet Paddy, you won't believe how good he is and all the things he knows about old buildings even though he has a limp. My Dad knows him forever. The two of them used to –'

She put her hand to her mouth and went as red as Tracy the Interflora girl had. Lucy looked at her in astonishment.

'I'm not supposed to say anything,' Sullivan said.

'About what?'

'About what they used to – anything. Just anything. It's private. It's past, it's nothing to do with me.'

I looked at Lucy, who shrugged. Neither of us had any interest in whatever Paddy with the Limp got up to in his younger days with Sullivan's father. Although her embarrassment suggested it hadn't been ordinary.

'Of course you can manage things,' Lucy said, going back to the main subject. 'You're managing the tower wonderfully. But you'll lose interest after a while.'

'Paddy says you should do event management,' I offered.

'You need someone to manage your career,' Lucy told her, relentlessly. 'Remember, Sullivan, if at the time you'd done the TV interviews you were invited to do, in order to justify how you'd ended up on the balcony of an apartment in your knickers after one of your boyfriends wrecked the other boyfriend's car deliberately, you would now be an unemployed and unemployable ex-banker, not to say slapper. As soon as you start appearing on TV, much of that negative coverage is going to surface again, and you'll need someone to filter out interviews with hostile journalists, to sue the bejasus out of anybody who libels you and generally to establish you not as what you were six months ago, but as what you are going to be for the next several decades.'

Sullivan began to perk up a bit.

'Furthermore, and arguably of more importance,' Lucy went on, 'is the fact that you have neither the experience nor the instinct to negotiate a contract.'

'That's true. I only ever worked in the bank and they tell you what you're going to do and what they're going to pay you and that's it. But I'd be afraid an agent wouldn't be interested in taking on someone who's never worked in TV before.'

'Sullivan. I will be your agent and manager.'

'You?'

'Me.'

'Would you?'

'Yes.'

Lucy Littleton suddenly got enveloped on the sofa. Briefly, the two of them looked like a gazelle trying to mate with a Pilates ball. Out of the melee came wild cries of delight and relief from Sullivan, who kept telling Lucy she'd be the new Gayle Somebody. Lucy eventually fought her off and patted her back into place at the other end of the sofa.

'Why would you want to be the new Gayle Whoever?' she wanted to know. 'I'd have thought you should be setting out to be the new Somebody Famous. Or maybe just be Sullivan Spencer. Would that be so bad?'

'No, you don't understand, I was saying that *you'll* be the new Gayle. Not me.'

Lucy looked across at me, opening her hands in the 'haven't a clue' move. I did it right back at her.

'I'll be the new Oprah.'

'You don't have the weight problems.'

'Who is Gayle, then?'

'Oprah's *friend*. They've worked together for yonks, and Oprah says she owes so much to Gayle, she could never, ever, repay her although she has made her a multi-millionnaire and the two of them, this is media again, have had to defend themselves *so* often against accusations of being lesbians, not that there's anything wrong with being a lesbian,' she added hastily.

'I'm not one,' Lucy said coolly. 'But I appreciate your logic.'

This threw Sullivan off a bit. Not a lot, though. When Sullivan channels the *National Enquirer*, not even a dropped lump hammer would stop her.

'It's so insulting, though, not just to the two of them but to Stedman as well,' she finished. It was obvious that Lucy not only didn't know who Stedman was, but she had no inclination to pursue enlightenment about him.

'I will draw up a contract,' she told Sullivan. 'I'll have it to you by close of business tomorrow. In fact, no, I'll be here at close of business tomorrow, along with a lawyer –'

'Isn't it an awful shame Mike is too busy this week, he would have been great to do it,' Sullivan put in, always eager to create her very own little golden circle and keep the business within it. I wasn't sure Mike Kearns, SC, had an overwhelming need of this particular level of business, but it seemed gratuitous to say so.

'We'll sign it together and after that, we'll be in business.'

'Fantastic. Brill.'

'You never asked her what she was going to charge you,' I prompted Sullivan.

'Oh, I couldn't ask a friend that.'

'The answer is that I'll have found out before I draw up the contract what the standard arrangement is, and that's what we'll apply.'

Sullivan stood up and did a dance around the room. She can't dance. I've tried to teach her, but she has the coordination of one of those wooden things our mothers used to dry clothes on. You know the ones where you spend ten minutes trying to get it to unfold, pinch your fingers in the process and end up with something that's all Xs.

'Make us some more coffee, would you, hon?' I asked. 'Lucy has to tell me all about the towers she visited in the last few days.'

As Sullivan headed willingly for the kitchen, Lucy shook her head.

'Out of time. Have to meet someone on the Quays in thirty minutes.'

'I'm really sorry,' Sullivan told me contritely. 'I shouldn't have gone banging on about my career when we should have been listening to the things Lucy found out about the other towers, because it's fascinating, she told me small bits of it when I'd check with her about other issues.'

'Is that guy Paddy going to be at the tower on Saturday, or do they not work weekends?' Lucy asked.

'That's the question on everybody's lips today,' I responded. 'Yeah, he will be there and no, they *do* work weekends. Saturdays, anyway.'

'Who else's lips?'

'Sorry?'

'You said someone else wanted to know about Paddy with the Limp and if he worked – '

'Oh, it was Daragh. His ankle is better and he wants to wander out there at the weekend.'

'Good,' Lucy said.

I agree with you, Ms Littleton, I thought. Just not sure our agreement is based on the same reasons.

'Because I think what I found out about other towers would be most time-effectively shared with you if this guy Paddy were present and if Daragh was there too, so much the better. So forget about today – no problem, Sullivan, what we covered was useful – and I'll get out of your hair.'

We thanked her profusely for the lunch and saw her to the door, before Sullivan went running upstairs to take off her make-up and finery (nobody but Sullivan would dress up to attend a training course) and to sing one song after another in a rolling cascade of new-found happiness I hoped Bryan would share when he heard about it.

CHAPTER TWENTY-THREE

The Boarded-up Years

*T*hat Friday proved the rule that the day you think is going to be calm and peaceful, not to say dull, never is. It started calmly enough, with each of us on our computers, coffee by our sides, checking on our e-mails. Admittedly, Sullivan was on such a high that she overturned her coffee onto her keyboard, but she used her hairdryer, diffuser and all, on it and it seemed to recover pretty well, except that if you hit the letter p it repeated itself ten times. She said she could manage that without difficulty. I think if every key on the keyboard had decided to do a sustained stammer, Sullivan would not even have seen it as a minor problem.

She put out our wheelie bin in between e-mailing instructions and checking up on tower project people by phone. I felt guilty, on the other side of the room, drinking coffee and doing little more than gossiping. The first mail in my inbox came from Mike Kearns.

Patricia, my dear,

My villains have stayed upright today, which is as much as anybody could expect of them. To ask them to *be* upright would be bootless. I cannot wait for this week to be over and to get out to the tower at the weekend. Even if there's nobody else out there, the sea, sky and that marvellously stolid structure will calm my soul.

Lichen is pronounced 'Like N'.

Will Eric take my advice about his Heaney Period? Probably. Because I have always seen in him the potential he failed to see in himself and it's the next logical step for his profound talent.

And therein lies the time bomb.

Mike

I looked at my watch, then realised time-checking was pointless since I had no clue as to what time a court case started in the morning, ergo no clue as to what time Mike was likely to leave his home. I send him a response anyway.

Mike,

All God's children are going to be out at The Tower at the weekend. (I have, as you will note, taken to capitalising it. Dunno whether this underscores my growing love for the bloody thing or my sense of *its* sense of historic importance. Or it may be, more venally, that I figure we should all get into the habit of saying The Tower so that documents going into the Revenue Commissioners impress them with its importance in every sentence.)

Lucy plans to be there, as does Sullivan, who will regale you, whether you want to be regaled or unregaled, with the TV training she's undertaking at the moment. She's just gone out to collect our wheelie the minute the bin collectors arrived and I swear to God they're out there, unable to move a step because she's glowing at them like a lamp. Daragh's going to be there. I don't know if he'll bring Tracy with him.

I don't think you've met Paddy, have you? He'll be there too. If you want to calm your soul, you may need to go for a long walk along the water's edge, because Lucy will be in full flight, telling us about the towers she's visited around the country.

I probably shouldn't ask you, because it's none of my business, but the reference to a time bomb intrigues me.

Patricia

Once I'd pressed send, I checked my phone and was irrationally pleased to find a text from Daragh amid the detritus.

Trish, I have this dull job. Called acctcy. Give me news, gossip or scandal 2 keep me afloat. D

No better woman than me today for news, although gossip and scandal are thin on the ground, I thought.

D, Sullivan is as high as a k over her TV prspcts + hs apptd Lucy as her agmt/mngr. Mike'll b @ Twr Sat. Ankl holding its own? P

Quick as lightning, came the response.

> Who else's wd it hold? It's ace. I, on other hand, am
> rubbish. Have given up cigarettes.X

I looked at my own phone to see if he could have typed X when
he meant to type P. How pathetic is that? Then I went back to
my e-mails to find Mike's reply.

> My darling Patricia,
> I have a misplaced genius for spotting and developing
> talent. For finding the crushed and almost destroyed and
> identifying within them the seeds of at least ability, but
> sometimes, as in the case of my beautiful Eric, greatness.
> It is a chronic asset and a dire liability, inevitably creat-
> ing an emotional dependency from which I profit in the
> short term while striving to extirpate in the longer term.
> The pattern is impregnable and will, I fear, play out in
> Eric's case as it has twice before. He will come to the
> full flowering of his genius, and shortly thereafter to the
> realisation that his genius is in his ownership, rather than
> driven into him by me, as at this point in our shared lives
> he probably still believes. And with that flowering and
> that realisation will come a waning of his need for me.
> I do not know which is worse, the final sundering,
> which Eric will cause to be violently disruptive because
> that is how life has trained him, or these months and
> perhaps years of fragile fearfulness as I relish every
> moment with him, yet find it tainted by the certainty
> of its transience.

I will bring Eric to The Tower on Saturday, in the full
confidence that you will have compartmentalised this
information in one section of your oversized brain.
Love, Mike.

As I sat wondering how or whether to respond, Sullivan came
back from answering the door, leading Clare, the TV producer.
Clare nodded at me but didn't say anything. She looked like a
hamster with its cheeks full of hidden nuts. Then she electri-
fied us by doing a Tom Cruise. She didn't actually leap onto
the couch and start bouncing on it, feet first, but she bounced
where she stood and punched the air.

'We have it, we did it!'

'They're taking the programme?'

'The entire kit and caboodle. Including Sullivan as presenter.'

Sullivan stood as still as a stone. As if moving would make
the dream go away. I leaned across and grabbed one French-
manicured hand.

'Are you thrilled?'

Weirdly, her eyes filled up with tears.

'Well, I know I should be.'

'But you're not?' Clare asked, perplexed.

'It's just this afternoon it hit me that maybe they would want
me, all right, but they wouldn't want me for talent, they would
want me because of the controversy. The minute the programme
went on the air, all the newspapers would be running stories
about me on the balcony and Hugo's ex wife would come out
of the woodwork all over again and they wouldn't mind because
it would up the ratings for the programmes, but I would mind,
Patricia. I really would.'

She began to cry. Clare looked at her, mouth open. No squirrelled-away nuts in her cheeks, now.

'I mean, when you think about it,' Sullivan went on, hiccuping on sobs, 'why else would they pick me?'

A key turned in the hall door. I was halfway out of my chair when Bryan appeared. Oh, yes, of course, he had a key from way back. He halted at the sight of Sullivan in tears, looking from Clare to me as if one of us must have – oh, I don't know – assaulted Sullivan, maybe?

'Sullivan thinks RTÉ picked her because she's notorious,' I said.

'Picked her for what?'

'They've bought Clare's TV programme. With Sullivan as presenter.'

'They can shove it,' Bryan said.

'No,' Clare told him firmly. 'They can't. I've invested a lot of time and hard sell in this.'

'Fuck your hard sell,' he told her.

For just a split second, she looked astonished. Which was understandable, since the Bryan she had met was the post-Jaguar-destruction Bryan, all damped down by his brother's anger-management counselling. Then she advanced on him.

'I don't know what's eating you,' she hissed at him. 'But I run a business and I'm not going to have my business screwed by an outsider who knows nothing about it.'

'Fuck your business.'

I began to write a little memo in my head to the famous Derek. Telling him his anger management didn't seem to have taken that well with his brother. Bryan stepped past Clare and grabbed Sullivan by the wrist.

'We're out of here,' he told her, and started to drag her towards the door.

I stopped writing memos in my head and stood up, poking him in the back with an index finger.

'Cool it.'

This distracted him for long enough for Sullivan to yank her arm out of his grasp and start massaging the red skin where he'd clutched it so tightly. Bryan swung around to me and I ducked. Ducked because I was expecting his fist to connect with my head.

The fact that I ducked seemed to bring him to his senses. He walked away from me to the window and looked out in silence.

'Everybody sit down,' I said.

Nobody moved.

'Now,' I said, speaking more loudly because I was afraid my voice would shake.

Sullivan teetered backwards until her legs met the couch and collapsed onto it. Clare sat beside her.

'Bryan,' I told his back. 'Come and sit down.'

'I'm sorry,' he said in Clare's direction.

Because he wasn't looking at her, he didn't see the narrowed eyes she favoured him with.

'Clare,' I said, as if I was chairing a meeting and she was the next item.

'Sullivan was accepted as presenter by RTÉ because I told them how good she is,' said Clare. 'They picked her because I snuck them a DVD of her training exercises. They picked her because she's alive under her skin and looks as if she's permanently delighted with everything. The camera loves that. Viewers love it, too.'

The girl who was supposed to be permanently delighted with everything was staring into nothing, her tears drying on her face, her sobs dying down to the occasional tremor.

'And I'll tell you something else for nothing,' she continued. 'They trust me to pick someone who will be professional and not go off the deep end emotionally because they imagine something awful in their heads. Of course the newspapers are going to go back to the old story. So what? Get over it.'

'I'm not having Sullivan subjected to that shit all over again,' Bryan said carefully.

'It was you who subjected her to that shit in the first place,' I said, as calmly as I could.

'Not true.'

'Oh, what planet do you live on?' Clare demanded. 'This girl's career was ended by your craziness and now you're trying to destroy her future.'

'Fuck you.'

'Bryan,' Sullivan whispered. 'Remember what Derek said.'

'Fuck Derek.'

Now, I might agree with that. In fact, I *did* agree with it. But I couldn't see how it would move anything on.

'Be very clear,' Clare said quietly to Sullivan. 'I will not move forward on this project if this kind of thing is going to happen. You may not have a reputation to protect, but I do.'

'How *dare* you say Sullivan has no reputation to protect.' Bryan demanded.

Clare rolled her eyes: O. My. God.

'If there is the smallest possibility that my programme would be damaged by your uncontrolled outbursts, I will not do the programme.

'You think that frightens me?'

'No,' I said. 'But it sure as hell frightens me. This programme is important to me in giving some payback to the consortium financing my tower. It's even more important to Sullivan.'

Bryan examined his hands with great attention.

'Did they really think I was good?' Sullivan tremulously asked Clare, who nodded.

'Isn't that great?' Sullivan asked Bryan, who continued to examine his hands. Suit you better, I thought, to examine the red welt on Sullier's arm left by you grasping it like a jailer.

My phone went off. I clicked it on and told the caller to wait.

'Bryan, go make us all coffee and tea,' I told him. 'Sullivan, go wash your face. Clare, stay where you are.'

'What's wrong?' Daragh's voice asked me.

'Good to hear from you,' I said, neutrally.

'Do you need me to get over there?'

Oh, please, yes, Daragh. Your quiet thoughtfulness would be calming in itself, even if you said nothing.

'Not at all.'

'Can I help in any way?'

A crash from the kitchen lifted me a foot off the chair. Clare went running.

'What the hell was that?' Daragh wanted to know.

'I don't know. Something in the kitchen. Bryan.'

'Has he gone off the deep end again?'

'Yes.'

'I'll be over straight away.'

'Where are you?'

'Moate.'

'*Moate*? And you're going to be over straight away? By helicopter?'

The two of us began to laugh. Clare put her head around the door.

'Bryan dropped the tray,' she told me. 'By accident. He says he'll replace everything.'

'Have we anything left to drink coffee out of?'

'Yes.'

She disappeared.

'I heard that,' Daragh said.

Sullivan arrived back, with a shiny clean face on her and a long-sleeved t-shirt. God love you, I thought. Concealing the red marks on your arm.

'My flowers are still beautiful,' I said to Daragh.

'I'm glad.'

'How are you doing without the cigarettes?'

'Badly. My brain is on strike.'

'Have you telephoned the smokers' helpline?'

'No, I find talking to you more helpful.'

'Yeah, well, you've had your dose for the day. Bryan's here with the teas and coffees.'

'Don't take any crap from him.'

'I won't.'

'Trish?'

'Yes?'

'Look, I – Listen, maybe we'll talk later.'

'Sure. Bye.'

Sullivan poured coffee into mugs that had been at the back of the cupboard so long, I'd forgotten we had them.

'The thing is,' she announced, sitting down on the chair

so Bryan and Clare had no choice but to sit side-by-side on the couch. Small couch. The kind they call a love seat. In this case, wildly inappropriate, because Clare clearly thought Bryan was for the birds and the sooner the birds collected him, the better.

'The thing is, Bryan was meeting Hugo this morning.'

'Who's Hugo?' Clare asked.

'Clare, you don't want to know. Trust me on this,' I said. She devoted herself to getting foil off a Viscount. It was in bits. Must have been on the crashed tray.

'Go on, Bryan, tell them,' she encouraged.

He looked at her despairingly.

'Listen, this is none of my business,' I said.

'He was really great, wait'll you hear.'

Bryan, now promo'ed as a hero, looked even more uncomfortable.

'In working through our issues,' he began, 'it was established that I should make recompense to Hugo.'

'What about his insurance?'

'Natural justice,' Sullivan said. It was clearly a quote.

'It was felt that it would be…' Bryan took a deep breath. Clare took another Viscount, but this time opened it upside down so the foil retained the bits.

'It was felt that it would be beneficial for the process in which I was engaged if I met the man and offered him – provided him with – you know, apologised and stuff.'

'Where'd you meet him?'

'The Shelbourne. He chose the Shelbourne. Not me.'

Wasn't accusing you of anything, Bryan, but not going to argue with you. I could end up drinking my coffee out of a jam jar.

'Bryan brought a cheque with him,' Sullivan said, nodding anxiously. 'A *blank* cheque.'

'So what was the meeting like?' I asked. Clare looked as if she didn't care. Bryan was clearly a write-off as far as she was concerned.

'Very interesting. I got the history of Jaguars. I heard about the way he had re-covered the seats in champagne-coloured calfskin. Calfskin, my arse. He took me through the sound system and the phone system and the frigging GPS system.'

'Sure you just lift out a GPS,' Sullivan said. 'It wouldn't have been damaged in the– the– It would have been perfectly OK.'

So Sullivan, I thought, you get righteous about the one thing Bryan had listed that hadn't cost more than forty euro in the first place.

'I also got how I had destroyed his career and his relationship – you're not going to believe this – his relationship with that voluble bitch, who he described, repeatedly, as "My Lovely Wife". Like she was a brand. Or the title of a reality TV show.'

'What did you say to all this?'

'Nothing. I did an hour and a fucking half of active listening. I did more active listening than I'd done in my entire life, up to that point. I actively listened the fucker to death, so I did. Any time the wanker paused, which wasn't often, I'd look reflective and raise my eyebrows to encourage him to get going again. Or I'd say "I quite understand" or "go on". Because that's what my brother the psychologist had told me was the best way to handle it. It helped that I was doing the relaxation exercises Derek taught me at the same time.'

'It helped who?'

'Me in the first place, him in the second place, because it prevented me getting so pissed off at him that I'd've taken the Shelbourne's pretty little china effing teapot and broken it over his big bald bullet head.'

Sullivan was shaking her head, suggesting that Bryan was an incorrigible rogue, but sweet at the same time.

'What value did he put on the car?' Clare wanted to know.

'Ninety K.'

'So that's what you filled in on the cheque?'

Bryan shifted in his chair.

'No, I finished off the meeting by telling him he had been very open with me.'

Nod, nod, nod from Sullivan.

'I told him that before the meeting, I had been convinced he was a complete self-absorbed shit.'

Sullivan's head froze in position.

'And I told him that as a result of the meeting, I was now absolutely certain that he was a complete self-absorbed shit. I took out the cheque and I showed it to him and I tore it up and I leaned across the table and shoved the bits into the pocket of his jacket.'

Clare silently got up, took her handbag and left the room. I could hear the front door opening and closing before Bryan spoke again.

'And I told him he could pay the effing Shelbourne bill, too, since he was so stinking rich and such an absolute shithead. And I walked out.'

'Have you told Derek about this?' I asked after a long pause.

He shook his head, still focused on Hugo.

'That bastard never mentioned Sullivan by name. Never mentioned her. Never asked after her, never expressed concern for her.'

Did you? I wanted to ask, but didn't. I figured he might break one of the remaining mugs and stuff the bits into the pocket of my t-shirt.

'But the whole purpose,' Sullivan began and trailed off.

'The whole purpose was for me to get up to my gills in borrowings.'

'Oh, Bryan, you know it was repatriation.'

'Reparation.'

'Whatever.'

'Why should I do reparation for that bastard?'

'But you said when Derek was talking to you –'

'Why should I offer this son of a bitch a penny? He couldn't make me, either. He didn't report me to the guards at the time of the incident, so he doesn't have a fucking leg to fucking stand on.'

'But you *said*. It was part of the *process*.'

Bryan sat and went mulish. Sullivan began to cry. I began to wish I had moved into the tower. Even sleeping in the rubble and using a chamber pot would be more fun than this.

My phone indicated it had a text for me. I poked it.

I want a cigarette. I want a cigarette. I want a cigarette. I want a cigarette. D

I had a little debate with myself. If a man (troubled by anger) and his former girlfriend (troubled by everything) are muling and crying at each other in your sitting room, having already destroyed the contents of your kitchen, is it rude to text in front of them?

Hang in there. It's worse here. It really really is.

What's wrong there?

Bryan has regressed.

Who'd he hit?

Nobody, yet. He did break all my crockery, though.

I'll kill him.

Not deliberately.

I'll kill him VERY deliberately.

He's sulking three feet away from me and Sullivan's crying on the couch.

So you can't tell me the story.

No, but you could get a bit of it from Clare. D'you have her number?

No. Text it to me.

OK.

By this time, Sullivan had gathered herself together and had replaced pathos with determination.

'Bryan, you should go now.'

He looked startled.

'We're having dinner together.'

'No, we're not. You're going home.'

I began to struggle out of the chair, gesturing that I was willing to leave them to fight this out between them. Bryan flapped his hand at me in a way that said 'a) You're irrelevant, b) Shut up, and c) Sit down.' Just to spite him, I should have continued to get up, but I was comfortable, so I slumped back.

'Oh, so now I'm the worst in the world,' Bryan began.

'I didn't say that.'

'Don't give me that sweetie-pie shite.'

'Don't swear at me.'

'I'll swear at you if I fucking want to swear at you.'

There are times when, slumped in a comfortable armchair in a warm room, it's quite pleasing to admit to being single and celibate. This was one of those times. If this is happiness, if this is the joy of coupledom, I thought, who needs it?

'Bryan, this is not fair on Patricia.'

'Oh, and it's fair on me? I'm suddenly told all bets are off, schedule's changed, everything's cancelled, go home.'

'Derek would tell you that you're kitchen-sinking,' Sullivan told him sadly.

I assumed 'kitchen-sinking' was throwing all accusations at once. Much more fun than letting them march in single file.

'Don't you ever, *ever* quote Derek at me,' he yelled, coming out of his chair like an aggrieved rhino.

'Bryan,' I said.

'What?'

'I don't care where you go, just go. Now.'

'You're coming with me,' he told her. 'We have a date.'

He grabbed her and it was then I fecked the contents of my mug, my remaining mug, over him. He was so startled that he let her go, and she ran out of the room.

I held out my mobile phone like a remote control.

'One more move out of you and I call the guards.'

'What did I do? I didn't do anything.'

'Out.'

My phone rang and I put it to my ear.

'From what Clare says, I'm worried,' Daragh's voice said. 'Is Bryan still there?'

'Bryan is leaving right this minute, Daragh,' I said. 'I just need him to give me the spare keys to my house.'

Bryan looked as though I had smacked him and for a moment I was deeply sorry for him. The sorry-for-him wore off when he dragged the keys from his pocket and flung them, full force, at the fireplace, where they knocked over my father's only golf trophy, a Cavan crystal horror I've always wanted to break. It didn't break this time, either. Just rolled back and forth in the hearth making musical noises to itself: showtime.

'Thank you *so* much,' I said sweetly, and stood waiting for him to go.

'The sound of banging doors suggests Bryan has left?' Daragh said hopefully.

And to my great surprise, I began to cry.

CHAPTER TWENTY-FOUR

Where There's a Will

I don't do crying well. You know how some girls cry beauti-fully? I don't. I cry like it's a disease. I drool, I slobber. I get fits of coughing, alternating with snorts. I did my best to tilt the phone so Daragh didn't get the full sodden blast, but I could still hear him murmuring 'Poor Trish. Poor Trish'. The truly disgusting thing was that at a certain point, when I was all cried out, I tried to keep it going just to keep him going.

'Are you still in Moate?' I eventually asked.

No, he said, he was five minutes away. Was there anything he could pick up? A set of china, maybe? No, I said, just him-self. I mopped the floor where Bryan had dripped some of the thrown coffee and headed into the kitchen to make fresh stuff. When the doorbell rang, there was Daragh, and Clare was with him, a complicating disappointment I didn't need, but I was nice about it.

'When Daragh said Bryan was gone, I thought I'd come back and finish what we were supposed to be doing,' she told me.

I couldn't remember what we were supposed to be doing.

Sullivan came bouncing barefoot down the stairs and hugged the two of them.

'You're in better form than I'd have expected,' Daragh told her as we sat down. Correction. As I sat down. He picked up my father's trophy and replaced it on its little plinth, flicking it with a fingernail to make it ring. It rang.

'I'm sorted,' Sullivan said.

'In which direction?' Clare asked carefully.

'Bryan. We're done and dusted.'

Bryan, I thought, was done and soaked, but this was a mere detail.

'Because he didn't pay the bald guy for the car?'

'No. Because he's filled with anger and it's not my problem.'

'I don't buy that anger thing,' Daragh said, standing in front of the fireplace, hands in pockets. 'It's just bad temper.'

'He did try with Derek, but it didn't work,' Sullivan said.

'I'm confused,' Clare said. 'Do I need to know who Derek is?'

'No,' I assured her. 'You don't. He's a therapist I suspect made Bryan worse and a pain in the arse to boot.'

'Bryan does have his good points,' Daragh said fairmindedly.

'He does,' Sullivan said.

'He nearly tore your arm out of its socket,' I said. 'Don't gimme that good points crap. He's borderline domestically violent and you shouldn't have anything to do with him.'

'I won't.'

'Yeah, right.'

'No, I won't. That's it. Not seeing him again, ever.'

Her phone rang. She took it up, looked at it, and clicked a button.

'That's him. Gone.'

Daragh offered everybody Nicorette chewing gum and then took three squares himself.

'Now,' Sullivan said, all business, 'the tower.'

'Wait a second,' I said. 'You bring him back here, you have a dinner date with him, you have a bloody fine row with him, he breaks all my cups and saucers, plus, I've now discovered, the coffee grinder –'

'And, based on the Hugo experience, your chance of getting a cheque to replace them are small,' Daragh said.

'He effs and blinds and tries to physically drag you across the floor, I throw coffee over him, he tries to break that lump of lead crystal, and you want us to move seamlessly on?'

'What do you want to do? Hold a wake?'

This, coming from Clare, startled me into laughter.

'Look, Patricia,' Sullivan said. 'I'm like Daragh.'

I looked from one to the other and shook my head.

'Daragh's giving up the fags, right?'

'How did you know?' Daragh asked defensively, as if she'd accused him of being bad-tempered.

'Three Nicorette at one go might be a clue,' Clare offered.

'And I bet you he's tried before. Haven't you, Daragh?'

He nodded, miserably, holding up three fingers.

'Three times. But you know what the research says? It says that his chances of kicking them this time are actually improved by him having tried and failed before. Same with me and Bryan. I've tried leaving him a couple of times before. And I've gone back. And I've tried everything to make it work. And it didn't. I have nothing to blame myself with. I'm sorry for him, but I know now that's a danger. It's being sorry for him that pulls me into harming him all over again, so I've stopped.

I hope he has a long and happy life. Someplace else.'

'We must hope,' Daragh observed, one cheek bulging with secreted Nicorette, 'that his next girlfriend has a black belt in some applicable martial arts.'

We all considered that and then decided there was nothing any of us could do about it.

'Right,' Clare said. 'The tower programme. Daragh's come up with the title.'

Daragh looked mortified and started chewing as if he was eating his own leg.

'Trish's Tower,' Clare told me.

'Who said I was Trish?'

'He did.'

'Nobody's ever called me Trish other than him.'

'So?'

'OK.'

Clare began to outline the programme. My tower was going to be central, but Lucy had already set up good relationships with tower-owners around the country, and some filming would be done at their towers. With imported footage of over-seas towers.

'Apparently there's one in the Florida Keys,' Daragh said. 'For some reason, I find that funny. Can you imagine? Pink flamingoes on the roof and a perfectly turquoise kidney-shaped swimming pool at the base.'

'But our tower exemplifies all of the towers,' Clare went on. 'We illustrate them as variants on a theme established by this example, and that will be greatly helped by the fact that, other than breaking out the wall, nobody's done anything to this tower since it was built. I have to find ways to connect the viewer, to make the viewer realise, "Gosh, I'm seeing those blocks the way labourers left them in 1802. This is not a replay. This is the real thing." I have to find ways of conveying the dread, the unhappiness in that tower.'

'The what?'

'Dread? Unhappiness? Can you not feel it when you walk under that great black-grey arched ceiling?'

I felt kind of self-conscious, as the owner of the thing, that none of these emanations had been registered by me. I just thought it was a building. Big roundy building with an interesting past. But stones with fear and dread seeping through them? I'd missed that bit. Must be short on the right historic sensitivities. Oh dear God, now Sullivan's recently tear-stained face was turned reproachfully to me.

'How could you not get the sadness off every stone?' she asked.

'Well, I haven't had the chance to personally get to know every stone. I have been a bit distracted by trying to dig friends out from under those stones and get frozen peas through the stones to them –'

'And having lump hammers and metal staircases fall on you,' Clare finished.

'But there was never a baby's cry in that tower,' Sullivan protested. '*Never.* In two hundred years.'

'There was never a baby's cry in a lot of buildings,' Daragh said mildly, 'but it doesn't make those buildings seep sadness.'

'What buildings would never have had a baby cry in them?'

'God, so many. Museums. Art galleries.'

'Nobody ever brought a baby into the National Art Gallery?' Clare asked, rowing in on Sullivan's thesis.

'Government buildings. Leinster House, for example.'

'TDs have babies, you know. And anyway, that was the home of the Duke of Leinster before it became the Dáil so there were oodles of babies in it down through the years.'

'Well, there have to be…'

'You see?' Sullivan wasn't triumphant. More surprised to find herself so comprehensively right. 'They built the tower and then they closed it up. At some point, workmen broke out the wall, and then they boarded it up again.'

'OK,' Daragh said, baffled as to how he had got into the baby prevention business but amused at the same time. 'No babies. You better get pregnant fast, Patricia. Or else get the tower exorcised or something.'

The reference to getting me pregnant wiped the smile off my face. It carried such an assumption that whoever got me pregnant would be someone other than him.

'But there's something else,' Clare said. 'And you may not like this, Patricia, but I'm dealing with it in the programme.'

I drank my coffee in silence, waiting.

'In the 1920s, the State started to divest itself of the Martello towers in a fairly haphazard way, because they could see no sign of any possibility that they could be useful as defensive structures in the rest of the twentieth century. So they sold many of them off for buttons. Including your tower, Patricia. It was bought by a man named Archibald Keller, who had the wall broken out in preparation for the ambitious transformation of the building he planned. It was gong to be his castle, the castle to which he was going to bring his bride. He was engaged to a nineteen-year-old from an old Anglo-Irish family in Kildare.'

'He must have had a lot of money, if he was going to transform it into a living place.'

'Not sure he'd have needed that much money back then,' Daragh put in. 'The 1920s were no boom time in Ireland. Constant emigration. Constant supplies of cheap labour. And remember, he wouldn't have shared your views of what constitutes decent living standards, Patricia. His bride wouldn't have expected American fridge-freezers or washer-dryers. Not even electricity, probably. So the task would have looked a lot easier and cheaper, back then.'

'So what happened?'

Clare was rifling through printouts. She found what she was looking for, read through it, and then resumed.

'Keller was in his early thirties and he had one seriously bad habit for a long time. He gambled. Like all gambling addicts, he wasn't as good at card games as he believed he was, and he didn't know when to call it a day. So one night he got into a card game in a shebeen – a little country pub that didn't pay much attention to the licensing laws and was too out of the way to be bothered by the police. An all-nighter. Drink flowing and confidence flowing through Keller, too, because he was at least ten years older than a smart obnoxious young fellow who was betting high on every poker hand. Daring him. Even though the younger guy did very badly in the first few rounds. Halfway through the night, though, everything changed. Other players fell away, leaving only a hard core. With the two men pushing each other, staring each other out, going so far that the rest of the men went silent. The air thick with cigarette smoke, the white sudsy stains on the pint glasses left to one side while everybody watched. Watched as Archibald Keller came to the point where he had a choice. He could bet his last big possession, or he could call it quits.'

'But he'd already lost a lot of money, had he?' Sullivan wanted to know.

'He'd lost so much money that he had nothing left to rebuild the tower. Nothing left to create a home for him and his bride. But he still could have walked away and earned the money over time. He couldn't bear to do it. Or maybe he believed he could win it all back in one ambitious play.'

'He wagered the tower,' Daragh guessed.

Clare nodded.

'He wagered the tower. And he lost. The smart young fellow, in one night's work, had taken it from him. Not only that, but he paid some of the other players to make sure Keller didn't leave. They let him sleep it off for a few hours and then, when morning came, they took him into the city to a solicitor's office and stood over him while he signed over the tower, lock stock and barrel, to the young gambler. Your grandfather, Patricia.'

I thought about my grandfather, trying to remember if I had ever seen him go into a bookie's or play a game of cards. Never. Not that this proved anything, since the only time I saw my grandfather was on family occasions where dealing poker hands and playing for high stakes are not the way to go.

'Two days later, your grandfather and one of his friends made the journey out to look at his new possession. The rubble was piled outside, much as it is now. The big wooden door was half open. The two of them got out of the motor car they had borrowed, and made their way into the tower via the half-open door. Because they were smokers, they had matches, and they both struck up a match. But it burned out so quickly, your grandfather lit another and set fire to the end of a newspaper he had brought with him, so that the rolled-up paper would serve as a torch. And in the light of that make-shift torch, they saw Archibald Keller. Hanging lifeless from one of those great iron hoops that stick out from the wall.'

I drank cold coffee and gestured at Daragh to sit back down when he made to get up to make some more: stay. Let's get through this.

'I can't find any evidence, but the word at the time was that Keller had left a note for your grandfather. What we do know is that he had taken a ladder, climbed up to where he could tie the rope to the iron hoop, worked his neck into the noose and kicked away the ladder.'

The four of us sat in silence.

'After that, everything seemed to stop. Somebody got workmen to put the rubble back inside the tower, the door was bolted and locked, and that was the end of it. Your grandfather owned it for the rest of his life, but did nothing with it.'

'He probably felt so bad about it he just wanted to forget all about it,' Sullivan told me, instinctively trying to do PR for my grandfather. She leaned across and rubbed my shoulder.

'Sullier? You don't have to console me about my grandfather. He probably left me the tower because he liked me least of all his grandchildren and wanted to hand me a problem. Or maybe not. What does it matter? I don't buy any of this ghostly inheritance stuff. Inheriting this tower has been the best experience of my life. It has precipitated a clutch of great possibilities and introduced me to new friends.'

Sullivan looked simultaneously relieved and disappointed. A little more angst would have gone down a treat, you could tell.

'Clare, the only person whose knickers will *really* be knotted about my grandfather's story being told is my first cousin

Goretti, about whom I do not give a rat's ass. She can laugh it or cry it. All the same to me. It does strike me, though, that this is the angle that will make your programmes really work. It's not going to be a series about how a group of people fell in love with a tower and put plumbing and memory foam beds into it. It's about a tower that for most of its time stood for fear and then, for fifty years, stood in silent testimony to a foolish gambler and a clever gambler who won something he could not bring himself to do anything with.'

She gathered up her papers.

'The later programmes will fill that tower with love and laughter and beauty,' she summed up. 'We're going to sell this sucker worldwide.'

'You might need some advice on tax,' Daragh said tentatively.

I'd like some advice on tax, Daragh, I thought. Or on anything else. But Tracy the Interflora girl obviously had to be met and fed. Or worse. Because he hugged and kissed Sullivan, kissed me like a brother (for Chrissake) and left along with Clare.

For the rest of the evening, Sullivan hovered around me as if she thought I'd get late-onset vapours or throw a quick nervous breakdown. Not about Daragh. About my tainted inheritance. Even me laughing at her didn't remove her need to take care of me.

'Sullivan, this is a triumphant night for you,' I told her. 'Would you ever forget about my grandfather and poor Keller and remember that it all happened nearly a hundred years ago, to people who are long dead.'

'You're right, of course,' she agreed. 'Would you not like some hot chocolate, though?'

To placate her, I said I wanted to get into bed and send e-mails to all the consortium and builder and advisors about what we'd just learned, and that, yes, a big mug of hot chocolate would be just the ticket. Once she knew I was going to tell everybody else, that seemed to lift her burden, and I could hear her in the kitchen, whipping hot milk so that the chocolate would be properly frothy.

'D'you know what you could do?' she asked, as she put it down beside me along with two biscotti for dunking. 'You could attach the agenda for the meeting at the Tower in the morning to whatever you're sending the folks. It's the only document on this. Save me having to send separately.'

She handed me a flash drive and said goodnight. I inputted the story as best I could remember it so that I could attach the same document to all the e-mails I was sending. Then I did notes to each of the people and sent them off, one by one. Before I was halfway through the transmissions, I got a note back from Daragh. The Interflora girl must be out on a hen's night, I thought.

Isn't it fantastic how people assume you should feel guilty about your grandfather? None of us is responsible for what the rest of our family do, and anyway all he did was out-gamble a gobshite. You're way too sensible to believe the building holds some psychic echoes. My arse to that. If all the old buildings in Dublin where kids died of diphtheria, measles and whooping cough while their elders were puking up their lungs from TB held psychic echoes, the capital city would be a desert

and we'd never have had a property boom. I'd live in
that tower in the morning. X Daragh.

I sent off the rest of the e-mails and logged off. I'd expected
Friday to be a dullish day and it had turned out to be anything
but. I expected Saturday to be a busy day. It turned out to be a
lot more than that.

CHAPTER TWENTY-FIVE

The Start of the Weekend

I dreamed about my grandfather, which of course woke me
up early. The unconscious has a great way out of playing
ball with unpleasant memories. It just jolts you out of sleep and
more or less tells you: that's enough of that. I got up, showered,
dressed and left a note for Sullivan, telling her I was headed to
the tower and she should text me with instructions on anything
I was to do when I got there. I knew Lucy was coming around
to pick her up, so I was not abandoning her without transport.
I took my computer. Sullivan already had broadband installed
in the tower.

In the dark of a winter morning, the tower looked hugely
dramatic. I climbed up the wooden staircase, let myself in
and groped for the switch I'd been told was on the right of
the entrance. Found it. Flooded the interior with light. Good
on you, Paddy and your boys, I thought, for rigging up the
generator so we have power.

Down the stone steps to where a table was neatly set out
with clean cups, a kettle, coffee and milk. I sniffed the milk

while the coffee was boiling. Fresh as could be. The tower was acting as a refrigerator. This reminded me to switch on the ceramic blow heaters the work team used, to surround myself with a noisy hurricane of warm air. Coffee made, I sat on one picnic chair and put my feet up on the other.

High above me on the right was one of the rusted iron hoops Keller had used for his hanging rope. Must ask Professor Gibbons if he knows what they were originally intended for...

Bang, bang, bang on the doorway. I leaped out of my skin, threw coffee everywhere, screamed at the scalding heat of it and ended up standing beside the table, pulling my jeans away from my thighs to stop the hot liquid they'd absorbed reaching my skin.

Bang, bang, bang again. I put the mug on the table and ran up the stairs.

'Who is it?'

'Mike Kearns.'

I pulled back the bolt and opened the door.

'You scared the crap out of me,' I told him.

'I thought I might. What happened to your jeans?'

'I spilled coffee on them in fright.'

He stepped into the tower and hugged me, one-armed. He was carrying a huge oblong parcel wrapped in brown paper under the other.

'I'm really sorry, Sweetheart. I shouldn't have knocked.'

'Forget it. I've been spilling and throwing coffee so much in the last few days, I stink of the stuff. Jesus, let's go down where it's warm, the bloody coffee's freezing the legs off me.'

We went down the stairs and I used a tea towel to mop coffee off every surface before offering him a cup.

'Oh, yes,' he said. 'Oh, yes please.'

I poured and he sat in the chair I'd had my feet on earlier. The two of us sat in the ceramic-heater hurricane in amicable silence.

'Bit early for the meeting, aren't you, Mike?'

'I couldn't sleep, so it seemed like a good idea to come on out here. I was going to do a run on the beach or, if it was too dark, just sit in the car until someone else arrived. When I saw light in the window, it was like all my Christmases had come together. Oh, and thank you for the e-mail about your grandfather.'

'Was that what gave you insomnia?'

'No.'

Sometimes you know someone doesn't have to be asked to explain. They'll do it in their own good time. He looked up and around the tower, his gaze fixing briefly on the rusted iron hoop, then moving on. I looked at my watch.

'Dawn should be happening soon. Will we go up on the roof to watch it?'

'Now, that's a great idea. After another mug of coffee.'

'Sorry I don't have a Danish or anything. I wasn't expecting company.'

'Coffee's hitting the spot.'

'Did you like the plans the architect drew up?'

'Very much so. Particularly the way she's making sure you'll be able to see the vaulted roof from the ground floor.'

'She's working hard not to cover up the stone walls, which is quite difficult, because, since there's not that much space in the interior, it's tempting to stick everything on the walls. Hey, what's in the big package?'

'A small gift.'

He lifted the package and handed it to me. It was surprisingly light. I undid the twine and unwrapped the brown paper. Inside was a layer of bubble-wrap. I folded it back and found myself looking at a blank expanse of canvas framed in wood. Turning it over, I discovered a painting of a great dark field, littered with specks of colour. He took it from me and propped it on a jutting-out block in the wall. I stood back to get a better perspective.

'It's a battlefield!'

'In Napoleonic times,' he nodded.

The painting evoked the detritus of a day at war, nothing stirring on the muddied ground, the specks of colour the uniforms of downed soldiers. I walked to the other side of the tower and looked at it from there. It was spectacularly beautiful and so right for the tower. He came over and stood beside me.

'This is Eric's work?'

'This is one of his recurring themes. The aftermath of violence. The sensual peace when the fight is over.'

'It's superb.'

'I think so. You'll note that it has no frame. Eric's paintings don't have frames. He learned that from a painter he met briefly a long time ago, named Tom Cullen. I thought it would work particularly well against the rough textures of the stone wall.'

'And the lichen,' I said, pronouncing it carefully.

'And the lichen,' he agreed.

'Thank you.'

'You'll hang it?'

'Of course I will. The Tower should be filled with his work.'

He looked at his watch.

'Better go up on the roof, if we're to see the spectacular dawn they've laid on for us.'

He rooted in a pile of workmen's clothes, came up with two bright yellow hooded waterproof coats and held one of them out for me to insert my arms into.

'It's not raining.'

'No, but these'll keep the warmth in us.'

He led the way up the spiral staircase, now illuminated from the top by an electric lamp hung overhead. Did the usual small struggle with the small door leading to the roof. Got it open, climbed the two deep steps and leaned down to give me a hand up into a world of darkness and occasional bird calls against a background of a fussing incoming tide. The smell of the sea was clean and pleasurable. He switched on a torch.

The conical roof of the tower had been cleaned, and, presumably for ease of getting from one side to another, two of the big railway-sleeper planks that now covered the ground floor in its entirety had been laid on either side of the cannon-mount in the centre, providing two narrow raised walkways from the raised step on one side to the raised step on the other. I tested one of the planks and found it as firm as the roof itself.

The two of us went across the planks, one foot in front of the other, until we were on the raised step at the side of the roof overlooking the sea. Mike turned off the torch and we leaned on the edge of the roof. As our eyes got used to the darkness, it stopped being complete darkness. To the right, we could see the red glow of the city, and nearer, on either side, we could see the odd spot of light indicating a house. Grey-pink light to the east, low to the sea, marked the horizon and the start of the dawn.

'Warm enough?'

'Yes, thanks. This coat is great.'

The white edges of the incoming waves marked where dark sand met the sea. Looking to the land on the left, I could see the lights of a car trailing in and out of sight behind stands of trees.

'Eric isn't coming today.'

'No?'

The light where sea met sky was warming into horizontal streaks of coral pink. Birds were beginning to fly, dipping and wheeling over the sea.

'He didn't want to meet so many strangers.'

'I can understand that. Is he shy with new people?'

He shook his head. I stayed silent, sliding my cold hands into the sleeves of my jumper to warm them against the skin of my forearms.

'To get to know the friends surrounding another person is to commit, in some way, to that person. To be known by those friends as part of a couple. To embrace them as part of the other person's life. It can be safer to steer clear of them. It allows for eventual escape with fewer emotional binds.'

'Except that you don't think his leaving is going to be eventual.'

He folded his big arms on the edge of the roof and rested his chin on them. In the growing light, I silently watched this big, handsome, clever man mourn for what he was about to lose.

'You're not going to fight for him to stay with you?' I demanded, suddenly furious.

He turned his head and smiled at me tranquilly.

'You're a great fighter, Patricia. I'm not.'

'Coulda fooled me. You fight pretty well in court.'

'That's true. But in court, it's about facts and it's about the law. It's not about personal need. The best I can do, Patricia, is let my love go in the gentlest way I can manage so that at least there will be contact and friendship. The access points to good memories.'

The sky in front of us was ablaze with blues, with pinks, with reds. Clear of clouds, creating a rippled echo in the ocean below. Mike, still leaning over so he was at my height, put his arm around my shoulders and drew me closer to him. We stood together as the dawn drew the noises of the day from the land. In the distance, a rooster called, and from somewhere else came the sound – the distant sound – of a man shouting a greeting. To the south of the tower, far out at sea, we could see one of the ferry ships moving slowly towards its berth in Dublin Port. The tide washed over the rocks, edging nearer and nearer to the line of seaweed along the the foreshore. The sweeping light from Dublin Airport, so noticeable in its contrast with the dark sky, faded into invisibility. The gaudy dawn colours in the east began to fade as full blue infused the arc of the sky over us and fussy little birds began to chatter to each other in trees nearby.

It was day.

'Consider this possibility,' Mike said, freeing me and straightening up. 'I get into the car and go find Danishes in the benighted hinterland of this magnificent tower, and you set about making fresh coffee.'

'Sounds good to me.'

CHAPTER TWENTY-SIX

Bryan and Sullivan

I was congratulating myself on my timing when the car pulled up outside, with such aplomb I could hear it even over the noise of the ceramic heater. I turned to the small door, coffee pot in hand, to greet Lucy and Sullivan.

'How'd you know we were going to arrive?' Lucy asked.

'Gosh, it's not freezing in here,' Sullivan said. 'Those heaters really work.'

'Indeed they do. I didn't know when you were coming. I made the coffee for me and Mike Kearns. He was here, earlier. He went off to see if he could find a shop selling Danish pastries.'

'Hope he gets enough for four.'

'Of course I did,' Mike said, opening the door. 'Hi, Gorgeous.'

Sullivan embraced him. Lucy unfolded two more of the picnic chairs and raised an index finger to her.

'I'll do any work you want done twenty minutes from now. But right now, my priority is coffee and carbs.'

'Warm carbs,' Mike told him. 'I see Gorgeous has installed a microwave.'

In seconds, the cinnamon sugar smell was wafting briskly around the tower on the streams of hot hair from the heaters.

'This coffee is so good,' Sullivan said, shaking her head at the proffered Danish and pulling a banana out of the pocket of her ski jacket.

Lucy took the other Danish and shoved it in the microwave for a couple of seconds. It sparked and complained.

'You must have silver paper on it somewhere,' Sullivan said.

Lucy took it out and peeled the foil off the bottom, then started to eat it.

'Will Bryan be with us?' Mike wanted to know.

I told him the story of the Shelbourne meeting, culminating in me fecking coffee over Bryan to prevent him manhandling Sullivan.

Sullivan listened without comment. I was struck by her restraint. It was a fair guess that she had hand-shaped bruises on her forearm, but it would never occur to her to show them off as evidence against Bryan.

'As an outsider to this,' Mike said thoughtfully, 'I am, of course, not entitled to have an opinion. However, were I permitted to express an opinion or two, the first would be sympathy with Bryan's stance regarding poor Hugo. The second would be that when someone has a history of furious response to any challenge, you're not going to replace that response with pacific sweetness and light in three weeks of brotherly counselling.'

We would probably have heard more from Mike if Sullivan, already bored with the Bryan saga, hadn't gone for a wander and noticed the painting. She went wild about it. Mike filled the two of them in on Eric's work while I began to tidy up after breakfast and went up the stairs to say hello to whoever was arriving. It was Paddy Stapleton and his crew. The big white-haired man hauled himself, mainly by arm power, up the staircase, and I met him in the doorway with my hands up in surrender.

'Not a hard hat on anybody in there. Not a boot.'

'That's OK,' he smiled. 'As long as you haven't been doing any work, you're perfectly safe.'

He turned on the platform and hand-signalled a lorry to come ahead up to the tower.

'Changing the Portaloos,' he explained to me, before calling instructions down to the rest of his team as they got out of their separate cars.

I led him inside the tower. He knew Sullivan, but needed to be introduced to Mike. Lucy had disappeared. Mike and Paddy stood, the two of them, nearly the same height if it wasn't for Paddy's slight crouch, talking in the middle of the tower's main room, Paddy pointing to structural points Mike needed explained.

Sullivan tugged at the yellow coat I still had on.

'You going to help me set up the tables for the meeting?'

'Do I have a choice?'

'No.'

'OK, then, instruct me.'

For the next fifteen minutes, it was all activity. I was a gopher for anybody who needed one, responding to calls from Paddy with the Limp's team and to Sullivan with equal willingness. The architect arrived, and he helped her find a way to affix her drawings to the wall of the tower and tilted lights so they shone on them. She fell in love with Eric's painting and kept coming back to take another look at it, which, given that she didn't know the connection between Eric and Mike, allowed the latter to take quiet pleasure, earwigging on her well-informed comments. This was a woman who knew her art.

I have to hand it to Sullivan, she had everything superbly organised. Right down to bales of briquettes and bags of logs she got Mike to carry in. He lined them up beside the big fireplace and carefully built a fire. Added to the ceramic heaters, it made the tower positively toasty, and mingled warm hues into the otherwise cold lighting. Must remember, I thought, when we get this place wired, to get light bulbs that are pink and softer than the bright white.

The meeting was due to start about fifteen minutes from that point. Sullivan was laying out pads and pencils and jugs of water drawn from some oversized Tipperary Water blue plastic dispensers up against the wall. Lucy came back in – obviously from her car – and picked where she was going to sit during the meeting, piling up documents at that position and lining up three pens in a neat row.

'Oh, Lucy, you haven't met the man in charge of the building works.'

'Paddy with the Limp.'

'The very man. They're up on the roof looking at something. Come on and I'll introduce you to him.'

Lucy put her windcheater back on and followed me up the spiral staircase. When we emerged into the wintry sunshine, I turned and hauled her up the two big steps. The guys were all lined up at the wall on the other side of the roof, leaning over, looking down at something on the outside of the tower.

'Paddy?' I called.

He pulled himself up, back of the hand to his lower back as he straightened, and turned around, as did the others.

'Paddy, I want to introduce you to Lucy Littleton, a good friend to me and Sullivan and the tower. Lucy –'

I got no further. Not only could I not speak, I couldn't breathe. The two of them looked at each other across the distance of the big round roof. Looked at each other as if the world was just about to end. Or just about to begin. Looked at each other so intently, the rest of us were diminished, drained away to nothing. He pushed himself away from the wall and came limping across the railway sleeper bridge until he was in front of her, towering over her, and put out his great gnarled hand. She put her hand in his and he brought the other big hand down on it in gentle imprisonment. I stood, not understanding anything, but knowing better than to speak.

'Lucy.'

'Padhraic.'

Never were two names uttered with such soft conviction. The conviction of knowing the entirety of what each name meant.

'You sent me such a kind letter,' he said, still holding her hand. 'Such a kind letter.'

Togso suddenly passed me and went down the stairs ahead of Redmond and the third man. I was frozen on the spot, afraid to go, knowing I should not stay.

'Padhraic,' she said again.

I turned and went down those stairs, not seeing anything for the tears.

Sullivan glanced up and looked concerned.

'It's all right,' I said, shaking my head and trying to smile.

'It's all right. It's just Paddy and Lucy know each other. Used to know each other.'

'I know that,' she said smugly. 'My dad knows Paddy since he was a kid. He warned me not to mention Lucy. I nearly did, once, but I stopped myself in time. How are they doing?'

I held out my hands helplessly to her. She straightened up and stared at me and then said nobody should go up on the roof for a while, right?

'Right,' I said. 'Right.'

She flitted around among the groups chatting in advance of the meeting and got a series of puzzled nods from them.

It was a good fifteen minutes later, in the mêlée as people found their seats and Sullivan handed out the agenda, that Padhraic Stapleton came down the spiral staircase, clumsy because of his limp, and spoke quietly to Redmond, indicating that Jim should take over for him at the meeting. Lucy appeared, slid her paperwork to the architect, muttered something and went out the big wooden door of the tower, followed by the big white-haired man.

We went on with the meeting as if nothing had happened, since of course only I (and Sullivan) knew anything about what was going on between the two of them. Jim Redmond glanced at me in a way that suggested he might know something, even if he didn't know the full story. We discussed and signed off details of plumbing, heating, the shape of the extension, what should be done with the roof and a million other details, and I got through the discussions on autopilot, with half my mind on the pair whose empty chairs were a constant distraction. It was much later that I found out what had happened when the two of them left the tower.

Padhraic had shepherded her carefully through the sloping gardens of the tower towards the beach and past the outcropping of rocks until they were on hard-packed dry sand, walking north. Walking in silence, she looking ahead, he looking down at her.

'I had to send the letter.'

He said nothing.

'Did your wife suffer?'

'She did. Not at the end. But yes, she suffered. She was a trooper.'

They came to one of those whitewashed beach shelters with a bench inside and without asking each other, stepped on to its concrete floor and sat down, half facing each other, on the bench. He took her two hands in his.

'I wrote back to you, Lucy.'

Her eyes searched his face, learning him anew.

'I told you I hoped to see you soon.'

She said nothing.

'I have missed you all the days of my life,' he told her. 'Missed you with a grinding ache.'

The silence grew and grew. The sky had turned grey and glowering, and spatters of rain began to star the hard, dry sand in front of the shelter.

'Never a single day did I not think about you,' she said simply, and he gathered her into his arms with the sureness of an old memory and held her while she wept. Held her and stroked the hair he had stroked when it was the silky blonde of youth. Ran his big bent fingers through it and patted it smooth, putting his head down to hers and making the wordless noises of long silenced love.

She wept her way past the need for explanations or apologies, washing away the hard protective shell so stringently built, so rigorously sustained. She wept away the years of a life half-lived, knowing now that it had been a preparation of a sort. When the weeping was done and she was limp with exhaustion, he pulled her onto his lap, folding her into him and murmuring like a lullaby.

'My Lucy. My girl. My little Lucy.'

The rain drilled the sand in front of the shelter, creating runnels and rivers washing back to the sea's edge, the sound of it joining the sound of his voice, and she slept in his arms as she had when they were teenagers. When he heard the soft breathing of her, he leaned back. And he sang against the rain. Sang the songs of generations back, the songs they had danced to, the songs they had sung around bonfires with friends on the long midge-tormented warm summer evenings of their shared past. Songs he had not sung since the day he had left her to fend for herself at a party. Songs he had never sung since. Nor thought he ever would.

The rain eased and the sound outside the shelter diminished slowly. Over to the left, a truncated section of a rainbow showed against the breaking clouds. He was stiff from holding her, but knew he could hold her forever.

When she woke, she went through no moment of confusion, no 'where am I?'. She put her hands to his face and to the hair that had whitened in the decades that had come between. He slid her gently onto her feet on the bench and pointed to the sky.

'I'd've thought we were worth a full rainbow.'

'Even a bit of a rainbow will do.'

He rooted inside his jacket and held out a scruff of crumpled tissue paper dwarfed by his big hand. She looked at him.

'No matter where I went in the world, I carried that with me, every livelong day,' he told her.

She took the tiny crumple from his palm and opened it. Centred in the ragged grey paper was her engagement ring. She put her face down into the palms of his hands and wept again.

'Not a day without it. Not a day without taking it out and letting the hard light of it tell me what a fool I'd been.'

She came up and he wiped her face with a big clean cotton hanky. She tried to put the ring on and gave a shaky laugh.

'My finger's too fat, now.'

With dextrous big hands, he put it on her little finger, where it fit perfectly.

'Will you wear it?'

'I'll wear it.'

'We're set, so.'

She laughed and flailed at him.

'Set!'

He pulled her to her feet and they walked out on to the wet sand. The wind tore at them, making her face cold where the tears had been.

'I always loved you, Lucy,' he told her, holding her two hands low between them. 'I always did. The drink made me forget how to show it, how to be good to you. It made me betray you. But the drink didn't take me. I can't blame it. I took the drink myself. Because I was a fool. I haven't taken a drink in twenty-one years. Lucy, that's a long time sober. A long time to know what I did to you.'

She said nothing, just looking at him.

'A long time to live a life without you and to try not to destroy other people the way I destroyed you. I did my best, Lucy. I did my best. Every day lived decently, every sober day lining up behind every other day in a path I always hoped I could walk back to you.'

'Limp back to me.'

He turned her towards the tower and the two of them began to walk towards it.

'I used to have to run a few steps to catch up with you.'

'The oul' leg slows me down. I'm no bargain, Lucy.'

'Never wanted a bargain.'

They walked in a silence filled with understanding.

'We –' he began and stopped.

'Just "we" she told him. 'That's all there is to it.'

'Till death do us part?'

She shook her head fiercely.

'All the days of our lives.'

He looked down at her, his eyes glittering with tears.

'Shake on it?'

The two of them stood on the grey sand and shook hands before they began to climb the sloped garden of the tower.

'Took you long enough,' she told him, giving him a dig.

'Sure you'd have been too busy, earlier,' he responded, lifting her over the low wall.

'Kiss me,' she instructed, and he did.

'You never lost it,' she said when she came up for air.

'Thanks be to God for small mercies,' he said.

CHAPTER TWENTY-SEVEN

A Letter From Sullivan

*O*f course, by the time they got back, the tower was almost empty. The meeting had concluded, decisions noted, actions allocated. The architect was about to take down her drawings when I asked her if it was possible to leave them where they were, because I'd like Lucy to see them when she could give them her full attention. Not a bother, the architect said. She could run off copies back at the office any time she needed them. In fact, she said she'd e-mail copies to everybody involved. Sullivan ran her off a sheet of e-mail addresses and sent her on her way.

The two of us tidied up.

'Pity Daragh couldn't make it,' Sullivan said. 'I think he was mortified. But some client had a crisis.'

She carried a rubbish bag out to the boot of the car. The skip at the front of the tower was already overflowing. Padhraic Stapleton's team said it would be collected in the morning and an empty one put in its place. But in the meantime, we were our own rubbish collection service. If necessary I would get up on the top of our wheelie bin in Ranelagh and jump on the rubbish until it compacted.

'Lucy didn't say much when she came back.'

'Paddy wasn't exactly overflowing with chat, either.'

'Did you notice her when she came in this morning?'

'You mean with her documentation?'

Sullivan nodded.

'Well, I was talking to her, so of course I saw her.'

'Yeah, but you probably didn't really *look* at her.'

'Thanks. Your point being?'

'When she came back she had a new ring on. It wasn't on her ring finger, though.'

I leaned against the wall and laughed.

'Sullivan, you are a great bit of stuff.'

Who'd have thought that telling Sullivan Spencer she was a great bit of stuff would provoke such a response? The next day when I woke up, I spotted a big brown envelope at the door of my bedroom. I sat in the bed, looking at it, trying to figure out why I might have left an envelope there. Then realised I hadn't. Definitely.

I slid out of bed, padded across the floor and opened the door.

'Sullivan?'

No answer. I picked up the envelope and retreated to the bed with it. Inside was a printed letter:

Dear Patricia,

I know it's ridiculous to be writing you a letter, I never did before, ever, I think, except emails, not that they count. But when you said I was a great bit of stuff,

I actually was chuffed. I know you think everybody compliments me but the thing is they just tell me I look great and you're the only one that I think sees more in me and it means a lot to me.

By the time you wake up, I'll be on my way to see my mother. My Dad is picking me up. So you'll have a couple of days peace. Plus I won't be around when you read this letter because I'd be mortified.

I'll probably be mortified anyway because I may not say it right. But I think I should try.

I realised something important after what you said. I realised I didn't care about all the criticisms my mother would throw at me when I visit her. It'll be like I have a wet suit on me for the first time – usually she chills me. She really does. She always has. All the time growing up I felt I was only useful for her to show other people what a good dressmaker she was because I would look good in the clothes she made for me. It was all smiles in the street and then the minute we got in the door it was 'Take that off you before you destroy it.'

Probably that's why I always think the next man is the right one, not for sex but just to be held and admired and feel warm. And to be perfectly honest with you, I don't think that's going to change. I don't think people change much. I know girls who get complete makeovers done and they know what to wear afterwards and after a few months you'd never know they'd ever had the makeover, they've just gone back to what they always wore.

I don't think I'm ever going to convert to someone

else. But the thing I wanted you to know is that being your friend lets me kind of borrow bits of you and they help me to be the best version of me I can be. I think I've been the best version of me over the Tower. I honestly think I made you get more courage about keeping it, because I have this reckless go-for-it personality and you don't, usually.

You're going to say I have a goddam nerve, but I think you should borrow from me the way I borrow from you. I saw how much you liked Darragh from the first day you met him. I honestly think you fell in love with him that day although I know you'd reject that because you'd be logical and say he was just attractive and knew about tax. But it was more than that. He was like an old friend you'd just met. You knew him by heart before you ever met him.

And if you're saying "Sullivan, puh-lease" you shouldn't. Because it would be smart and cynical and safe and if I'd let you be smart and cynical and safe you wouldn't own a Tower. You've spent the last few months pretending not to be in love and you probably felt you were winning. You were losing, Patricia. You weren't smacking Darragh in the face, but you were like that bitch in school who used to pinch me but never did it hard enough to make me squeal so the teacher would know. I'm not saying his girlfriend isn't nice, I only met her once and she was, but she doesn't seem to be around much and it could be your destiny. (I know that's confused, but you know what I mean. Sometimes you should just go for it.)

I just have this sense that years from now the two of us will be sitting with our backs up against the wall of the tower on a warm summer day watching our children play. Please don't laugh. Please don't. It will happen. And each of us will be better as a mother because of the other.

I keep re-reading this and it's like trying to catch a floater in my eyes – you know when you can see this dot but when you look at it it floats up out of sight? I knew what I wanted to say when I started to write this but it keeps floating out of my reach.

I'm probably not clever enough to do this right. Still, you'll be able to capture it because you always know what I'm trying to say even when I don't say it the right way.

The best way I can put it is to tell you that you're the thing that's made sense out of my life so far and I hope you'll always be there to help me make sense of my future. I don't know much about love, so I probably should mind my own business about you and Darragh. But I'm an expert at friendship. So are you. Because when you're just being friends, you take risks and don't stay safe. Paddy and Lucy have a second chance at happiness because you weren't cautious with Lucy.

I think we'll look back at renovating the Tower all the rest of our lives, and at the friends we made. How the two of us made a big old bleak lump of stone where a man killed himself into a fortress for friendship and happiness.

This letter is no shagging good but I tried.
Love, Sullier.

I got into the shower and read it again wrapped in towelling. If I accepted its marvellously confused message, it seemed I had no choice but to get dressed in the most glamorous thing I owned, get the heels on, get the face paint on, go locate Darragh, fling him to the ground and have my way with him. Or at least tell him the embarrassing simple truth.

I thought about it. Long and hard, I thought about it. Long, as in up to lunchtime, when I ate something and put clothes in the washing machine. At one point, I even took the car keys off the hook in the hall.

But, of course, I put them back. On the pretext that I needed to re-read the letter. The real reason was that I was retreating into my shell like a tortoise. Because Sullivan is right. People don't change that much. I was in a safe place, even if I was on my own in it. If Darragh had fallen in love with me the way I'd fallen for him, he'd have done something about it. Right? Right.

I looked at my watch. Seven o'clock in the evening and all I'd done was one load of washing and read a letter. For some reason, though, I was exhausted. Too exhausted to even dry the washing. I went to bed, fell asleep and dreamed about Sullivan as a grandmother. She was the best-looking grandmother you ever imagined.

CHAPTER TWENTY- EIGHT

Dawn and Darragh

*B*ecause I had gone to sleep at about eight, I was awake at a quarter to six. Bright-eyed and anything but bushy-tailed. Who needs to be awake on a winter morning at that early hour? I showered and messed around a bit and then submitted to the urge to go out to the tower for another dawn-watching session, taking a carton of milk with me because Sullivan had cleared out all the leftovers from the makeshift kitchen.

The door at the top of the wooden stairs yielded like it was welcoming me, and my hand found the light switch without a grope. Eric's painting was propped in my line of vision and I stood for a long moment enjoying it. Then I went down the narrow stone steps to put the ceramic heaters on. On impulse, I poked the fire, to discover glowing turf embers still alive. I took down one of the architect's drawings, making a mental apology to her, and stuffed it, together with more turf and the smallest logs I could find, into the hearth. After a few moments, it began to give signs of life. The kettle boiled and I made a pot of coffee. Note to self: this means you're going to hang around this white elephant for half the morning. Just a possibility, methinks, you may be falling in love with it.

'More than lichen it,' I said aloud and laughed at my own pathetic joke.

Then I doctored the mug of coffee, put the yellow water-proof coat on, and got myself up onto the roof of the tower. The dawn was more advanced than the previous day's, and less pink. I leaned on the eight-foot-deep ledge and breathed in that marvellous air, drank my coffee and thought about how near I had come to abandoning the tower. Something moved in the distance to my left and I swivelled to look.

A dot moving on the beach. Purposeful. A runner. No, a walker. Tiny, in the dark distance, covering the hard sand close to the water's edge. The light was coming into the sky and seeping onto the beach as the walker came towards the tower. Regular footfalls, still silent because of distance. Setting himself a hell of a pace.

The walker seemed to almost pull the light with him, so that as he materialised into a mop-haired slim tall man in black shorts and white top, the brightening surroundings attracted his attention, and he looked to the left and right of him. Then up at the tower. Face up to me. Bearded face. Mephistopheles.

He went slightly out of step as he registered a figure on the top of the tower, waved and came on. Breaking into a run. Slowing to negotiate the outcropping of rocks, running into the bay in front of the tower. Halting and hanging over from his waist so the tips of his fingers touched the sand. Coming back up, putting hands on hips to catch his breath.

'Trespassers will be prosecuted,' I called down.

'I own. A bit of this. Place.'

'Not the bit you're standing on, though.'

He laughed up at me, the teeth startlingly white against the black beard and moustache.

'Listen, you. What about coffee?'

'Ready and waiting.'

I retreated down the stairs and met him in the interior. I threw him a tea towel and he mopped himself.

'Fire lit and all,' he said admiringly.

I did his coffee the way I knew he liked it and joined him at the fire. Never goes away, the wonder of an open fire. The two of us, hot-faced from its warmth, sat across from each other in silence for a long time.

'How's the ankle?'

'Not painful any more. Next week I'll start running.'

'Now you're off the fags.'

He crossed his fingers at me.

'I made that guy pay, yesterday, for keeping me away from the Tower when all the folks were there. The client I had to deal with. Bored the arse off him about this tower in particular and Martello towers in general.'

'I'm getting that way. I'm beginning to want to actually attract tourists to come here. Even tell them the story of how my grandfather won it.'

'It's a great story.'

'It is, isn't it?'

I told him the story of Lucy and Padhraic Stapleton. He patted some of the rough-hewn stone near him, as if it was responsible for that happy ending.

'You going to live here?'

'Oh, yes.'

'Is Sullivan?'

'Who knows?'

By the end of that silence, the two cups needed refilling. I was just about to move away when he caught hold of my wrist.

'Patricia.'

'Yeah?'

'I really like you.'

'Grand,' I said. 'Fine.'

'No, I mean, I *really* like you.'

'Daragh, I did hear you the first time and no offence, but my left leg is scorching.'

He released my wrist and I went to put the coffee pot back on the table, with an irrational urge to stay over there. Away from him. I resisted it.

'I'm in danger of loving you.'

'Well, *there's* a compliment. In danger?'

'In danger because I just don't know if there's any point.'

The old rage burst willingly into flame like the architect's drawing in the fireplace had. All spark and crackle and scorch.

'You have a bloody nerve,' I yelled at him. 'Playing both sides off against the middle.'

He looked mystified.

'I don't follow you.'

'Don't play Mr Innocent Boy with me. You have a girlfriend. Tracy the Interflora girl.'

'The who?'

'Interflora girl – the girl you sent with the flowers. And she's lovely.'

317

He began to laugh and I gave consideration to using the poker on him.

'I know she's lovely.'

'Well bully for her. As God made the two of you, he matched you.'

'Not really. She likes Australia. I don't.'

'What's that got to do with anything?'

'Tracy lives in Melbourne. We parted more than a year ago. We keep in constant touch because we are the best friends in the world – I'd trust her with my life. She happened to be home for a fortnight when we all got half-killed in the tower. Looked after me. Delivered flowers to you. Visited the tower.'

'And went back to Australia?'

'The day after she visited the tower.'

'Well, why didn't you tell me?' I asked, trying to keep my rage going without quite knowing why.

'Tell you what?'

'That she's – that Tracy's not your girlfriend any more.'

'I don't recall you asking me.'

'Well, you should have known.'

He stood up and folded up the tea towel he had mopped himself with.

'We were on the wrong footing from the start, then,' he said.

I looked up at him with dread.

'Maybe we should start over.'

'Like how?' I asked, standing up.

He held out his right hand.

'You must be Patricia. I'm Mike's friend, Daragh Gibbons.'

'Call me Trish.'

'With pleasure. Trish of Trish's Tower? Always wanted to meet you.'

I shook hands with him, feeling ridiculous.

'How do you do?' he asked with grave politeness.

'This is silly. A handshake at this stage.'

'Yeah, but the problem is I reek with sweat.'

'So?'

'You can't hug a girl when you're sodden.'

I proved him wrong. I proved him *so* wrong.

And then I proved him wrong again.

The End